CHANJORI HOUSE

By

Joy Wood

Best wishes
Joy Wood

To my husband, John
Not only do I love you, but you're my best friend.

Acknowledgements

The hardest part of writing the book for me is the back cover and the acknowledgments. I want to write something special that will draw people in to read my book, and I want to thank everyone for their contribution and not leave anyone out. Both I always find a significant challenge.

Firstly, I am truly grateful to have fabulous friends in my corner who I love dearly. They know who they are – without them, life would be a pretty dull place. They eagerly await a new book, and are unstinting in their praise for each story. It isn't just about the writing though, I'm blessed to have them in my life…particularly when it's their round!

I have wonderful support from my beta readers, Julie Popplewell and Maxine McCormick, and my proof reader and formatter, Sallyann Cole, who diligently spots my word blindness and alerts me to any errors. Special mention to the wonderful Tracy Smith Comerford who helps me with the launch of my books, designs fabulous teasers, and just about puts me right on all the bits I get stuck with. She knows everything 'booky' there is to know, and I'm so thankful to have her available at the click of a button.

To my brilliant author friends, Lynette Creswell, Siobhan Daiko and Lynette Rees who are always there to offer advice. Their wisdom is needed on so many occasions, and I'm indebted to each of them for their wise words, encouragement and generous support. Thank goodness for their experience in the 'book world'.

Once again it's praise for my amazing editor John Hudspith – Johnny works so hard cutting all the fluff away, keeping continuity in check, and of course ensuring the sex scenes . . . *work!* Thank you, Johnny, you never let me down.

A special mention must go to Jane Dixon-Smith (JD Smith Design) for the beautiful cover she has designed for Chanjori House. This is the third cover she has done for me and I love them all. The 'mock ups' she sends me initially present a dilemma as I always end up falling in love with each of them which makes choosing a specific one extremely difficult. So thank you to all my friends and family who 'voted' for their favourite, and as always, I went with the most popular.

I continue to be blessed with fantastic support from readers. Each email, review or message to say they have enjoyed one of my stories, means the world to me. I'm truly humbled by their continuous enthusiasm and genuine desire for me to do well.

Finally, my husband who is much better at English grammar than I am, and agreed to do a last proof read of my book if he was suitably rewarded. I hope you enjoyed your roast beef dinner, John!

Table of Contents

1

The brilliant sunlight streaming through the patio doors brightened up the lounge and signalled a beautiful *come out and enjoy me* day, but the silence in the room was dark and uncomfortable. Bruce Smyth's bleak eyes said everything. The practised doctor in his senior years focussed his sympathetic eyes directly on her husband.

"I'm sorry, Chester. The cancer is advancing much quicker than we first thought . . . I'm afraid it's just a question of time now."

Although the prognosis was no surprise, the actual words still had the ability to shock as they'd expected longer. Eve reached across the sofa for her husband's hand. It seemed the right thing to do, but he pushed it away and uttered two small words requiring a mammoth response, "How long?"

The doctor's lips creased, "Weeks at the most."

Despite the finality of Bruce's tone, Eve didn't want to believe it. She felt sick to the pit of her stomach. Nobody deserved this. While their marriage wasn't a great love match, it was a respect match and she felt Chester's pain. How does anyone cope with such terrible news?

"What happens now?" Eve asked, "I know you've explained things before . . . would you mind reminding us of what," she paused searching for the right words, "you know, what to expect next."

When Chester was first diagnosed with a brain tumour, Bruce had spent some time going over things with them, but right now she needed him to keep on talking. Anything to give them time to comprehend that Chester's death was no longer further down the line, it was now imminent.

Bruce nodded compassionately. He was an experienced doctor so must have delivered news such as this so many times before.

"The next few days as the cancer advances, you'll become bedbound sleeping for long periods of time. I know you want to stay in your own home as opposed to going into hospital," he looked enquiringly at her husband to see if this still was the case. Chester nodded.

"We can make the necessary arrangements for you to be nursed here at Chanjori. I'll contact the agency and make sure you have a nurse here all the time. I take it you want someone here overnight as well as days?" Bruce hesitated, "As long as you are aware of the cost . . ."

"I know about that," Chester interjected sharply, "and I'm staying here. When the time comes, I want to be in my own home not in a bloody hospital bed."

Eve nodded also. She knew absolutely nothing about caring for a terminally ill person, and Chester would not be a compliant patient so a nurse was an absolute necessity.

The sorrow in Bruce's eyes was evident. He'd been Chester's doctor and friend since he'd started in general practice. He'd also been the physician for Chester's first wife Ann up until her death.

"We will of course do everything we can to make sure you're comfortable and pain free. There are so many drugs we can use to help."

Chester stood up and walked slowly to the window. No doubt for self-preservation, but it almost seemed to Eve, now that he knew, the doctor was of no further use and he was dismissing him.

She needed something, anything, to divert from having to deal with the news they'd just been given, even if it was only a temporary reprieve.

"Would you like some tea, Bruce . . . or maybe something stronger?" She turned towards her husband hoping he too would encourage the doctor to stay with them a bit longer, but he continued to stare out of the window overlooking the garden.

Bruce picked up his bag, "No thank you, Eve, I've another visit to make. I'll call you later when I've made the necessary arrangements and give you the name of the person co-ordinating the nursing staff. I think," he looked across at her husband who still had his back to them, "in view of how Chester is, we need to start the nursing staff as soon as possible, even if it's just for a few hours each day at first to get to know you all."

"Yes," she agreed, "thank you. I'll walk you out."

She stood up, "Bruce is leaving now, Chester." Although thanks weren't required in circumstances such as these, Chester didn't turn around, but she understood. How do you come to terms with the realisation that your death is looming?

Bruce made his way to the door and shook his head as if to say *leave him,* and held it open for her. As they made their way down the long hallway towards the front of the house, she was grateful for Bruce breaking the silence between them.

"He's strong Eve, he could well surprise us all and have a little bit longer than I've predicted," he paused and his voice softened slightly, "but you need to be prepared it could be sooner. The cancer is somewhat advanced. He must have been unwell for quite a while before he was diagnosed."

"I'm sure you're right," she agreed, "but you know him better than any of us. He'd never give in to anything such as illness; he'd see that as a definite weakness."

"Yes, he would."

She frowned, "I can't understand why it didn't show up at his annual check, that was only last year."

"I'm afraid the type of brain tumour he has is a rapidly growing one so may not have been there last year. I know he would have had symptoms long before he came to me with them though, but I'm not sure even then that surgery would have been an option. It would have most probably been radiotherapy which would only prolong his life by months and I'm guessing he would have refused that anyway."

"Probably," she nodded, "I'm sure he would have suspected what was wrong long before he sought your advice."

They paused at the door, and she took his coat from him and held so he could slip his arms into it. He fastened the buttons, "I'll be back tomorrow around midday to speak to him. He may want to be on his own for a while now, so let him. He'll speak when he's ready."

"Thank you, Bruce. I am . . . we both are, grateful for your support. Perhaps tomorrow you could stay and have some lunch with us?"

He leant forward and kissed her cheek, "Maybe not. I'll be wearing my professional hat from now on," the disappointment must have shown on her face because he took her hand, "but you'll still be seeing a lot of me over the coming weeks, we'll just skip the lunches." He smiled gently at her, "If that's okay?"

"Yes of course, I do understand."

He stepped out of the house onto the porch and hesitated before clearing his throat, "I think it's time, Eve."

She tilted her head, deliberately giving the impression she didn't understand, "For what?"

But she knew. It had always been the elephant in the room. Her pulse tripped over itself, and her tummy muscles clenched. She could pretend and feign confusion all she wanted, but Bruce was still going to deliver the blow almost as devastating as her husband's prognosis.

"Someone needs to inform, Rick," his gaze was determined and none negotiable, "it's time he came home."

2

Eve closed the front door and staggered towards the chaise longue in the hallway. Her legs suddenly felt weak, and the knot in her abdomen was tightening by the second. She began to breathe in and out through her mouth, a technique she'd adopted years ago to calm herself when she suffered from nerves and was susceptible to fainting episodes.

Rick Forrest. The man she'd worshipped and given her virginity to . . . the man who'd adored her and shown her how beautiful lovemaking could be . . . the man she'd planned a future with. But he'd lied and disappeared when she needed him most of all. Every breath of her youthful body had loved him, but he'd crushed that by leaving without even so much as a goodbye.

An image of his handsome face flashed in her mind. The face she had tried so hard to not think about, but could recall in a second. It seemed a lifetime ago she'd desperately willed him to come back and prevent her marrying his father when there was no other option. But he never came.

Eleven years had rolled by. She kept herself busy and thought about him much less now, but she couldn't totally wipe him from her mind however hard she tried. He'd been her first love, her only love, and try as she might, she could never erase that. In the daytime she was fine, but at night, still after all these years, she thought about him. They were the nights she'd wake up and wonder if he was happy, or if he ever dreamt about her.

She breathed in deeply hating the unsettled feeling that had gripped her. Her life was not exactly of her choosing, but it was a steady life and she'd become an accomplished actress in the last eleven years. Chester had often said their marriage had been a great success, but that was largely due to her compliance and support towards him. Anyone that knew them as a couple would have no idea she was playing a part . . . nobody would as she did it so well.

She accompanied Chester on social occasions and hosted numerous charity events, garden parties and afternoon teas. He was a wealthy man with his own oil company, and influential as President of the National Institute of Petroleum. As a husband, he was extremely generous towards her. Her wardrobe was full of designer clothes and shoes, and the safe in the house was secure for her beautiful diamonds and watches. Her hair was cut at an expensive salon, and the food she ate was of the highest quality. There were staff at the house so the most she was ever involved in was saying yes and no to the housekeeper Gilly if there were any domestic issues. She had a chauffeur, Niall, to drive her anywhere she wanted to go. Life was good, and she refused to dwell on what was lacking from it. She had a husband she respected and a dear friend in Jo, Chester's daughter. The greatest joy in her life was her precious son, Oliver. He was her everything. All the love she had was for him, and all she ever did in life, was with him in mind. His happiness was her happiness.

The only real sadness in her life was her dear mother, but even she was ensconced in an excellent care facility which Chester funded so she had no reason other than the misery of her terrible dementia to worry about. So there was no time in her life for regrets or what ifs. She was content and very fortunate compared to some.

Chester's diagnosis had been a terrible blow though and had forced her to consider selfishly, the thought that eventually she'd have to leave her home of the last eleven years. Chanjori House would eventually belong to Rick as it went through the generations to the oldest child, so she would have to leave when the time came. That wouldn't be such a problem for her despite loving the house, but the thought of uprooting Oliver and how upset he would be did unsettle her. He was only a little boy and Chanjori was his home.

"Are you alright Mrs Forrest?" Gilly, their trusted housekeeper interrupted her train of thought. It must have looked odd that she was sat in the hall of all places on a sofa that was fundamentally designed as a piece of furniture to enhance the décor as opposed to sitting on for relaxation.

"Yes, I'm fine," she reassured with a fake smile. Chester always said that staff should be kept out of family business. He was emphatic they were employees and should be treated as such, and only involving them in the tasks they were employed for. On most occasions she adhered to that, but Gilly was special and one of those wise women that seemed to know everything and had an innate sense when things weren't right.

She swallowed, "Could you bring some tea for Mr Forrest and I to the library please?"

"Of course I will." Gilly's eyes were piercing, she knew there was more, but she was too practiced to presume anything would be shared with her.

"Would you like some of the freshly baked scones that Mrs Abbot made this morning? I know she's done them especially for Mr Forrest as he's partial to them."

"Not right now, I think just tea would be fine." Chester wouldn't want to eat anything. Who would after hearing about their death sentence?

She wanted rid of Gilly so she could compose herself before she went back to Chester. "I'll be through in a minute, thank you."

She watched the housekeeper make her way to the kitchen area of the house, and waited until she was out of sight before exhaling deeply.

Would Rick come home?

3

The court usher cleared his throat, "All stand," and the packed courtroom followed the instruction. Rick watched as Judge Digby came into the courtroom and took his seat which was the cue for them all to follow and sit down.

This was it. He looked up at the defendant, Patrick Diffey linked by handcuffs to a police officer. His jaw was tight and a twitch under his right eye indicated he was nervous which he had every right to be. Whatever words were spoken next in the courtroom would seal his fate. He was either going to prison for a long stretch, or he was going to walk free. Rick was confident in his ability to defend his client, and that in the next few minutes, the latter would prevail.

Rick Forrest's successes in the courtroom were highly publicised. He thrived on the drama of a showdown with rigid rules where he had to match his wits against the best the opposition could offer. And he'd done exactly that during the trial. His cross examination of witnesses had been almost theatrical, and timing was everything. He'd concentrated his efforts on the leader of the jury, knowing he could swing the outcome in his client's favour. He didn't doubt for one minute today's victory would be his; he'd wager his life on it.

The usher walked up to the judge and handed him a slip of paper, which he along with every other person in the courtroom watched him read over the top of his half-rimmed glasses. He folded the paper and looked across at the speaker representing the jury.

"Has the jury reached a majority verdict?"

"Yes, your Honour, we have."

The judge looked at Rick's client.

"Will the defendant please stand."

Patrick Diffey got to his feet.

The judge addressed the jury, "Do you find the defendant guilty or not guilty to the charge of murder?"

It wasn't even a second before the spokesperson uttered the two words that confirmed every second of Rick's preparation had been worth it. His endless plotting of his opponent's strategy had paid off.

"Not guilty."

He'd done it again. Another victory.

The courtroom was in uproar. The family of the deceased man were on their feet shouting obscenities at the jury, and the defendant's family were doing fist pumps and hugging each other. It was always the same with these high profile cases. Winners and losers, side by side. He'd become indifferent to it all now.

It took the judge several minutes to get things under control so that he could inform Patrick Diffey he was a free man.

Rick opened his briefcase to pack away his paperwork. The prosecuting barrister, Derek Burrows approached him with an angry and twisted face which smacked of a sore loser.

Fed up at being beaten again in the courtroom, no doubt.

His smile displaying his expensive veneered teeth couldn't quite hide his anger at losing.

"You sonofabitch, Forrest." He over-emphasised his words shaking his head from side to side as if implying no, no, no. "I don't know how you do it, that bastard has guilty running through him like a stick of Blackpool rock and you know it."

"Be careful Derek, watch your blood pressure," he replied, enjoying his victory.

"He's just going to go back out there and murder some other innocent bastard you know. It's in his blood."

"Not my problem," Rick shrugged dismissively, "I was paid to defend him and that's what I've done. End of."

The organisation behind Patrick Diffey had engaged his services at an exorbitant rate. That toe-rag didn't deserve his freedom as far as he was concerned, but he'd just been doing what he was paid to do. He accepted early in his career, it didn't pay to have an opinion.

Rick placed the papers in his briefcase and closed it.

He gave his colleague the usual firm but fake handshake, "See you around, buddy," and walked away to the holding room to complete the paperwork for his client's release. He glanced across at the empty public gallery. They'd all filed out now.

Why had Saul Boylen been there for the verdict? A notorious gangster surrounded by a glut of saps who did his handiwork for him. It was a mystery as to why he'd been in the courtroom some of the days as Patrick Diffey didn't work for his organisation, so there was no reason for him to be there. If reputations were anything to go by, Saul Boylen didn't do anything without a reason, and he certainly didn't do support. So why had he been there for parts of the trial? There had to be a reason.

He believed his client when he said he had no idea why he'd been in the courtroom, but the very mention of Saul's name seemed to unnerve him. He became twitchy and evasive.

Rick made his way towards the court exit. Saul Boylen niggled him. His legal brain was programmed to solve puzzles, not have pieces left over that didn't fit.

About a dozen press rushed towards him as he exited the courtroom and attempted to make his way down the steps.

"Has justice been served, Mr Forrest?"

"Was your client framed?"

"Who did murder Bashara Dierne?"

He hated the press. They were a bunch of pariahs but there was no way in his profession he could avoid them. He had to say something so he could be on his way and get that victory drink he'd promised himself.

He leant towards the closest microphone to his face. "Following a lengthy trial, Patrick Diffey has been acquitted today of the charge of murder. The jury reached a unanimous verdict of not guilty. My client is now on his way home to spend some time with his family, having spent nine months in jail awaiting the trial. There'll be no further statements today. Thank you."

Patrick Diffey had been led out of the back of the court. No doubt there would still be a handful of photographers' eager to get a picture of him for tomorrow's tabloids. They'd hired a car with blacked out windows to ensure he wasn't photographed, and had the driver reverse it close to the building so he could get straight inside.

Even though he'd been found not guilty, today wasn't a day for celebrating. Rick had warned him not to give a statement. Tension was particularly high in the Asian community and there was nothing to be gained by giving the press any more than they currently had.

Rick headed down the steps and briskly walked away. There was no way he was going to explain anything to the press. It wasn't for him to discuss the intricacies of the law and how he'd successfully defended a man most certainly who would have been sent down for a long time with anyone other than him. It wasn't arrogance, it was confidence in his own ability to exploit any loophole in proceedings that he could. Exposing the inadequacies of a police investigation was his field of expertise, and he thrived on the exhilaration of winning. Today he'd done just that. He'd thrashed the opposition yet again.

He parked his car underneath the plush Canary Warf building and used the lift to the offices. The receptionist, speaking on the phone as he walked past, beckoned him over.

"I've got an urgent phone call for you. They've rung once today already."

He frowned, "Who is it?"

"It's Peter," she glanced down at her notepad, "Whitlam."

His father's lawyer. Why would he be ringing him?

"Give me a minute."

Rick opened his office door with a feeling of doom flooding through him. He'd been high minutes earlier with his success. The last thing he wanted was to spoil that by being reminded about the past. And Peter Whitlam was his past, so there could only be one reason he was contacting him. The old man must be dead? But why hadn't his sister contacted him? When they'd last met, she hadn't indicated there was anything wrong with him, but then again, he wasn't a topic they discussed as she knew how much he hated him.

He poured himself a large Glenfiddich whisky from the vast array lined up, and added some ice before walking to his desk. The celebratory drink was less appealing now he'd been reminded of Chanjori. He never liked to think of that place.

He picked up the phone, "Put him through, Jessica." He waited until he heard the line transfer.

"Good afternoon, Peter. What can I do for you?"

"Hello Rick. Nothing to cause immediate alarm, but I'm afraid I have some rather unpleasant news which you need to know about."

Minutes later, Rick put the phone down and swivelled his chair away from the desk towards the window. He stared out at the view of London. It was just another day. People were rushing about, trying to shelter from the sudden torrential downpour. He swirled the ice in his glass as he considered the news he'd been given.

Up until the phone call, the day had been great. He'd made love to Louise, his fiancée with a promise of dinner to go over yet more wedding ideas. His early morning starts always included an hour's workout in his gym with weights, and then he'd had the court victory. So it was all good. As soon as he heard his father's lawyer Peter Whitlam's voice, he knew something was wrong. Peter hadn't contacted him in eleven years since he'd left Chanjori, so he wasn't ringing for a social chat.

He breathed in deeply absorbing the information he'd been given. So the old bastard wasn't dead, but he was dying. Good. It felt strange to be talking to Peter after all these years. Not only had he been the old man's lawyer for as long as he could remember, he'd also been a close friend of the family.

The old man only had two friends if you could call them that, Peter and his doctor, Bruce. Maybe *men he trusted* might be a better way to describe them as an image of his father having friends like a normal human being was elusive. Nobody ever got close to Chester Forrest, not even his own children.

Rick took a slug of whisky, enjoying the heat as it travelled through his chest. He didn't particularly want to think of his old life, he'd well and truly assigned that in his mind to the closed pile, but he couldn't stop himself now.

His memories drifted back to what seemed a lifetime ago when his bastard of a father had physically had him removed from Chanjori House and put on a plane to Australia. What a cunt he was. Why would Peter think he was going to be dashing to see him just because he was dying? Not-a-chance. He'd vowed never to set foot in the place again while the old man was still alive, and he'd meant it. There was no way he would ever go back. If he did, he would come face to face with *her* again, and that was something he couldn't do even after all this time.

A picture of the smiling assassin, Evie Henshaw flashed in his mind. Why, after all these years did that still happen? He never thought about her anymore, she was another memory that he'd filed in the closed pile. He'd loved her once, but what a scheming bitch she'd turned out to be. No sooner had he left Chanjori, she'd married his father. It made him feel physically sick to think about the two of them together. His father was at least thirty years older than her. It was clear exactly what the old man would see in her, but Christ almighty, what the hell would she see in him? Pound signs that's what. And now, all her wildest dreams were about to come true. She'd be a rich jolly widow dancing on his grave. Well, there was no way he was being part of that. No way was he going to see her again. What was the point when all he'd want to do was fasten his hands around that beautiful neck of hers and squeeze the very last breath out of her?

4

"At least try a bit, Chester, you need to eat," Eve coaxed. "Can I get you something lighter, maybe an omelette?"

"For Christ's sake woman, stop fussing. I don't need building up where I'm going. This constant harping on about food is getting on my fucking nerves so cut it out."

She took an audible deep breath in. He knew she hated him cursing at her but he still did it regardless. Her embarrassment was heightened because Chester's trusted friend and lawyer, Peter had joined them for lunch and he was sat opposite her in silence, looking highly uncomfortable and all because she was trying to be kind. What was she supposed to do, watch him wither away in front of her?

"I'm only trying to help."

"Well don't." He threw his napkin down, "If I need your help, I'll ask for it. Until then, stop bloody nagging at me."

There was no point in saying any more, she knew him too well. But trying to make allowances was hard and she hated having to.

"In that case," she stood up and looked at Peter, "if you'll excuse me, I need to visit my mother."

Peter stood also, "Of course, Eve." He hesitated and she knew why. How do you enquire about a woman that has advanced dementia? It's not an illness to which you improve or get better from.

"How is your mother, any change?" he asked politely.

She smiled at his thoughtfulness, "No, none at all, I'm afraid."

Chester butted in, "Nor will there be. If she was an animal they'd put her out of her misery."

"Well she isn't," Eve snapped, "so I'd appreciate it if you kept that sort of comment to yourself."

She nodded to an acutely embarrassed Peter and walked towards the door as Gilly knocked and entered. "Are you ready for dessert, Mrs Forrest?"

"No dessert for me, thank you. Perhaps the men would like some, or maybe coffee," she didn't bother turning to ask them. "I'm leaving shortly to visit my mother. Could you ask Niall to have the car ready," she glanced down at her Rolex, "for two o'clock please?"

"Yes of course."

Eve left the dining room and made her way upstairs to her bedroom. How unbearable Chester could be. He'd always been a difficult man to live with, but since his terminal diagnosis, he'd become insufferable. Bruce had said he would become more aggressive as the disease manifested itself. He must have meant *more aggressive than usual*. She was trying to be sympathetic but it was becoming increasingly difficult each day.

She entered the sanctuary of her bedroom, grateful for her own private space. Chester never visited her there, which she was thankful for. Since they'd married, this had been her room, her refuge where she could kick off her shoes and be Evie Henshaw instead of Mrs Chester Forrest.

It was a beautiful room which she'd had decorated in subtle relaxing pastel colours. Facing south, the room was dominated by a gorgeous bay window with a delightful window seat. The sun shone through most of the afternoon and early evening, and she liked nothing better than to escape to it at various times of the day to relax and read. Although Chanjori had a sitting room and a snug to relax in, she still preferred the tranquillity of her room where she could unwind with a good book, or fiddle with her iPad.

There was also a library in the house with a couple of PC's which always looked inviting with the vast array of books, but Chester's daughter Jo monopolised it. She was a successful novelist and used it for her research and writing. Eve always felt when she was in there the same time as Jo, she was disturbing her, and she much preferred the tranquillity of her own room anyway.

Eve loved Jo as if she was her own sibling. When Chester first brought her to Chanjori as an eighteen year old, she'd felt vulnerable, almost like an injured bird. Her father had died, and her mother had been admitted into a care home. Jo initially felt like a kindred spirit with an air of vulnerability about her also. She'd been born with a congenital deformity of the hip and had undergone numerous operations as a child and young adult. The corrective surgery hadn't been terribly successful, and as a result, she walked with a significant limp which had hugely affected every aspect of her young life.

Jo was a lovely woman, inside and out. She was highly educated and successful with her writing. Everyone loved her, but she led a quiet solitary life at Chanjori with her head stuck in books and research most days. Jo had low self esteem, although she disguised it well, and Eve tried over the years to encourage her with her personal appearance, but to no avail. Jo was a pony tail and jeans kind of girl, and rarely went out socialising.

It hadn't always been that way. Before Eve arrived, apparently Jo accompanied Chester to functions after her mother died, but it seemed a relief to her not to have to continue with that when Eve slipped effortlessly into the role.

Eve stepped into her dressing room and took a moment to inhale and enjoy the freshly laundered smell. It was citrusy and reminded her of a time in her life when she'd been content and happy. As a child, she'd been the centre of her mother and father's world, and the only thing she had to worry about in her young life was passing her next piano exam.

Rick had told her once he found the smell of her attractive. Those simple words were the beginning of her sexual awareness. The innocent dreams about him kissing her, and what that would be like to experience for real, turned into sexier dreams, and eventually into a desperate longing. She wasn't sure what to do about the sexual feelings that were emerging, and had no idea about giving herself sexual pleasure. She knew about the sex act for procreation, but not the pleasure that could be gained from it. That was until a couple of girlfriends persuaded her to go to the cinema under the pretence to her mother of a romantic comedy, when in fact they went to a completely different cinema across the other side of town and watched a French film with subtitles which demonstrated quite graphically self gratification and masturbation. At home, in the privacy of her bedroom, she began exploring herself with her fingers. With her eyes closed, she visualised it was Rick kissing her and *his* fingers delivering the pleasure instead of her own. That night, she had her first orgasm.

It was months of using her fingers before Rick turned her pubescent dreams into reality, and when it happened, the sex had been amazing. She couldn't get enough of him, he used to tease her and call her ever ready, like a battery that went on forever.

The heat between her legs brought her back to reality. She inwardly chastised herself. Getting all steamed up about Rick now after all these years, was just plain silly.

She pulled out a couple of dresses from the vast selection hung on the rail, eventually opting for a light blue dress and white flat shoes. It was a gorgeous day and her mother's room would be hot. She checked her watch. Just enough time to go and pick some wild flowers from the garden. Eve always liked her mother to have some sort of pretty flora in her room, and flowers always made her mum smile.

Eve adjusted the blind at the window to block the sun from her mother's eyes. The room in the care home overlooked the pretty pond in the garden, and her mother's needs were met more than adequately at the enclosed institution. She was satisfied her mother was comfortable, even though she could never vocalise that; the poor dear had no idea where she was living. Her world was one of restless confusion.

The staff encouraged her mother to join in the facilitated group activities, and reported she actively participated, but seemingly was much happier and calmer on the occasions Eve visited. As far as Eve was concerned, the specialist residential dementia centre was a godsend and worth every penny of the extortionate monthly fee. It gave her peace of mind that her mother was being cared for and she was grateful to Chester for paying the fees. Without that, she'd most probably have ended up her mother's carer and living with them as she couldn't be left unattended.

As always, she had to acknowledge Chester's generosity towards her mother. He might be a difficult man to live with, and some may dislike the forceful way he expressed himself and went about his business, but she'd always respected him for supporting her with her mother. She'd never regretted marrying Chester. He'd offered her a future when she couldn't see one, and as her mother's needs were her own needs, she was thankful Chester had met them full on.

Eve insisted both Chester and Oliver visited her mother at the residential home on occasions such as her birthday or Christmas time, but it was a useless exercise really. Oliver didn't like going as she referred to him as Hughie, who was the little boy who'd lived next door to them when she was a child. For some reason, she was always delighted to see to Chester though. She'd gone to school with Chester and his first wife and could recall fondly those times as if they were yesterday. Not for long though, but whenever he first arrived, her little face would light up, and she'd ask him about Ann, his late wife as if she was still alive. Then after a few minutes of him humouring her, her mind would drift off into the little enclosed world she resided in. The previous Christmas was the first time Chester had refused point blank to visit and she knew it wouldn't be long before Oliver would do the same.

She read a few more chapters out loud from the paperback novel she had in her hand. It was a very old Mills and Boon paperback from the days when the most couples got up to between the pages was a passionate kiss. It was hard to imagine what her mother would make of the modern contemporary stories with intimate descriptions of sexual activity on every page; she wouldn't dare bring any of those.

Eve would quite happily read aloud as it helped pass the time away. Conversation was jumbled, and it was so hard just sitting there. Occasionally when none of the staff were about, she would sing quietly to her mother. That brought joy to her confused mind. She would close her eyes and tap her leg gently. On those occasions, Eve could almost believe she was normal and not the shrunken, bewildered lady in front of her.

Her mother had been so proud of her singing voice, even as a small child. In those days, she would ferry Eve around the country to various talent contests, delighted if she won singing trophies. Music had once been Eve's life, but that all changed when she was seventeen.

She placed the book in her mother's bedside drawer knowing it wouldn't see the light of day again until she next visited.

"Thank you, dear. I hope it's got a happy ending, I only like those."

"It will have, Mum, I only get stories like that for you."

Unbeknown to her mother, Gilly very kindly raked around the charity shops getting them for her.

Her mother smiled and Eve knew that conversation was now over. She moved from one topic to another like it was a hundred metre race.

"I think we'll have lamb for dinner, it's your father's favourite."

Eve hadn't the heart to tell her that her dad had been dead eleven years. The latest research she'd read suggested not to startle a person with dementia by telling them the truth. It only added to their confusion.

"That'll be nice," she agreed.

"I'll do Yorkshire puddings as well. I know they don't go with lamb, but your dad is very partial to them, and you like them too, don't you, darling?"

"Yes, I love anything you cook Mum, you know that."

Her mum looked pleased, "You're such a sweetheart. Now you'll have to excuse me while I use the bathroom."

"Do you want me to give you a hand?"

"No, I can manage, dear, thank you. You could help and start peeling some vegetables though, if you wouldn't mind?"

Eve sat back in the chair. *This just gets harder and harder.*

Her mother closed the door to the ensuite and Eve gazed around the small cosy room that was her home. She'd made it as snug as she could with warm-coloured fluffy cushions and a beautiful Scottish tartan throw, and various knickknacks from their house before it had been sold. She'd framed bright photographs of herself with her parents, and amongst them, she'd put some of Oliver as a baby, and a couple of family ones of her, Chester, and Oliver together. She knew her mother looked at them, as each time she visited, they'd be shuffled around in a different order which gave her some comfort.

She stared at the photograph of Oliver on the terrace of their retreat in Florida. He was a definite Forrest; his eyes were the giveaway. It was the rich brownness of them with the long thick curly lashes. Jo and Rick had them too. Sadly, though, Chester's once vibrant eyes were now becoming dim and faded, with sleep dominating the days now just as Bruce had said it would.

Were Rick's eyes still vibrant and alive? Despite vowing not to, she allowed him to penetrate her thoughts yet again. It was because of Chester's illness she told herself and nothing to do with the dreams she'd had about a different life if she'd married him instead of his father. What did it matter how many children they would have had, or where they would have lived? Who'd ever cared that her teenage dream had been to study music and marrying Rick? It never worked out anyway. He'd gone away . . . and the music had well and truly stopped.

From an early age, music had been her life, eagerly facilitated by her ambitious mother. Rick would argue it wasn't encouragement, it was enforcement as her own musical career had been thwarted. There was no question that her mother had been very talented musically, but opportunities weren't available for her when she was young, as money was tight in her family, so when she left school in the seventies, she'd gone straight into clerical work.

Eve could remember beginning singing lessons as soon as she started school. Then came the piano which she never liked but continued with as her mother wanted her to, and she liked to make her father proud. On the occasions he was at home, he loved to listen to her play and sing to him. It was quite a rarity for him to be home though, her memories were mostly of just her and her mother as he was absent for long periods of time, travelling extensively with his work.

Rick used to say it was her mother's frustration pushing her down the music route. That wasn't totally true, she did love it, but once she'd met him, even as a young girl when they were only friends, her priorities changed. Instead of music being her total life, he became it.

She chastised herself for thinking about him again and checked her watch. If she was quick the chauffeur could pick her up and she could go with him to get Oliver from school. That would be a nice surprise for her son, he'd like that. She picked up her mobile and rang Niall. Normally he would fetch Oliver from school on his own, but today she wanted to be there. Any time spent with her son always lifted her spirits. He'd begged her to let him travel on the school bus and for Niall to meet him at the end of the drive, but she wouldn't allow that. She liked him to be picked up from outside of the school gates. It was safer that way.

She smiled lovingly as her mother came back into the room. Alice Henshaw was still a beautiful woman. She was much thinner now, but her complexion was flawless, and even though her hair was now dull and lacklustre, it still had a mind of its own. Eve lifted one of the wayward curls covering her eye, leant forward and cupped her face in her hands.

"I love you Mum," she kissed her forehead, "always. I've got to go now to pick Oliver up from school."

"Oh, yes, you mustn't be late. Don't miss your piano lesson this evening."

Bless her, she still thinks I'm at school.

"I won't," she smiled tenderly, "I'll be back on Wednesday and I can read a bit more of the story."

"Tell Miss Munroe, Daddy will write a cheque for the lessons at the end of the month as usual."

"I will do Mum. See you soon."

"Bye dear."

She slung her handbag over her shoulder and left the room. A tear escaped from the corner of her eye and ran down her cheek. Visiting her mother was always sad, but it ceased to bring tears anymore. Today though, she felt exposed. Chester's illness was impacting on them all, and the thought that Rick might come back had her nerves in tatters.

Please don't let him come. I couldn't face him.

The fresh air was welcoming as she exited the building. She took a deep breath in, filling her lungs as she came down the steps towards Niall who was waiting patiently. He opened the car door for her and she got in the back. Ten minutes to school and she'd see her precious son. That's all she needed to brighten the day.

Why was she torturing herself worrying about Rick? She needed to get a grip. Jo knew him better than anyone and said repeatedly he'd never return to Chanjori, and Peter had spoken to him on the telephone and had almost apologised on his behalf as he'd refused to see his father before he died.

So there was no way he was coming back. No way at all.

5

The air stewardess topped up his champagne. "Anything else I can get for you, sir?"

Rick breathed in deeply. There was, but he wasn't sure what he needed was part of the service. The premier private airline certainly used the best flight attendants; this one was stunning with her ample breasts tightly ensconced in a tailored jacket.

"No thanks, I'm fine."

She smiled, "We'll be taking off shortly. The captain says he's waiting for a slot, but it could be about ten minutes."

"Good, thank you."

He focussed on her ass as she walked away. He wouldn't mind having some of that to kill time during the flight. His mobile buzzed interrupting his salacious thoughts.

"Forrest."

"Just the man," a male voice replied. A familiar voice that had called him before. The voice of a man he'd seen more recently in the courtroom.

Rick cleared his throat, "Hello Saul."

"Great job in court last week."

Saul Boylen wasn't ringing to praise him about court, that was for sure.

"Thank you. Forgive me for being brief, my plane's about to take off. What can I do for you?"

"I've got a job for you . . . a job that would suit a man with your skills."

Here we go again.

"I've already got a job."

As you well know . . . you've watched me do it the last few weeks.

"I know you have, but this one pays a lot more than what you get right now."

Rick laughed out loud, "I can only live in one house and sleep in one bed, Saul, and I already earn plenty of money."

"Ah, but what about the extra benefits you'd get working for me?"

"I already get all the *extra* benefits I need working for myself."

It was the same banter each time between them. Saul would ask him to do a job, and each time he would refuse. One day, surely, he would give up asking.

"I'm disappointed to hear that, Rick, I want you onboard. You're making a big mistake turning me down you know."

"Then it's a mistake I'll have to live with," he answered, hopefully with humour in his voice.

There was a pause, maybe a pause of acceptance . . . for now?

"One of these days, I'll get you to change your mind."

"You never know," Rick answered evasively, wanting rid of him. "I'm getting the signal to turn my phone off, so I'm going to have to go. Take care, Saul."

"You too, my friend."

The line went dead.

Rick called his secretary and waited for her to pick up. It would be an enormous error of judgement to get on the wrong side of Saul Boylen.

"Amy, can you send another box of Cuban cigars to Saul Boylen please."

"Yes, of course. Do you want to include a message?"

Rick paused. His intention wasn't to insult Saul, but there was no way he was ever going to *come on board* that particular ship, figuratively speaking.

"Put, *thanks but no thanks, I'm not a good sailor*."

"Consider it done, Rick. Enjoy your trip."

He switched his phone onto flight mode. Enjoy wasn't exactly the right word for what he was about to do. He associated the word enjoy with dining out and eating fine food, savouring a delicious vintage bottle of red, or fucking Louise all night long. No, it wasn't a word he could associate with this trip.

He looked out of the window as the plane started to taxi towards the runway. In less than two hours, he'd be back in Edinburgh where he'd grown up with his mother and sister. Despite all the vows to never to set foot on Chanjori soil again, he was going back.

Up until the previous day, he was determined not to, but he needed closure. He had time before he started another case, and impulsively decided that before he married Louise he wanted to totally eradicate the house and everything it stood for out of his mind for good.

The old man would be dead soon. It was still a surprise, even though he'd had time to think about it. The old bugger seemed invincible. There was no question of him not inheriting Chanjori, it had been in his late mother's family for years, and passed onto the eldest child, him.

His thoughts drifted fondly back to his mother telling him and his sister as children about renaming the house to incorporate all their names. She'd taken the first two letters of each of their Christian names and come up with Chanjori. CH for Chester, AN for her, Ann, JO for his sister Josephine and RI for himself. Only a woman as beautiful as his mother would think of something special like that.

He recalled his greedy old man challenging him in court to take his inheritance from him, but he lost. That's what comes with having a lawyer for a son. He was legally proficient to totally screw him. Of all his victories, none was sweeter than that particular judge finding in *his* favour.

So, Chanjori House would soon be his. The irony was, he didn't particularly want it. After his mother died, he hated it there, and when his father packed him off when he was nineteen, he hated *him* even more.

But right now, there was a reason he wanted the house.

He wanted revenge.

And he'd get it by ousting her, his father's slut. She's sworn she loved him, yet the scheming cow had married his father within weeks of him leaving, and according to his sister, had given birth to a brat.

He'd long ago ceased to think of the old man as being anything other than a bastard his mother had had the misfortune to marry.

Images of the dirty old git touching Eve made him sick to the stomach. All the promises they'd made together, the life they'd planned when deep down she was after the main chance, his father. Well, she'd be sorry about that. Wife or no wife, she was going to be out of that house as soon as the old man took his last breath, and she could take her bloody offspring with her.

6

"Why haven't I ever met Rick?" Oliver asked, opening his mouth and filling it with a huge spoonful of pancake covered in maple syrup.

"Because he left before you were born to start a new life in Australia. Don't put so much into your mouth like that."

"But Jo said he lives in London."

"Yes, he does now. He came back from Australia."

"Why?"

"Because he wanted to, that's why. There were more opportunities for his type of work."

"What work?"

This was getting too much. Eve didn't want to be talking any more than she had to about Rick Forrest. She didn't even want to think about him right now.

"You'll have to ask Jo, she'll tell you all about him. He's her brother, after all."

"Jo says he's my brother too and he's really clever. She says he has lots and lots of money," he placed his spoon down on the empty plate, "what sort of car does he have?"

"I have no idea, Oliver. Come on now, Niall will be waiting to get you to school."

"When can I go on the bus with the others? I hate going with Niall. Everyone keeps calling me a baby being driven to school every day and having to be picked up."

She sighed, kids could be horrible sometimes.

"I've said you can when you're older, but just not yet."

"When I'm twelve can I?"

"We'll have to see. Now go up and brush your teeth. Be sure to knock on your father's door and say goodbye."

"Do I have to?"

"Yes, you do. Remember I told you that he is very poorly so we need to be extra kind to him."

"'Cause he's going to die?"

"Who told you that?"

"Jo. She said the doctors had told him he. . . erm . . . " Oliver scowled, clearly trying to remember the right words, "he's not got long for this world." He scrunched his face, "Think that's what she said."

"Did she now." Blast Jo, she had no business being so direct. She'd needed to have a word with her. The last thing she wanted was for Oliver to be worrying. He'd be upset enough when the time came so there was no sense in adding to that in the weeks leading up to it.

"Go on up, quickly now, and make sure you clean your teeth properly for three minutes."

Oliver stood up from the table, "Is he going to die?"

She sighed, "We'll talk about this after school. Like I said, he's a poorly man."

"Okay," he huffed.

She stared at the door as it closed behind him. Trust Jo to be talking to him about Rick. It made her on edge. He'd dominated her thoughts too much the last few days. She really didn't want reminding about the man she'd promised to love and honour for the rest of their days, and then pledged that in a legal ceremony to his father. But try as she might, she couldn't get him out of her mind.

Had there ever been a time when she didn't love him? Her thoughts drifted to the first time she came to have any real contact with him.

She'd travelled to Highgate Grammar all-girls school on the same bus as Rick each day as he attended the 6th form grammar all-boys school. The previous house her family had lived in had been much closer to the school so she was able to walk or cycle, but since her father's business had taken a nose dive, they'd had to move out of town to a much smaller house and that meant catching the bus.

She didn't really have much to do with the rowdy boys that sat at the back of the bus. Hers was one of the last pick-ups and she would get on and sit at the front near the driver. Quite what she would have done if the seat adjacent to the driver hadn't been free she didn't know, but thankfully everyday it was. She always sat with her book and earphones to try and block out the noise coming from the back.

The other girls on the bus attended the comprehensive school and were much more affable with the boys. They seemed so much more relaxed than she was, and their language was suggestive and filled with loads of effing and blinding.

Tormenting and name-calling was a frequent occurrence, but she kept her head down. One particular day, her book was swiped out of her hand and thrown around. It was a library book so she needed it back, but she was scared to go down the back of the bus to retrieve it. She remembered the jeers of '*come and get it, Evie, Evie, lemon squeezy'*, in reference to the fragrance of her clothes which was down to her mother's obsession with lemon fragrance wash powders.

That particular day was imprinted on her mind. It was the day her life changed. While she was deliberating exactly what to do about the book, simply because she'd be fined if it wasn't returned to the school library, Rick walked towards where she was sitting clutching it in his hand to background taunts of, 'trying to get in her knickers, Forrest'. Unaccustomed to dealing with boys, she was nervous about what he was going to do when he got to her seat.

He handed her the book, "You'll have to excuse those morons, they've escaped from the zoo and it's feeding time," which made her smile but only caused them to squeal louder, whistle and make monkey noises.

Rick Forrest was gorgeous looking even then. He was really tall, but not gangly. He suited tall and had a thin athletic body, which she later found out was due to all the sport he played. She wasn't quite sure what to say as she wasn't accustomed to chatting to boys, her mother made sure of that.

"Thank you," she smiled, concerned that he might want something in return for the book. Another opportunity to ridicule her, maybe?

He gestured with his head towards the others, "They're all knob-heads."

That had made her more relaxed, and as her eyes met his chocolate warm ones, something shifted deep within her. She didn't understand then, but the look they exchanged, changed her life significantly. It was the day her young heart fell in love.

"Are you reading it because you like Thomas Hardy or as part of your GCSE course?" he asked as if she was a regular friend of his. Her mouth was dry, was he taking the Mickey? Why was he interested in what she was reading?

She cleared her throat, "As part of the course." She looked back down at the book, not quite knowing what else to say, and he surprised her by sitting down next to her, "We read it too, in year ten. I really liked it."

They continued to discuss Thomas Hardy all the way to school. Recalling their conversation in her bedroom that night, she concluded it was the best journey to school she'd ever had. She thanked God for Thomas Hardy as she relived every word, every sentence, and every mannerism of Rick. He was everything her teenage heart dreamt about in a boy. She'd known who he was, growing up in the village, but she'd never had anything to do with him. Her parents knew his parents as her mother had gone to school with them both.

She'd never been interested in boys. Her future had been completely mapped out for her and certainly didn't include them. Each day she had to concentrate on music. After school and at weekends, she had her singing lessons, music tuition and hours of practice. Her mother would never allow her to go to anything that wasn't related to school activities or music. Some of her friends at school had boyfriends and some even had sex, but she never did.

Until Rick Forrest.

The family had a gorgeous Labrador dog, Bess, and she used the dog as an excuse for getting out of the house. She explained she wanted to do more exercise to keep trim, which thrilled her mother whose whole ethos in life was devoted to appearance.

She would attach the dog's lead and wave to her mother as she left the house for the 'so called' exercise, when in fact the whole purpose of the dog-walking was to meet Rick on a Saturday afternoon in the woods by the lake, as he liked to fish.

Their friendship blossomed. She wasn't naive enough to think he didn't have girlfriends. For long periods of time, he didn't meet with her and it was during those times that she guessed he was in a relationship with a girl. And not once did he ever give her a hint that he thought of her as anything other than his friend, even though she would have jumped at something more from him, but it was never forthcoming.

Until her sixteenth birthday.

It was a gorgeous sunny day and they were laid by the pond. Rick supported himself on his elbow and looked so gorgeous with his khaki shorts showing off his muscular legs. Even his tee-shirt looked good on him, but maybe that was something to do with the quality. Rick Forrest's family were rich, so he always wore clothes with a label attached to them, yet he never made her feel inferior.

"Is your birthday this Friday?" he asked.

"Yes. How did you know that?"

"You told me."

"No I didn't."

He cocked his head to one side, "Well how do I know then?"

"I don't know. You've found out somehow because I didn't tell you."

His cheeky grin gave him away. He'd been snooping.

"What have you got planned?" he asked.

She rolled her eyes, "A thrilling evening with my parents and friend to the cinema, and then for a meal afterwards."

"Is that what you want to do?"

"No, but there's really no choice. My parents aren't the sort to let me go clubbing."

"Would they let you come out with me?"

"You?" She smiled incredulously, "You must be joking. My mother would faint. I don't think boys feature in her plans for me."

"I'd like to take you out . . . properly."

Her little heart was bursting, "I'd like that too, but it isn't going to happen. They'd never allow it."

"Why not?"

"They wouldn't, Rick. Their whole life is focussed on me getting into Harlow to study music. Nothing's allowed to get in the way of that."

"Don't you want to go out . . . you know have a boyfriend?"

"I've never thought much about it to be honest."

Liar, liar, pants on fire.

"Would you like to go out with me?"

All sorts of emotions were whirling around inside of her, particularly between her legs. Thank God, he had no idea how she was feeling. He must have taken her silence as a yes, as he continued, "I'd like us to . . . you know . . . be together more than we are."

She was gobsmacked. He felt the same way she did? That made her youthful heart sing, but it was no good, she'd never be allowed.

She shook her head dismissively, "That isn't going to happen. My mum's not well for a start so I'm needed at home when my father's away on business. Anyway, I'm sure you've got plenty of opportunities with other girls."

"I have," he answered honestly, not at all with arrogance, "but they're not you." And then he did something that she dreamt about since the day he'd rescued her book for her. He bent his head and kissed her. She could have moved away, but there was about as much chance of that happening as running the London marathon. She wanted to feel his lips on her and to taste him. She'd dreamt about it for so long. This kiss was everything she imagined it would be, and more. His lips were so soft and she matched their movement with her own. She wasn't greatly experienced in the art of kissing, although she had done before at a couple of parties she'd been to celebrating friends' birthdays, but this was completely different. With him she never wanted the kissing to stop.

He pulled away far too soon.

"I've wanted to do that for ages."

"Me too."

He laughed out loud at her, "You're so different from other girls. I like us being friends, but now," he hesitated, and something warm fluttered in her belly as his eyes softened, "I . . . want more."

God, she wanted more too.

She took a deep breath in, "I'd never be allowed. If they found me here now with you, I'd be frogmarched home and grounded until I graduated from college."

Rick leaned forward and came really close, "Then we won't tell them, how about that?"

And so, the deceit began. The sneaking out, meeting him when she should have been studying. She missed piano and singing lessons, shamelessly citing her mother's illness to the tutors who would politely smile with sympathy, which gave her confidence knowing they wouldn't contact her mother about her frequent absences. She wasn't lying about her mother. Her mind was spiralling from forgetful to completely confused. Her father was limiting his time away so he could watch over her, and as a result, she actually gained more freedom as her father was not as intense about her studying music. That said, he wouldn't have allowed her so much freedom if he had known a boy was involved.

She loved her mother and knew eventually she would end up in care. All the assessments had indicated that, but her and her father tried between them to manage her. It was heart-breaking to see her mother's deterioration. Dreams of studying music became just that. Her father still wanted her to pursue it, but they'd decided between them for her to defer her application for a year while her father scaled down his travel, and then they would regroup on her future. Her dad had talked of retiring early, but said he couldn't afford to do that due to the monies he was owed. He had to carry on working.

When her father was away on business, Rick would sneak into her room and they'd share wonderful nights making love. He was a skilled lover, and she suspected he must have been involved with an older woman at some stage as he certainly knew which buttons to press. He denied it of course, in a cheeky way, but she didn't believe him. He brought such joy into her bleak young life, she didn't care about his past, she only thought of the future, and not once did she think of it on her own. Rick Forrest was her future.

They made promises to each other, and somehow the happiness he brought to her life compensated for the deterioration of her mother's mind. It was like having a child around. Yes, she could manage tasks such as washing herself, or cooking a meal, but she was deteriorating and it was apparent that even those tasks were becoming harder and harder. The only relief Eve felt was when her mother was asleep in bed. And on the nights when her father was away, she got to have the most amazing sex with Rick.

A voice interrupted her reminiscent daydream, "I'm ready."

Her precious son stood in the doorway in his navy blue school blazer, boasting the school emblem on its pocket, and his peaked cap fitting snugly on his perfect head. All thoughts of Rick were pushed from her mind as she smiled lovingly at him. The most important person in her life now was Oliver. Rick Forrest was history.

"Right then, sweetheart, you've got your homework folder today, haven't you?"

He patted his bag, "Yep, I've got it."

"Good. Let's go and find Niall."

They made their way towards the side entrance of the house where Niall waited each morning.

"I'll be glad when I don't have to go to school," Oliver puffed.

"There's a long way to go before that," she reminded him, "you've got college and university yet."

"I don't want to go to university," he dismissed, looking so cute with his turned-up nose, "I'd rather be in the Olympic swimming team."

Eve opened the back door and gave Niall an acknowledging nod.

She loved her son's childlike aspirations. She used to have those once upon a time.

"That would be nice, sweetie, but all great Olympians have to have a plan B as they might get injured and can't compete. So you need to work hard at school," she smiled and straightened his tie, "just in case?"

She hugged him as much as he would allow these days.

"Promise me you'll do your best?" she said, kissing his cheek.

"Okaaaay," he drawled, "see you later."

She watched him climb in the back of the car and waved at him.

You most definitely will, my darling, you can be sure of that.

7

Eve was sitting with Chester in his room. It was nice he was in a chair by the open window and getting some fresh air, but she knew being out of bed would soon be a thing of the past. He looked very poorly.

"What time is it?" he asked.

"Ten thirty. Why?"

"I just wondered," he shrugged, "I don't even know what day it is."

"It's Friday, but it doesn't matter."

"No, I don't suppose it does anymore." He looked exhausted, and was it her imagination that his colouring had changed that morning. He seemed almost grey.

"Peter's calling round later. I've suggested after two o clock when you've had a bit of lunch and a rest."

"Right," he replied wearily. He looked as if he was about to say more, but his heavy eyelids seem to have a will of their own, and she watched as they gently closed. Seconds later, his head fell forward as if his neck was no longer strong enough to hold it. She reached across to adjust his pillow and make him more comfortable. Whether he was aware, she wasn't sure, as his eyes remained closed.

It was becoming increasingly difficult to witness his deterioration. His decline was becoming more evident each day, and Eve had a secret wish to run away and not come back until it was all over. His mind when he was awake was still sharp, but his desolate eyes said it all. He was in God's waiting room.

Chester had been such a strong, energetic man, and never really ailed from anything. As long as she'd known him, he'd never taken any time off work for illness. It was hard prising him away for a holiday even, and on the occasions she did, it was her that entertained Oliver while he had his phone permanently stuck to his ear, or sat staring at a laptop.

She had so many photographs of her and Oliver, but very few of them as a family. Their annual trip to the US and the Disney theme parks were just her and Oliver. Much as she loved being with her son, it was sad there wasn't anyone to share the fun and see the places from a child's perspective. Her gaze was often drawn enviously towards mums and dads on holiday with their children, and she couldn't help but feel a pang of jealousy at their family dynamics, and wished her life had been like that with Oliver having a dad that wanted to be with them. She knew how fortunate she was with her lifestyle, having money to enable them to do anything they wanted to, but she'd trade that in an instant to have a man she loved by her side and someone truly caring for her.

A low groan snapped her out of her melancholy thoughts and back into the room. Chester was becoming too sleepy to stay upright, and the concern must have been evident on her face because the nurse suggested they got him back to bed. Once he was lying comfortably, she explained that he was more sleepy than usual because his pain relief had been increased.

Sleep was probably the best thing for him; he'd be more alert when Peter called later. She knew nothing about Chester's business affairs so it was left to Peter to sort out the company which she knew would be terribly difficult for her husband. He'd built the company from nothing and now it had to be dissolved. Peter would be selling off the assets for a fraction of their true value, and you didn't have to be a financial expert to know the vultures in the oil industry would be swooping.

Eve left Chester with the nurse and made her way to the library to speak to Jo. It was a surprise to see Niall the chauffeur stood beside her as she sat at the mahogany desk in the corner of the room. It was unusual for Niall to be inside the house. He had a rota each week for his duties, and if anything changed, they rang him.

Jo nodded an acknowledgment as Eve closed the door. Jo's usual attire was jeans and a tee shirt, especially if she was writing, but today she was wearing a nice pair of black trousers with a pretty pale blue blouse. Her hair for once wasn't scraped back in a pony tail either; it was loose, which really suited her.

Jo wound up her conversation with Niall. "If that's everything then, I'll be ready at midday."

"Yes, of course," he nodded, recognising her dismissal and made his way to the door. He paused, "How is Chester today, Mrs Forrest?"

"About the same. Very tired."

"Send him my best wishes."

"Thank you, Niall, I will."

Niall had been their chauffeur for only a few months and she really liked him as did Chester. He resided in a small cottage at the entrance to the grounds of Chanjori as Chester preferred the convenience of having his chauffeur on hand rather than use an agency driver.

It didn't sit comfortably with Eve that Niall would soon have to be looking for another position. If Rick sold the house, sadly all the staff would have to find new jobs which she didn't like the thought of. They were all trusted employees and each of them having to leave through no fault of their own, caused her more distress. These days her tummy seemed to be in constant turmoil about every little thing, which she knew she had no control over, but nevertheless worried about.

Niall smiled at her and Jo before closing the door behind him.

"Why was he here?" Eve asked, taking a seat at the side of Jo's desk.

"He wants some extra time off to fly to the States for his sister's wedding. He didn't want to trouble you."

"He should really sort that out with Gilly, she manages the staff holidays. Why's he asking you?"

"I think he was worried about asking for more time off than two weeks . . . you know with Dad being so poorly."

"Ah, I see. I suppose it makes sense having a bit more time if he's going all that way to the States," she agreed, "but I don't understand why he's worried about asking."

"He probably felt a bit awkward, that's all."

"Mmm, maybe you're right."

Eve wasn't there to talk about Niall. She wasn't happy about Jo's directness with Oliver concerning Chester's illness, but she needed to tread carefully. The last thing she wanted to do was upset her more than she already was. As difficult and obnoxious Chester could sometimes be, he was her dad and she loved him dearly.

"I wanted to have a word with you about Oliver and what you've said to him about your dad."

Jo gave a puzzled frown, "What have I said?"

"Something along the lines of, he's not got long for this world." Jo looked a bit sheepish as she carried on, "I didn't particularly want him knowing the details about exactly how ill he is. I think it was better to say he was poorly rather than tell him outright he was going to die."

Jo leaned back in her chair and pulled an apologetic face, "Aw, I am sorry. I didn't think there was any point in skirting around it," she shook her head, "we can't protect him from it forever and he was asking. You know what he's like."

Eve knew exactly what Oliver was like with his endless questions, "Yes," she sighed, "but it seems such a lot for a little boy to take in."

"He needs to know, Eve, it is his father after all." Jo's voice softened, "We're all going to have to deal with the grief sooner or later."

"I know, but we're hardly a conventional family, are we, with Chester doting on Oliver. Your dad's not played a huge part in his upbringing; he's more like an uncle figure to him. If the truth be known, Oliver's a bit scared of him to be honest."

A wave of sadness passed across Jo's face, "I know what Dad's like, you don't need to tell me. I've had twenty-eight years of his parenting style. Rick and I both have."

"Yes, but at least he was the right age to be a dad for you. When Oliver was born, he was fifty and I think a bit too old for it all." She tilted her head to one side, "Please don't think I'm being critical. We're all having to deal with this in our own way, it's just . . . I don't want to put too much on Oliver's young shoulders."

"Okay," Jo nodded, "point taken. I'll try and tread a bit more carefully."

Eve smiled kindly at her, "Thank you."

Since she'd come to Chanjori, Jo had been such a support and friend to her. She loved her and it would break her heart to fall out with her. Now she'd said her piece, she wanted to quickly change the subject, "Anyway, how's the new book coming on, is it almost finished?"

Jo grimaced, "I wish. My agent understands what's happening and is sympathetic," she raised her eyes towards the ceiling indicating Chester's bedroom, "well, she said she does, but the publisher has a deadline and as they keep reminding me," she gestured finger quotes, *"they are running a business."* Jo took a deep breath in, "They'd like me to finish the second part of the trilogy as soon as I'm able," her eyes filled up, "but right now . . ."

"Hey," Eve took hold of her hand, "you don't need to do anything right now but concentrate on your dad. There'll be plenty of time to write later. As soon as you're ready, you'll do it."

"You're right, I know," she pulled a tissue from her pocket, "thank you. I've been feeling guilty, but I know deep down, I shouldn't."

"No, you shouldn't. Your dad is the most important person at the moment; your writing will still be here . . ."

The roar of an engine and a blaze of colour flashed past the library window. The sound of screeching tyres ripping up the tarmac indicated someone had arrived.

"Who on earth is this?" Jo frowned and walked to the window which overlooked the front of the house, "someone in a rather nice car," she added craning her neck to see who got out.

Eve slowly eased herself out of the chair and into a standing position. She didn't need to look who was in the flash car. She knew exactly who it was.

He might have been away eleven long years, but today, the prodigal son had come home.

"It's Rick!" Jo squealed.

Eve's stomach plummeted as if she'd dropped from the top a rollercoaster. Rick had dominated her thoughts and invaded her dreams for as long as she could remember, and despite all the protests that he wouldn't come back, she'd always known deep down, he would. This was the moment she'd dreaded since Bruce had suggested bringing him home. Any minute now, she was going to come face to face with him again after all these years.

Her heart was racing. What would he be like?

Please God, not still gorgeous, let him have aged and be ordinary.

Jo's limp was as pronounced as ever as she moved towards the door and flung it open, which gave them both a view across the hall towards the front door.

Eve remained frozen to the spot. Her hands went clammy, and she could feel perspiration trickling down the back of her neck.

Gilly had obviously seen him approach the house and dashed towards the front door, but Rick beat her to it.

The door flung open and her nemesis stepped into the hall.

Breathe. Breathe.

"Rick!" Gilly flung her arms around him.

Eve watched him lift the housekeeper off the floor and spin her around the hall, "Stop it!" she squealed, "Put me down!" He spun her round a second time and eased her feet back to the ground and let her go. She tapped his arm playfully with the back of her hand.

"What are you like, Rick Forrest, that's all I need to aggravate my vertigo." Even though she was reprimanding him, she was smiling fondly. Clearly the old charm was still there. As a young man he'd been like a magnet attracting the females, but in those days he'd only wanted her.

Stop it, she chastised herself.

"Rick," Jo called from the doorway.

He quickly strode across the hall and threw his arms around his sister. They hugged, rocking from side to side in a playful way. Eve couldn't have looked away. She was so close to seeing him after all these years. Her heart rate accelerated to a level that must surely be dangerous.

Oh my God.

He pulled away from Jo and held her at arm's length, "Now then beautiful, how the hell are you?"

Jo titled her head and grinned, "Still not beautiful, but thank you anyway."

She leant forward and gave him another quick hug, "I'm so pleased you're here, Rick."

Damn. He wasn't ugly. Rick Forrest was as overtly masculine and hot as he'd always been. More so in fact.

Jo pulled away from him, "Come on in, Eve's here."

She stood still. Helpless. Motionless.

A shiver ran across her body as he turned his head to look at her. Their eyes locked and goose bumps erupted all over her skin. It was like an impact of a blow, but without any pain.

"Well, well, well, if it isn't Evie Henshaw. Ooops, sorry, I forgot, you go by Forrest now, don't you?" He widened his eyes mockingly, "By my reckoning that must make you my stepmother."

Years of discipline, and training herself to be the perfect wife kicked in, and she clenched her jaw in an effort to ignore his sarcasm. "Welcome home, Rick. Please, come in."

He didn't move. His eyes were fixed on her face.

If you're trying to make me uncomfortable, you're doing a pretty good job.

"Come and take a seat and I'll get you something to drink. Would you like some tea?"

He raised an eyebrow, "Tea? How very civilised. You've turned into quite the little housewife." He was smiling at her, but it wasn't a genuine smile. The falseness was for his sister's benefit.

"I'll pass on the tea, thank you, but I wouldn't mind something a little stronger as I seem to have a foul taste in my mouth." His eyes scanned the room, "It must be from coming back here."

"Don't be like that, Rick," Jo interjected, "come and sit down and I'll go and get us all a drink."

Eve watched him move towards the sofa. He was stunningly handsome with his chiselled jaw, strong nose and day-old stubble. Time had been good to him. Her chest tightened as she surreptitiously caught sight of his jeans, clung to his long thighs as if they'd been sprayed on, and his white shirt hiding his lean torso.

Had he always been so hot?

He remained standing behind the sofa and ran his hand across the back of it. His eyes swept around the room.

Eve was rooted to the spot, desperately trying to think of a plausible excuse to get away. It would look odd if she left without exchanging a few pleasantries. Only five minutes, though . . . she couldn't manage any more than that. Her nerves were in shreds already.

She gave him what she hoped was an empathetic smile. "It must be hard coming back after all this time, but I'm sure you must be relieved to be here."

"Relieved as opposed to what?" he frowned.

It didn't surprise her he was deliberately being difficult. She somehow suspected he would be.

Jo was already eyeing them both up carefully so she really didn't want to be having any sort of conversation with him in front of her.

"I meant because of your father being ill and you being . . . estranged from him."

"Oh, right, yeah, I see." He'd wanted to say more, she could tell that, but wouldn't be able to because of Jo being there. Thank God, she was.

"Eve, you sit down with Rick," Jo smiled, "and I'll go and shout Gilly to fetch some drinks. A whisky you said, Rick?"

"If you wouldn't mind. A large one with plenty of ice," he answered, but his eyes were still focussed on her. Her heart thudded with nervous tension which was ridiculous. He wasn't back for her.

She needed to get out . . . now.

"Coming up." Jo started to move.

"I'll get it," Eve said and attempted to move across the room. But Jo stopped her. "No, it's okay. I need to ring Niall and tell him I'm delayed. I'll only be a minute."

It was pointless arguing when Jo was closer to the door than she was.

"Don't alter your plans for me, Jo," Rick said, "I can entertain myself, or maybe," he raised an eyebrow at her, "Eve will look after me?" That was a challenge if ever there was one, but she wasn't rising to that particular bait.

"I'm afraid I can't. Peter . . . your father's lawyer is coming, so I need to be there." It was a lie, he wasn't coming until the afternoon, but she'd say anything to get away.

"Yes, I know who Peter is," he sneered, "he was my mother's lawyer too."

That was below the belt.

"What can I get you to drink, Eve?" Jo asked.

Was Jo aware of the tension between her and Rick? There was no way she was sitting with him on her own, even for a few minutes. She couldn't.

"Nothing thank you, I'm fine. I'll go up to sit with your father until Peter gets here."

"Okay, but keep Rick company until I come back, would you?" she asked, walking through the door. Jo had absolutely no idea about the extent of her intimate relationship with Rick as teenagers, only Chester did, so she couldn't refuse. It would look as if something was wrong and that's the last thing Eve wanted.

The door closed behind Jo. In all the dreams he'd haunted, not once did she ever picture seeing him again in the library at Chanjori.

And now they were alone together for the first time in eleven years.

Silence.

As he stared at her, he still had the ability to make her feel painfully female. Just a look from those dark brooding eyes made her feel hot all over, reminding her sex wasn't part of her life anymore. She'd been right to dread him coming.

He was still standing much closer to the door than she was, and her mind was trying to think of a way to get him out of the way so she could excuse herself. She needed to be on her own to catch her breath and gather herself.

"Please, Rick, sit down. You must be tired."

"Tired?" A smirk found his lips.

"After your journey."

His eyebrows pulled together, "You can cut the hostess crap, Eve, I really don't need it from you."

"How would you like me to be?" she snapped, before putting on a sweet voice, "I'm so pleased you're back, Rick, how have you been all these years?" She widened her eyes, "Is that what you'd prefer?"

The level of discomfort in her chest magnified as his eyes continued to survey her, "Maybe I'd prefer you to tell me how it feels to be married to a man old enough to be your father? Is that what you were after all along? Your father died so you wanted a replacement and thought you'd have mine."

Anger raged within her. "How dare you be so rude?"

"Rude?" he scoffed, "You'll see exactly how *rude* I can be when he's popped his clogs and you're out on your ear with his brat."

"That's enough. I don't have to stay here and listen to this." She made her way towards the door, expecting he'd let her pass. He didn't.

He leant against it, barring her way.

"Open the door," she told him firmly. "I want to get out."

"Don't you want to say hello properly?" he asked insolently.

She didn't reply. Her heart was pounding in her ears.

He exaggerated the movement of his head from side to side, "No? That is a disappointment. I seem to remember a time when you couldn't wait to say hello to me, Evie."

They were both breathing heavily now. She could remember that too and the ache in her pussy did also.

His face was inches from her, and she felt his breath on her own face. He smelled of mint. Her pulse seemed to catch and trip over itself as he leaned forward and brought his perfect mouth down on hers. It was a demanding assault. His lips were raw and angry, punishing and particularly memorable. She fought to pull her mouth free.

She slapped him hard across his face.

"You bastard!" she spat, as she stepped back from him. "Who the hell do you think you are?"

The silence between them was edgy. *He deserved that.*

He brought his fingers up to his face and rubbed the cheek she'd slapped. He'd probably had that done to him dozens of times. His eyes seemed to have turned almost black. There'd be repercussions. That scared her. Not just of him, she was scared of herself.

She wrenched the door open to make her escape just as Jo was approaching.

"Gilly's on her way with your drink, Rick," Jo smiled, "she's fetching tea for me, Eve, so she's bringing you a cup as well. I said you didn't want one, but you know what she's like."

Eve couldn't speak. She was too busy trying to control her racing heart.

Rick spoke for her, "Thank you sweetheart, but I think our *stepmother* is leaving now."

The pupils of his eyes appeared to have dilated, and his cheek had a pink blotch where she'd slapped him. "I'll look forward to carrying on where we left off later, Eve. Perhaps we can reminisce some more about the old days," he raised an eyebrow, "I'd like that."

He was insufferable. Arrogant. Insolent. All of those things and plenty more.

She hated him. How dare he kiss her?

She deliberately turned her head towards Jo, and forced a smile, "I'll have my tea with your father. That'll give you and Rick a chance to catch up."

"Okay." Jo turned to Rick, "You'll want to go up and see Dad though, won't you?"

"Later, there's no rush," he answered matter-of-factly, "shall we have that drink first."

With as much dignity as she could muster, Eve walked away. Was the intolerable, conceited bastard still watching her?

8

After catching up with Jo, Rick excused himself and made his way upstairs to his room. He'd had to brush off Jo's questions as best he could about how well he and Eve had known each other as teenagers. Jo had no idea about the extent of their previous relationship. Their father had seen Jo as the more intelligent of his two children and afforded her a private school place where she boarded during the week, whereas he'd attended a state school.

He shouldn't have been careless speaking sarcastically to Eve in front of Jo. On the occasions he met with his sister in London, they never discussed her or his father. Jo knew he was disgusted with them both so she only ever mentioned Eve in reference to the house, but he always ignored it. He hated the very mention of her.

He cursed himself. He earned his living disguising his emotions in front of a jury, and yet here he was, five minutes in the company of Eve, and he was behaving like a bloody adolescent. It was her fault though for slapping him. She'd been lucky Jo came back when she did, otherwise she'd have paid dearly for that. And judging by the way she'd responded when he first kissed her, she'd be up for it too. What a cow.

He placed his travel bag on the bed of the room he'd occupied as a child. His gaze flicked around the charming room that held fond memories of his late mother. Images flashed in his mind of her reading a bedtime story to him, and when he was poorly and had a raging temperature, she'd sat with him, wiping his face with a cool flannel, and had given him ice lollies to suck.

A voice interrupted his pleasant reminiscing. "It's been decorated twice since you left."

He turned to see Gilly in the doorway, "Mrs Forrest chose the colours. She has a great eye for detail, don't you think?"

Oh, yeah. A great eye for detail . . . particularly for the money.

"Yes, she certainly does. It's lovely, Gil. He walked over to the window and stared across the vast lawn which would have made Capability Brown proud. He recalled playing cowboys and Indians, and running in between the trees with his toy gun. His childhood memories thumped at his gut. He needed to be alone.

"I've got a few emails I need to catch up on before I go and see the old man. Jo's given me the code so I can log on to the system here."

"Right, I'll leave you to it then," she smiled affectionately, "it's good to have you back Rick, but I'm sorry it's circumstances such as this that's brought you."

"Mmm, I know what you mean, but that's life, isn't it? Most of us bury our parents," he admitted with a nod, "it's better that way round."

"Of course, and at least you're here," she hesitated, "you know . . . to make your piece for when the time comes. Your dear mother would have been so proud of you."

The wily old bird made her way to the door. Not much at Chanjori got past her.

"You're sure there's nothing I can get you?" She asked.

"I'm fine, Gil, what time's dinner?"

"Same time as always, seven thirty, but they generally have drinks around six thirty in the sitting room." A wave of sadness passed across her face, "It's only recently your dad has stopped coming down. He has a tray in his room but his appetite is deteriorating now."

Christ, the less said about him the better.

"You can be sure I'll be down for drinks before dinner then. The malt I had earlier was particularly nice."

"Then I'll make sure the decanter is topped up for you," she winked. She hovered, but he really wanted to be on his own.

He unzipped his holdall and flipped it open. "You're still here then Gil, after all these years? I thought you might have retired by now."

"I daresay that'll be forced upon me very soon."

He smiled back at her and recognised the look on her face, the one she wore when she wanted to ask a question but already knew the answer.

"How long do you think you'll be staying?" she asked before quickly adding, "I'm not being nosy, I only want to know for housekeeping reasons."

Yeah, right. Like it mattered in a house as big as Chanjori if there was an extra person. It wasn't as if his room was needed for anyone else.

"I don't know, I'll have to see." He lifted some shirts out of his bag, "No more than a day or two I wouldn't have thought."

She opened the door to leave, "Well, it's good to have you back Rick, it really is."

He smiled at her as she left the room. It certainly didn't feel good to be back.

He sat at the ornate yew desk which had replaced his childhood one, and removed his laptop from his bag. He switched it on and leant back in the comfortable chair while it powered up.

What the fuck had got into him coming onto Eve when he loathed the woman? What in God's name made him get so close to her? Married women weren't his bag at all.

Eve was stunningly beautiful. Why the hell couldn't she be frumpy and overweight, instead of looking as if she's ready for a magazine front cover shoot? The years had been kind to her, assisted ably no doubt by his father's money. Everything about her smacked of wealth. The styled blonde hair, the perfectly manicured nails, the designer dress, but it wasn't just that. Evie Henshaw had that special something that couldn't be bought, it wasn't from a bottle or had a label attached to it, it was innate. The woman had class.

His mind drifted back to the times he'd made love to her. She'd only been young, but even then, she had the ability to make him feel like a king. She'd been so receptive to him. He used to wonder if she faked it as she was more than a match for his youthful sexual appetite.

Even now, he never liked fucking a woman face down. That's what *they* did. Eve loved to feel him on her back with his breath on her neck biting and kissing. He was happy to oblige and fuck her anyway she wanted. He didn't care as long as it was her. No other woman had made him feel like she did. Evie Henshaw was still the most beautiful woman he'd ever met. He'd been with stacks of women over the years, yet five minutes in a room with her, and he wanted to fuck her senseless and knock that prim mistress-of-the-house look right out of her. Nothing would give him greater pleasure than pounding his dick into her until she screamed *his* name over and over again, just like she used to.

Fuck, he was hard now. He needed to stop thinking about that money-grabbing bitch or he'd have to resort to jerking off. He laughed to himself remembering how many times he'd done that in this very room during puberty.

He pulled his iPhone out of his pocket. He'd better send Louise a text to let her know he'd arrived before some sort of drama from her. He'd ring her later. He couldn't face it right now.

9

Rick tapped on his father's bedroom door. He wasn't nervous, that probably had been half the trouble. His father had wanted him to be frightened of him, but he never was. Despite all the beatings he'd taken from him as a child and teenager, scared wasn't an emotion he felt towards him. But loathing was.

"Come in," Eve answered. Shit, he hadn't expected her to still be in there. He was bracing himself for seeing her at dinner, not before.

He opened the door and the old bastard was facing him in a huge brass bed propped up on a stack of pillows and looking much older and thinner than he remembered him. Eve was sat beside the bed with a kid sat next to her, which he deduced must be theirs.

He closed the door behind him as the old man beckoned him to the bed.

"Here, Rick, have this seat," Eve stood up, we're just going."

There was a look of trepidation on her face but his eyes were drawn to the child staring at him. He smiled back at the kid rather than look directly at his father. It was easier to acknowledge him than the old man.

He looked like a miniature replica of her, almost too beautiful to be male. But he was as dark as his mother was fair. That'd be the Forrest gene, they were all dark.

"You must be Ollie. Jo's told me all about you, I'm Rick."

The kid gave him a big grin, "Mum likes me to be called Oliver. She doesn't like my name shortened."

"Seriously?" He couldn't keep the scorn out of his voice, "And what do you prefer to be called?"

He looked uncomfortable, as though he might get told off, "The boys at school call me Ollie."

The old man huffed, "You run along now Oliver. Your mum, Rick and I need to have a chat."

Eve ruffled the boy's hair, "Go and find Gilly, she'll get you a snack and I'll be there shortly."

The kid made his way towards the door, "Will you be staying for a while?" he asked.

"Oliver," Eve's tone was reprimanding. The poor kid mustn't have read the latest edition of social etiquette.

"It's okay," his eyes glanced at his father, "I'll be here for a while."

"Great," the pleasure was evident in his young voice. Poor little sod, probably there weren't many visitors to the house. He remembered the feeling of isolation well.

His childlike face lit up, "We're doing about Australia at school. Would it be okay to ask you some questions?"

"No problem, Ollie," he emphasised the abbreviation, "I'll be happy to help." He was rewarded with a beaming smile. The kid had a really cute face.

"I'll see you at dinner. About six-thirty?"

"Yeah." His childlike excitement caused a twist deep inside his gut. He'd been that kid once upon a time. He winked at him as he left the room. Fancy having the old man for a father. Christ Almighty.

Rick moved towards the seat the kid had vacated next to Eve. *Bloody hell, as if I haven't had enough of her for one day.*

The old man glared at him, "You came then?"

"Yep."

"I wasn't sure you would."

"Me neither," he shrugged, "but I thought I'd have one last look around my mother's house."

"Your mother's been dead fifteen years."

"It was still *her* house," he snapped.

"It's my house till I die and you better remember that."

"Oh, I remember alright. How could I ever forget?"

Eve interjected, "I really don't think there's anything to be gained here by baiting each other." She glared at him, not the old man.

"What would you like us to do, *stepmother dear*? Sit and have afternoon tea together as if the last eleven years haven't happened?"

"No, of course not, but we need to be civilised. And why are you being so insulting? I'm hardly your stepmother in the broadest sense," she scowled.

"Perhaps you'd better leave too, Eve," his father interrupted, "so I can talk to Rick on my own."

She stood up, "Fine. But please, both of you, no arguing." Again, she glared at him and not the old man, "I don't want your father getting stressed, he's in enough discomfort as it is."

"Just get the hell out of here," the old man barked, "I've told you, I'm sick to bloody death of you fussing around me."

Eve's face had hurt and embarrassment written all over it and Rick had to suppress an urge to tell her not to take any notice of the insensitive old sod. . . he'd always been a bastard. But surely she must be used to him by now, and their marriage was between the two of them, not him.

With a straight back, she made her way towards the door. She held her head in the same dignified way she'd always done and still moved gracefully. His lustful groin kicked, and even though he hated her, as the door closed behind her, he felt bereft and wished she'd stayed. Christ. He needed to get out of this fucking place, she was already playing with his mind and he vowed that wouldn't happen again. Ever.

He snarled at the old man, "You've not changed then. Couldn't you try to be a bit more respectful to your *latest wife*, at least around other people?"

"The way I speak to *my* wife is none of your business," his tired eyes flickered with dislike, "how long are you here for?"

He shrugged indifferently, he wasn't answerable to him.

"Why did you come?" the old man asked.

"Why did you send for me?"

"I didn't. Peter sent for you."

"I came to see for myself if you really are on your last legs."

"Well as you can see, I am. You'll have the house soon enough."

"Good." *And then I can get rid, and all the crappy memories that go with it.*

"So, why's Peter sent for me? He does nothing without your approval so you must have wanted me here for something. What is it? You want to say sorry before you pop your clogs?"

"Sorry for what?"

"Christ, you want a bloody list? How about beating me black and blue all the way through my childhood, for sending me away from my home to the other side of the world, for marrying the girl I was in love with . . . his voice was louder now, "do you want me to go on?"

"I sent you away for a reason and it's not done you any harm. You've done well, much better than if you'd stayed round here. I knew my brother and his wife would give you a better life."

"You gave me no fucking choice," he said, "bundling me away in the middle of the bloody night across to the other side of the world. You never even bothered to ask if it was what I wanted. No, that's not your fucking style, is it? The almighty Chester Forrest makes all the decisions. He knows what's best. He's always fucking right."

"Stop bleating. I haven't got time for this crap. I got you here to talk about your sister, Josephine."

"What about her?"

"I want to make sure you'll take care of her. She'll be a wealthy young woman and will need help. I can imagine every low life in the world will be coming onto her when I've gone."

"I can't take care of her. My life isn't here anymore which you made sure of. I can't see her wanting to come and live in London with me somehow, can you?"

The old man hesitated as if he hadn't thought of that. "No, but you don't have to live with her to oversee her trust fund."

"You think I'm going to do anything to help you?"

"I'm not asking you to do anything for me, she's your sister. At least look after her."

He would gladly take care of Jo's finances if she wanted him to, but he wasn't going to tell him that, even though he agreed entirely. Every scumbag in the world would be falling in love with her.

He remained motionless while his father got over a coughing fit.

There's one other thing," the old man continued, clearing his throat.

If he dares to mention looking after her.

"Eve's mother is being cared for in a residential home and I pay for that. She has advanced dementia."

"Christ, is that domineering old bat, still alive?"

"Yes, and the care home she lives in is a specialist centre which is supposed to help. Costs a bloody fortune each month with zero results as far as I can see."

"But you still pay?"

He nodded. "I've set up a fund which will continue to pay for her treatment until she dies."

"And what about *your wife*? What financial provision have you made for her?"

"There's plenty of money for her to buy somewhere for herself. You'll get the house, of course, which no doubt you'll be selling?"

"Who knows? I might want to raise a family here myself."

"You've found someone to take you on then?"

"Yeah," Rick sniped back, "and let's hope when I have kids I'll do a better job than you did."

"Let's hope you do." He watched the old man close his eyes and waited, wondering if he'd fallen asleep.

He opened them again, "If you keep the house, you could let Josephine stay. I don't like the thought of her being uprooted. This is her home."

"It was my home too, but you weren't bothered about uprooting me."

"That was different," he sighed, "you were going down the wrong path and you know you were. If you'd have stayed here, you'd have ended up in jail. I did you a favour, and whatever you think of me, you know deep down that's true. And as for *my wife*, you shouldn't have been with her in the first place."

"Why not? What fucking business was it of yours?"

"I was a friend of her parents and the last thing I wanted was you knocking her up."

"You aren't God you know, playing with people's lives."

"She was a bright young thing and destined for a career in music. Her mother didn't want her getting involved with anyone. She was too young."

"So you thought you'd get rid of me, then the coast was clear for you."

"I did what I thought was best at the time."

"Best for you more like. What was it? You got fed up with paid whores, or did you see me with her and fancied a bit for yourself?" The old man didn't respond so he carried on, "Nothing to say? You make me sick . . . the pair of you do. Why would she marry a bloke old enough to be her father? If my mother was here she'd vouch you're hardly husband-of-the-year material, so it had to be for money."

"Shut the fuck up about her. Tell me you'll take care of Josephine and get the hell out of here. The last thing I need on my death bed is a conversation with you."

10

Eve stared at her face in the bathroom mirror. The warmth of the bath had made her cheeks pink. Did she look older than her twenty nine years? How did Rick see her? She wrapped her robe around her naked body and tied it. A wave of pleasure rippled through her from the sensual feel of the silk against her skin.

What on earth had got into Rick in the library earlier? She'd not seen him for almost eleven years, and within minutes of coming face to face with him, he was kissing her. She was livid, but fury nudged something deep within her she hadn't felt for years . . . it made her feel alive.

She selected her face products and began her skin care routine wondering how Rick and Chester had been after she'd left them together. Her husband might be ill, but testosterone had certainly kicked in when Rick came into the room. Jo said they'd always fought, from as far back as she could remember. Even as child, Rick couldn't do anything to please their dad, and because of that, he'd become a bit of a mummy's boy. Not in an effeminate way though. Apparently, their mother doted on him to compensate for Chester being horrible, and in return he worshipped her. Jo said he never came to terms with her death, and Eve remembered asking him several times about his mother when they were together as teenagers, but he always managed to evade any questions about her.

There was no doubt part of her died when she came to Chanjori House. She'd certainly become a different Eve over the years. Being a wife, a mother, and having the responsibility of her own mother's failing health had propelled her into maturity. But the problem right now causing acute muscle tension in her neck was Rick knew the old Eve. He knew Evie Henshaw, the happy young girl who'd heartily laughed when something amused her, who wore her hair loose rather than tied up all the time, and who used to sing at every opportunity she could. Mature Eve never sang anymore, unless it was quietly to her mother, and her hair was nearly always fixed securely. When was the last time she'd worn it down? She couldn't remember.

Did she laugh anymore? Very rarely. Even before Chester's diagnosis, laughter wasn't an emotion that came naturally to her. No, Eve Forrest was deliberately measured, and if she was honest with herself, a little bit dull. It had taken Rick coming home to make her realise how much she'd missed Evie Henshaw.

She moved from the ensuite into her bedroom and sat at her dressing table to apply her make-up. Her head was beginning to ache so she massaged her tense neck muscles hoping to relieve the pressure.

Her short-sleeved dress was laid out on her bed alongside a set of luxurious satin blue underwear she'd bought but never previously worn. There wasn't much need for sensual at Chanjori, not for her anyway, but she did like to buy quality underwear and loved the feel of it against her skin. It gave her pleasure knowing she looked as good underneath her fine designer clothes, as she did with them on. Somehow this evening, she was drawn towards the silky vibrant bra and panties. Was it him?

Of course not.

Without warning, the bedroom door opened, and she reeled backwards on the stool as Rick entered her room. From the look on his face, he was equally surprised to see her.

"What the hell are you doing?" she screeched, jumping to her feet.

The swing door closed behind him.

"I was coming to look at *my mother's* room."

"This is my room."

"I didn't know that. Don't you share a room with him?" he scowled.

"No. Not since he's been unwell," she added quickly.

He raised an eyebrow, "Ah, I see . . . so Evie Henshaw sleeps alone? Doesn't that get a little cold for a woman with your sexual appetite?" His eyes moved towards her bed, and hers followed his as he perused her underwear.

"Very nice," he drawled, his chocolate-brown eyes looking directly at her.

She was mesmerised by his dilated pupils, almost drowning in them. An image of her underwear in his hands caused a sudden ache to appear everywhere and nowhere all at once. She pressed her thighs together. Something strange was going on in her chest.

"You need to leave." He stood rooted to the spot. She raised her voice, "Now."

"Why? What are you scared of? That I might show you just what it's like to fuck someone nearer your own age rather than a wizened old man."

"I won't tell you again," she threw some venom into her voice, "get out."

"And what are you going to do if I don't . . . scream the place down? How do you think that will look, eh? Anybody hearing you will think you're in the throes of ecstasy."

"Stop it now, Rick. You're being totally inappropriate."

"Am I really?" His eyes darkened, "That's rich coming from you, married to a man old enough to be your bloody father. Just how appropriate is that?"

"You know exactly what I mean, and my marriage to your father is none of your business. It has nothing to do with you."

"Too right it doesn't," he snarled, "but we do have a past, however much you try and forget it. You were mad for me once. Can't you remember screaming my name over and over again when I fucked you? Doesn't Evie Henshaw want reminding of what a little vixen she was back then, is that it?"

"I'll tell you one more time, leave my room now, or I'll . . ."

"You'll what?" He spat. "Stop being so bloody high and mighty. You might call the shots round here now, but when he's gone, remember you won't own this house, I will. So don't start lording it over me."

She took a few paces towards him, intending to open the door.

It was déjàvu. He'd blocked her way in exactly the same way this morning in the library and look what happened then.

"You're a bastard. Do you know that? A complete bastard."

Fury registered on his face. His colour deepened, but she didn't care. She hated him, and her fingers itched to slap his arrogant face again.

He knew.

"Don't dare even think about it," he warned, "or you *will* be sorry."

"Get out!" she spat, with more conviction than she felt.

With no warning, he grabbed her and pushed her against the door.

"What the hell do you think you're doing?"

His fingers grabbed the nape of her neck and he yanked her head back, almost violently, bringing her throat to him, making her senses reel at his closeness and his breath on her face. "I'm doing exactly what you want me to."

Velvety lips crushed hers. She fought him, and fought herself harder, but there was no escaping him. He was too strong for her and she was lost in the feelings his punishing mouth was generating. Her heart was beating like a wild thing, and heat seeped through her veins as the onslaught continued and she greedily devoured him back. His tongue slid against her lips, and then dipped inside, tasting, filling, possessing.

He was kissing her like a man possessed.

Her robe tie came lose, and his hand found her breast. The lip onslaught continued, he licked and sucked and bit with abandon causing her nipple to pebble under his skilled hand.

His swelling erection nudged her tummy. "God, I want you," he groaned, "here, right now."

The movement of the door handle turning interrupted them, "Mum . . . I can't get in . . . the door won't open."

She pulled away and wiped her mouth with the back of her hand as if that somehow erased what had just happened. Rick moved slightly to the side, away from the door as she hastily tied her gown and eased it ajar. "It must have been stuck, darling, I'll have to get it looked at. Are you okay?"

"Jo sent me to look for you. I can't find Rick either. I've knocked on his door, but there's no answer."

"He's probably out for a walk. I'm sure he'll be back shortly. I'll just get myself ready and come down. Go and tell Jo I'll be there in five minutes."

"Okay."

She watched her son walk across the landing, and when he turned to go down the stairs, she closed the door.

"Don't you dare set foot in here again," she spat through clenched teeth, "God knows how it would have looked if he'd seen you in here?"

"I'm quite sure at his age he doesn't fully understand the ramifications of me being in your room and us about to have sex," he shrugged.

"Don't flatter yourself," she said, "as if I'd have sex with you when I'm married to your father." Judging by his expression, that reminder stung his male pride, "And I'm warning you. Keep away from me, and keep your hands to yourself, otherwise . . ."

"Otherwise what? You'll tell the old man, will you? Tell him how you're like putty in my hands. Another minute and you'd have been begging for it."

"Get out now, Rick. You disgust me. The sooner you leave this house, the better."

He gave a supercilious grin with mocking triumph at her outraged expression as he opened the door.

"See you at dinner then, Stepmother dear."

11

Rick had the phone on loud speaker while he quickly changed for dinner. He needed to get a move on and end the conversation with Louise, "I can't say how long. I'll know more tomorrow."

"Surely you have an idea," the frustration in her voice was evident, "a few more days, a week? You said it was only going to be a flying visit and then you'd be back."

"I know I did, but things change."

"What's changed? We have the Steadman's party on the twentieth, and the opening of Orion's. You'll be back for those, won't you?"

"I don't know, Lu," he wasn't answerable to her, not yet anyway. "Look, I'm going to have to go for dinner now. It's not the done thing to be late, so I'll speak to you tomorrow."

He knew her; she wouldn't be brushed off. "How is your father? Is it . . . you know, imminent?"

"I'm not sure it's imminent, but he's very ill."

"But you don't like him, Rick. I don't understand why you need to be there."

"I just do. Can't you bear with me?"

She exhaled heavily, "It looks like I'll have to." He could tell by her voice she was pissed with him, "But please think about coming home soon. It's lonely without you," her voice softened, "I miss you."

"I miss you too, but it's not for long. I'll be back soon, I promise."

"Okay," she sighed, "I love you."

"Love you too. Speak tomorrow." He ended the call before she had chance to say anymore.

Did he love her? He thought he did. Before returning today he did. His future was planned and he was finally settling down with a woman that would make him happy. So why was he suddenly irritated by her whining on the phone?

Only a day back at his childhood home and everything in his calm and ordered life seemed all of a sudden not to be quite so ordered. What would happen if he did decide he wanted to live in Chanjori and breathe some life back into the place? Louise wouldn't want to live here; her life was very much ensconced in the capital. Maybe they could use it as a weekend retreat, and for holidays? He tried to picture him and Louise living here after they were married but the image was elusive. She'd hate it, he knew she would.

Did Eve like the house? Once upon a time, he'd have known just by looking at her exactly what she was thinking, but if today had been anything to go by, she was much more guarded now.

Why in the space of a few hours, had he come onto her, not once, but twice? Bloody hell, he was like a buck rabbit. He really needed to control himself around her, but that was easier said than done. She still had the ability to make him feel so fucking horny every time he was within a few metres of her.

He made his way downstairs to the sitting room remembering his father's tradition of drinks before dinner.

This place is so archaic.

He was itching to see Eve again even though he disliked her. Christ knows what would have happened earlier in her bedroom if Ollie hadn't disturbed them. He knew she would be festering about it, and most likely putting on an 'everything is normal show' in front of Jo and her son.

He opened the sitting room door and Ollie rushed up to him. "I've got my stuff," he greeted excitedly, "so you can tell me about Australia."

Jo laughed, "Let him sit down first Oliver, you've got all night to quiz him."

A memory kicked in of a time way back when *he* was once a young child in this huge house. Any visitor was exciting.

Eve was sitting by the fireplace wearing the stunning blue dress that had been laid out on the bed earlier. The vibrant colour seemed to enhance the blue of her eyes. But it wasn't just her eyes that were so appealing; her legs which always had the power to turn him on were coiled around the sofa displaying her racehorse ankles. The dress was a respectful length so she wasn't flaunting them, it was the very fact he knew what they felt like wrapped around his neck. His dick twitched, particularly as he knew the navy silky underwear she had on underneath the dress.

Dinner was going to be a nightmare lusting after her all evening.

Get a grip. You're engaged to be married.

Always the hostess, Eve smiled politely at him, "What would you like to drink, Rick? Gilly's just getting ours."

"Scotch please," he smiled at Gilly.

"Coming right up," she replied, "Mrs Abbot has made lasagne for dinner. I told her it was your favourite with garlic bread."

Maybe it was his favourite fifteen years ago, but these days his preference was for sophisticated culinary delights, more often than not in Michelin-starred restaurants. "That'll be great, Gil, I'll enjoy that."

Gilly headed towards the bar area in the corner of the room looking pleased with herself. The wise old owl must be pushing sixty but looked exactly the same now as she'd always done, and obviously had a memory like an elephant remembering a meal he liked. He'd forgotten that completely.

Ollie had a *can we look now* impatient expression written all over his face.

"Right then Ollie, show me what you got."

He spent the next forty minutes looking at Ollie's Australian project and adding things of interest. The kid had done well but his work needed more detail to enhance its appeal and improve the grade. No sense in settling for a C or B when he could get an A.

It was an effort for him to keep his mind focused on Ollie's endless questions when Eve was sitting nearby. His antenna was fixed on her soft voice as she discussed his father with Jo.

Why does she have to be so bloody sexy?

His abdomen clenched as he reminded himself who she was married to. He concentrated on Ollie, explaining to him about the Harbour Bridge in Sydney and how the Australians ran out of steel and had more shipped from Middlesbrough.

Ollie appeared to have a genuine thirst for knowledge, and listened attentively as he explained about the Opera House designed by Jorn Utzon, who found his inspiration from looking at discarded orange peel on his plate, which gave him an idea for the roof of the iconic building. He discussed facts and figures about the construction of the building and encouraged Ollie to tap them into his iPad to substantiate their accuracy, even though he knew everything he told him was correct.

Ollie eagerly asked, "Have you been to the Opera House?"

"Yes I have, a few times."

"Cor. What about the bridge, have you seen that?"

"Yep," he smiled enjoying Ollie's youthful enthusiasm, "you can't see one without the other really. I've walked across it too."

"That's amazeballs," Oliver exclaimed, "I'd love to do that."

"You will when you're older. It's a must see for any adult."

Oliver turned to his mother, "Why haven't you ever been to the Opera House, Mum?"

Rick saw her tense up. Even though he'd been back less than twenty-four hours, he knew his presence unsettled her, however, it was apparent she'd become quite an accomplished actress. The composed smile she gave her son disguised her discomfort, "It would be hard to travel such a long way in case Grandma gets poorly."

Lord knows why he felt sorry for her, but he did. "Your Mum's right. It's quite a distance to fly, so when you do go, you need plenty of time to explore it all."

"Did you live in Sydney?" Ollie asked.

"No, I lived in Manley which is across the harbour. I travelled there each day on the ferry for university though."

"What's at Manley?"

"The most fantastic beaches with warm turquoise water; you can swim every day of the year if you want to."

"Did you used to go swimming?"

"Definitely. I love swimming."

"I do too. I've got through to the semi-finals of the school swimming competition. The county selectors are going to be there for the next race."

He patted him on his shoulder, "Good for you, mate. I used to swim for the county when I was your age."

"Did you? I hope I get picked," his face came alive at the mention of swimming. It was obvious he loved it. "I want to swim in the Olympics too."

Gilly announced dinner was ready. Ollie gathered his papers together and closed his project folder. Rick noticed a wave of disappointment pass across his face at the interruption. It thumped at his gut.

"We can do some more tomorrow if you want to? I'll have a look on my laptop for some photos we could print off. Real photos are much more vibrant than the internet; anybody can get those, whereas yours will be unique."

"Can we? That'd be great," Ollie answered enthusiastically, and turned to his mother, "Mum, Rick's going to print me some real photos of Australia for my project."

She smiled, one of those fake ones that didn't quite reach her eyes, "That's nice, darling."

They stood to make their way to the dining room. Rick gestured with his hand for Eve and Jo to go in front of him. His eyes drifted down towards Eve's feet in open-toe wedge shoes. Peeping out were cute painted pink toe nails.

Even her bloody toes are a turn on.

"Can I sit next to you, Rick?" Ollie asked, smiling as if he hero-worshipped him.

"Course you can, mate. Long as you don't pinch all the garlic bread," he winked.

Dinner was the usual gourmet affair at Chanjori. His mother had always insisted on a formal meal in the evening and the old man had obviously carried on the tradition.

They'd all interacted politely around the table and Eve put on quite a performance with her appropriate dinner talk questions about London, encouraging Ollie to join in the discussion with some of the tourist sights they'd seen on a visit.

Jo smiled at him, "I bet it's all flooding back, Rick, isn't it? Those awful dinners we had to sit through around this very table?" She turned to Ollie, "You're lucky, Oliver, your mum lets you off some nights and you can have your meal in the kitchen, whereas Rick and I were never let off. Come rain or shine, we had to sit here each night and eat meat, vegetables, and all the courses. I got a break in the week when I was away at school, but poor Rick never did." She turned to him, "Can you remember Rick how we used to protest to Mum, *do we have to have gravy dinners.*"

"God, yeah," he said, "those wretched vegetables night after night, when all we really wanted was sausage and chips. Friday was good though, when we used to take it in turns to choose. Sounds like I chose lasagne."

"Didn't you ever have burgers?" Ollie asked.

He grinned at the kid, "Yes, we had those, just not in this house. As soon as I was old enough, on a Saturday, I used to get the bus or cadge a lift to town and go to the Wimpy and stuff myself with burgers and fries with loads of ketchup."

Jo laughed, "The Wimpy. I'd forgotten all about that. Not that I went much, I was too busy studying." She turned to Eve, "Did you hang out at the Wimpy?"

Rick knew the answer to that before Eve spoke. She'd never have been allowed anywhere as downmarket as a burger bar. Eve's mother would never let her mix with the low life that she would insist congregated there. Eve had been safely tucked away in that all-girls grammar school where there was little chance of meeting boys, and any spare time was spent in solitary with her music.

"No," she answered, and her sad face somehow hit him in the gut. "It was very rare for me to be allowed to go to town, I'm afraid. My parents were very strict and wanted me to concentrate on my music."

Christ, they needed to lighten things up. Despite Eve putting on a show worthy of an award with her jolly hostess demeanour, he knew she was tense and rigid after their altercation in the bedroom.

He felt sorry for Ollie too. He was a likeable kid but it was hardly a fun house with the old man dying upstairs. He was at the age where he wasn't old enough to go out with friends, so must have spent pretty much all of his time cooped up with his mother and Jo. From what he'd already seen, Eve was overprotective to the point of stifling the boy.

He remembered the Friday nights after dinner when he, Jo and his mum used to play board games. They took it in turns to choose each week, and it became a ritual. On the occasions his father had dinner with them, he never joined in. No, playing board games with his kids certainly wasn't Chester Forrest's style.

Had old age mellowed him? Did he ever play board games with Ollie before he became ill?

Rick put his dessert spoon down. "What normally happens after dinner then, Ollie? What do you do for fun?"

"I sometimes watch television, or play on my Play Station," then he quickly added, "If I've finished my homework."

Rick glanced at his watch, "It's still early. Do you fancy playing a board game?"

Ollie's eyes lit up.

Eve's expression slipped into not-on-a-school-night mode. "It's a bit late for a board game, Rick. Usually Oliver does his own thing for an hour or so and then it's about time for bed." She must have seen something disparaging in his face as she added, "He might have a book or something to look at for homework."

Eve, have you heard yourself. How old are you?

"He's done some homework tonight on Australia," he glanced at Ollie, "haven't you, mate?"

"Yeah, Mum. I haven't got anything to look at, honestly."

"I still think it's best to have some quiet time before bed."

"Quiet time?" Rick couldn't keep the scorn out of his voice, "I think your mum's been reading too much Pride and Prejudice, Ollie. Who needs quiet time when we've got a game to win? Go and find us one, and you and me can thrash the women."

The kid didn't even look at his mother as he made a quick exit out of the room. Eve's face said everything, *here we go again.*

"I really wish you hadn't done that," she said through gritted teeth. "Oliver has a routine on school nights that I don't particularly want to be broken."

"Oh, come on Eve, for Christ's sake, loosen up a bit. It's a board game, not a night out on the town. Can you imagine what that kid's life is like locked away in Chanjori Towers? He needs a bit of fun, especially with what's going on with the old man."

She didn't look convinced.

He turned to his sister, "You want to play with your brother, don't you?"

"Hey, leave me out of this," Jo said, shaking her head.

"Come on, you two," he sighed, "let's live a bit. I promise we'll finish at ten, how about that?"

"Whatever game we play, he'll win, Eve," Jo sniggered, "I've never beaten him at a board game yet. We used to play them all the time with Mum. He swears he doesn't cheat, but it's funny how he always wins."

Oliver returned with a beaming smile on his face clutching three boxes. "Monopoly, Scrabble or Trivial Pursuit?"

Eve was still looking like she was chewing on a wasp. She cleared her throat, "I think I'll go and sit with your father, Oliver, and leave you to *play a game* with Rick."

As if I'm letting you get away.

Rick exaggerated the movement of his head from side to side. "Not yet, Mum. It's you and Jo against the mighty Forrest men. We need four of us," he winked at Ollie, "don't we, mate?"

"Yeah," Oliver answered excitedly, "Stop and play, Mum."

"Alright," she sighed heavily, "just this once."

Oliver's face was a picture. "Which game shall we play?"

Eve perked up, "How about Scrabble, that's educational."

"Nah," Rick dismissed, "who wants educational. I'm in the mood to win lots of cash, how about Monopoly?" He turned to Jo, "Do you fancy being banker, sis?"

"Good idea," Jo raised an eyebrow, "then I can make sure you don't cheat."

He winked at her. Hopefully a board game would keep his lustful thoughts about Eve in check. . . safety in numbers and all that.

Ollie's face was a picture as he began so sort through the box and placed the counters on the table. "You pick first, Mum. What do you want to be?"

She smiled warmly at her son, "Erm . . . I think I'll be the thimble." As she took the tiny icon from him, she gave him one of those, *if looks could kill* stares.

Rick reached for the top-hat counter and raised his eyes to Eve and Jo, "Right then, ladies . . . game on!"

Jo rolled her eyes but Eve actually smiled at him.

His dick reminded him of plenty of other games he'd rather play with her, and none of them involved a dice and two other people.

12

Eve couldn't believe what she was seeing. It was stupid hiding behind a tree in her own garden, but the sight in front of her was one she didn't want to disturb. Jo was in an embrace with Niall the chauffeur. What a shock.

She'd walked down to the garages for a bit of exercise and to see Niall who could usually be found there in the daytime. Her intention was to cancel one of her appointments he was taking her to.

Eve stared at them wrapped up in each other, oblivious to anything other than the two of them. As long as she'd been at Chanjori, she'd never even seen a hint of Jo with a man. It wasn't just her disability, she'd been badly hurt by a boy she'd been in love with and vowed she'd never get involved with anyone again. Seemingly, they were planning a future together after university and then according to Jo, he just disappeared. His parents informed her that he'd left the area and didn't want to be contacted.

She watched as Jo pulled away from Niall. They were both breathing heavily.

"I've got to go," she whispered with a look in her eyes that said she really didn't want to.

"I know." He brushed some hair off her face, "but when? We can't carry on like this. I want you, Jo, I want more than this."

"I want you too, but it's too quick."

"Why's it too quick? I seem to have been lurking around waiting for you for ages, and when I do get to see you, it's just a few stolen moments. We're both single, why can't we take things further?"

"I can't believe you want me," she shook her head, "nobody ever has. Why . . . why would you? You can have anyone you want. A normal woman . . ."

"You are normal, for God's sake. And I do want you," he pulled her towards him and kissed her passionately. "Come to the cottage tonight," he breathed, "please."

Jo pulled a face, "I'd have to make an excuse for missing dinner."

"Well do that. Just come."

It took her only a second to agree. "Okay, but I really have got to go now."

They kissed again, and then Eve quickly made her way through the trees back to the house.

Eve always felt Jo had gone into writing as it was solitary and she didn't need to mix with people as you would in a normal working environment. The most she ever saw her do was visit her agent and publisher in London. Apart from that, she was ensconced at Chanjori. Chester had told her that before they'd married, she used to accompany him on occasions to social functions, and was very able to hold her own socially, but had always had a preference to be on her own. The reason was evident to all that knew Jo why she lived the way she did. She had a massive hang-up about her disability. It was true she did have a prominent limp, which dozens of operations had failed to improve significantly, and while she wasn't the most beautiful girl, she had a lovely temperament and was so kind and caring.

Eve thought back to Jo's explanation about her boyfriend she'd been in love with when she was eighteen. In the eleven years since Eve had been at Chanjori, Jo had vowed not to get involved with anyone, and as far as she knew, she hadn't. Until today.

She smiled to herself. Jo and Niall had looked happy together, and by the sound of things, he wanted things to develop between them. How lovely for Jo.

Now she understood the slight changes she'd seen in her, the make-up and the curling wand she'd bought and started to curl the ends of her hair. That wasn't like her at all. Now Eve knew why, and it looked like tonight was going to be the night. She felt her pussy twitch at the thought of them making love. It had been such a long time since she'd done that.

Eve entered the house by the back door and discreetly went to her room. It was unusual for her to masturbate during the day, she saved that for night time when she was alone in bed, but right now, she needed to satisfy the overwhelming urge she had. She reached for a throw from the armchair and covered herself with it as she lay on the bed.

She moistened her fingers with saliva and slipped them inside her panties. Her clit throbbed and she gently began to massage it in circles. It felt so good. She pushed a finger inside herself and her pussy clenched around it.

An image of Rick making love to her caused her nipples to pucker. She added another finger pushing them both in and out, enjoying the tingling sensation that was building. With her spare hand, she reached for her nipple and squeezed it, adding to the pleasure her fingers were creating.

She was building towards her release, circling her throbbing clit with more pressure, and the tension was increasing inside of her. It was Rick's fingers tweaking her nipple, and then replaced by his mouth, sucking and biting, first one breast, then the other. It was *his* fingers inside her, *his* thumb rubbing her clit so hard.

Pleasure spiralled towards her pussy. She rubbed frantically. And then she was there, her fingers delivering a shuddering climax that rippled through her.

Eve languished in the contentment the orgasm had given her, and her eyes remained closed. Two minutes back in her life, and here she was fantasising about Rick Forrest as if he'd never been away.

Her thoughts drifted back to the night eleven years ago that changed the course of her life. The night she'd been totally desolate. Her mother's mind had deteriorated to the point that she couldn't be left alone and the authorities had placed her in a care home for respite and to carry out yet more assessments. Eve didn't know how she was going to manage when the week was over and she would be discharged. Their home was eventually going to be repossessed as she had no way of paying the outstanding debts attached to it, and she couldn't work and leave her mother on her own. Her father had died leaving massive debts. He'd been in business and instead of accepting it wasn't making a profit, he'd soldiered on borrowing money on the strength of things improving, but sadly he'd died suddenly before they did. No doubt the stress of it all had brought on his heart attack.

She'd no idea where she was going to live. She hadn't any money at all, and everyday life was becoming increasingly more difficult. The only joy in her young life was Rick, but for some reason he wasn't answering her calls that particular day.

She tried to call him again and left a pleading message, 'Please ring me, Rick, I need to speak to you'.

Over and over again, she searched for options that weren't there. She was running out of ideas, and even though she wasn't at all religious, she prayed for the first time since being at school. It was more talking out loud and begging for help really, until tiredness overcame her and she'd fallen asleep exhausted by the fear of the unknown.

A knock on the door woke her early evening. It must be Rick. She looked out of her bedroom window to check and was surprised to see Rick's father, Chester Forrest at the doorstep.

Please God, let Rick be alright.

She leapt down the stairs and hurriedly opened the door. Anxiety must have been written all over her face.

"Hello Eve. I hope I'm not disturbing you?"

"Is Rick alright?"

"Yes, he's fine. I'm sorry if I startled you calling round like this. I've just come from seeing your mother."

Oh, God, let her be okay. Surely the home would have contacted her if something was wrong?

"Your mother's fine," he quickly reassured, "would it be possible to have a word with you about her?"

He was a friend of her mother's going back since their school days so she had no worries about inviting him in. She was just puzzled as to why he was there.

"Please, sit down," she'd instructed Chester as they entered the lounge. "Can I get you something to drink?"

"No, thank you, I'm fine. Please, would you sit with me? I need to talk to you."

She took the chair opposite him. *What would he have to talk to her about?*

"As I said, I've just come from visiting your mother."

It was nice of him to take the time to visit her mum. That was genuine friendship.

"Thank you for calling to see her, did she recognise you?"

"She seemed to initially, but then started to confuse me with your father," a wave of sadness passed across his face, "it's terrible to see."

He had no idea. One visit. Imagine living with it every day of your life.

"Forgive me for being so direct," he said, "but I'm hoping I can help. The nurse was telling me she was coming home next week. Are you able to take care of her here?"

It was a relief to be able to speak to someone about the situation she'd agonised over for so long, even though it wasn't really any of his business.

"No, not really. I'll need to get a job, but that's easier said than done as I can't leave her on her own."

"She can't stay in the care home?"

"The assessments indicate that currently she can still live independently with support, but I haven't the finances for that. The authorities are currently looking at it all, but it's all taking time. . ."

"I can imagine it must be difficult. As far as I'm aware, these care home fees are a lot of money."

"They are," she agreed, "and I can't pay even for a short while," she gazed around the room of her parents' home, and tears threatened, "there's no money left, I'm afraid. Maybe if I could get a loan," . . . the penny suddenly dropped. He was rich, and he might be able to help? He was a friend of her mother's after all. She'd pay him back, of course, with interest as soon as something was sorted.

Dare she ask? She hardly knew him.

He nodded sympathetically as if he understood. "I saw your mother a while ago and she was pleased to see me, but today, I saw a real deterioration in her."

Eve breathed out. It was true, she had deteriorated rather quickly. The only good thing about that was, she didn't fully understand that her husband had died, or maybe she did and that had exacerbated her dementia?

"She slipped in the bathroom two days ago and I think it's really shaken her. She should have waited for the nurses but she tries to do things for herself."

It had upset Eve when the home rang to say she'd fallen. Weren't they supposed to be looking after her?

"Oh dear," he said with concern. "I'm wondering if you've heard of Springfield Lodge?"

Yes, she'd heard of it. It was a specialist centre for Alzheimer's patients. A sort of home from home, based on a Swedish model she'd read about. Seemingly there were shops inside the building, a library and hairdressers. It was meant to enable the residents' a degree of independence, even though they were confined. They could visit the shops and hairdressers and mix with others under the watchful eye of the staff. There were group activities also, and visits from drama and community groups to try and keep the residents' minds as active as possible.

Where was this going? She certainly couldn't afford Springfield Lodge.

He cleared his throat, "I'd like to help if you'll allow me?"

"How?" she frowned.

"I could pay for your mother's care, if you'll permit that. She could be moved to Springfield Lodge."

Now she was completely puzzled, "Why would you do that?"

"I have my reasons, and you can be assured I have your mother's best interests at heart."

"I can't take money from you; she could be in there indefinitely."

"You could. I have the money to continue to pay for as long as she needs it. I make substantial contributions to charity each year anyway, so I'd rather know some of my money was going to someone that really needs it."

"What would your family think? I'm sure they wouldn't be happy about you giving money to someone outside the family indefinitely."

"What I do with my money is my business, and I'd really like to help, if you'll allow me to, that is."

"No," she shook her head emphatically, "of course I won't. I know you're rich and everything, and you and my mum go back a long way, but why would you help me? Rick's told me you've found out about us and don't approve."

"You're right, I don't approve, but that's irrelevant now as Rick's gone away."

Her antenna flared up, "Gone away . . . what do you mean gone away?"

"Exactly that," he answered, "he's gone. So, you'll not be seeing him again."

"But . . . he can't . . . he can't have gone away. I need to see him." She reached for her phone from the coffee table and pressed his number. Rick said his father was a brute and would stop at nothing to get his own way. Was this some sort of move to split them up?

The familiar sound of Rick's ringtone started softly and then gained momentum. It seemed to be coming from the pocket of his father sitting in front of her.

"Why have you got his phone?" she glared accusingly.

"Because he doesn't need it anymore."

This is ridiculous. Why would he let his father have his phone? He hates his dad.

"I have to see him . . . please. It's important. Let me speak to him."

"He's gone, Eve, and he won't be coming back," he told her firmly.

How dare he come here telling her she wouldn't be seeing Rick again? They loved each other and Rick wouldn't just abandon her . . . he wouldn't do that.

She stood up, hoping he'd get the message she wanted rid of him. "Rick loves me, so wherever you've sent him, I know he'll be back. He wouldn't allow you to split us up." She wanted to hurt him for sending Rick away. "He doesn't even like you, so you can be sure he'll hate you after this."

"My dear girl, I've long since stopped worrying about what my son thinks about me. Now I suggest you sit back down, and we look at options to help you and your mother."

Yes, that was the priority. She'd ask him for a loan. Rick would be in touch later, she was sure of it.

"Would you be willing to lend me some money," she asked sitting down again, "to tide me over until the authorities sort out the finances? Once Mum's in a care home permanently, I could get a job and pay you back . . . with interest of course."

"No," he shook his head, "I've already told you what I'm proposing."

"What, that you're willing to pay my mother's care home fees and want nothing in return?"

"I don't believe I said that exactly," he blinked.

"Ah, so you do want something. What? I haven't got anything you could possibly want."

"I want you to consider carefully what I'm about to say. You don't need to make a decision now, you can think about it."

She was so weary. What could he possibly come up with that might help?

"I want you to think about marrying me and living at Chanjori House as my wife."

"Wife!" she shrieked, "are you out of your mind?" She tossed her head dismissively, "I'm not going to be your wife . . . what a stupid thing to say."

"I'm not out of my mind," he replied calmly, "I'm a practical man. I can pay for your mother's care, and provide a home for you. But for that to happen, you'll need to become my wife."

"What? Marry you? You're mad. Why would I marry you?" she asked disparagingly, "if I marry anyone, it'll be Rick not you."

"You won't be marrying Rick. He's gone, and as I've already said, he won't be coming back."

"Yes, he will. We love each other. He'll be back when he finds out what you're suggesting. It's . . . it's disgusting."

"I'm not going to repeat this again, but for the final time, Rick has gone away and won't be coming back. Now, I'll give you until tomorrow to think about my proposal. You can become my wife and enjoy all the privileges that come with that. You'll have a home, and your mother will be taken care of."

She looked at him closely. He must be over fifty. Did he want her for sex like one of those Thai brides? That must be it. Why else would he even be suggesting anything so outrageous? The thought of having sex with him made her stomach turn.

"And what's in it for you? You're . . . my father's age."

If he understood what she was getting at, he skirted over it. Or maybe he chose deliberately to ignore it.

"I will of course expect you to manage the smooth running of my home, and attend any functions with me as my wife, as well as supporting me with my business interests. I would hope you'll become a friend to my daughter Josephine. She gets lonely in the house all day on her own and could do with some female company."

She didn't answer so he carried on. "However, there is one caveat you need to think about. This marriage will be permanent. I'll not tolerate any affairs or scandals. There'll be no such thing as a divorce."

Was she dreaming and going to wake up any minute now? The man was mad.

"Why would you marry me? I could leave you anyway after so long. A marriage certificate doesn't keep people together."

"You could, yes. And if that was the case, there's very little I could do about it. We will of course have a tight prenuptial agreement, and if you do decide to leave me at any stage, maintenance payments would have to be thrashed out which would involve a long and protracted court case. And, of course I'd be forced to withdraw the funding for your mother's care."

"That's blackmail."

"Is it? I don't think it is. Think about it carefully. I'd suggest my offer is a way out of all your current problems. A very generous way out actually, but it's entirely up to you."

She looked at him incredulously, "What will people think about you marrying me and the age gap? It's going to look a bit odd when I'm young enough to be your daughter."

He shrugged, "I've long since ceased to care about what other people think. And rest assured, whatever scorn anyone may place upon a union between you and I, it would be rather tactless to vocalise it."

He stood, "I'll leave you now. Think about what I've said. I'll be back tomorrow for your answer.

Remember though, if it's yes, there'll be no going back. So, the sooner you stop thinking about Rick the better."

"Where has he gone to?" Tears had started streaming down her cheeks, "Please at least tell me that."

He reached for his trilby hat and placed it on his head, tilting the brim, "Until tomorrow," and quietly left her to contemplate the biggest decision of her eighteen-year-old life.

She'd spent the whole night crying, dozing and crying some more. Over and over again she asked the question, why would Chester Forrest be offering to marry her and fund her mother's care? What was that all about?

He'd been emphatic about Rick not coming back, so that must mean their promises of a future together meant nothing to him . . . it had all been a lie. He wouldn't have left if he loved her as much as she loved him. Surely, he wouldn't? The stabbing pain throbbed in her chest. He meant the world to her. He was her life. But he hadn't felt the same way about her, and as heart-wrenching as that was, she had to accept it.

Her whole body felt heavy. Weighed down by the terrible burden and trauma placed upon it. She ached for Rick.

Could she marry his father? It would solve all of her problems. She tried to imagine having sex with him. How could she have sex with *any* man after Rick? No. She'd rather be on her own for the rest of her life.

In the early hours of the morning, a sick feeling in the pit of her stomach woke her and she dashed to the bathroom and threw her guts up. Rick Forrest might have gone, but he'd left something behind growing inside her.

She married his father four weeks later.

13

Rick was in his room on the phone listening to Louise droning on about a social event he'd missed which she'd had to attend with her brother. He still hadn't made up his mind how long he was staying for.

He didn't want to admit it, but he was looking forward to spending some more time with Jo and Ollie. Not Eve, though, he definitely didn't want to be spending any more time in her company.

It was refreshingly different to be away from London and doing something other than research preparation for rich clients. Those who were fortunate to have money to buy a top-class defence, guilty or not guilty. His everyday life consisted of endless hours spent building up the strength of an effective argument strategy for the courtroom, and now for the first time since he'd started practicing law, it seemed to have lost a little of its appeal. Work had always been his driver, but that seemed to have shifted since coming back to Chanjori.

Why was that?

Why did the prospect of something as basic as Ollie's Australian project give him something to look forward to?

Ollie was a good kid, and seemed to enjoy playing Monopoly the previous evening and Rick had to admit, he had too. Children never featured in his organised high-life, and he wasn't entirely sure he would actually have any of his own. If Louise wanted them, then of course he would, but it had never been a burning desire he had. Yet, he liked this little fellow.

"Are you still there?" Louise asked.

"Yes, course I am."

"I thought for a minute the signal had gone. I was asking when to expect you back."

He scanned some emails on his laptop, "I'm not sure."

"But you must have an idea."

"No, not really. I've told you, the old man's dying, I can't put a date on when that's going to happen."

"But that could be weeks by the sound of things."

"Yes, it could be."

"Then why are you staying there when you could be at home? You told me you hated that place."

"I do, but I'm needed here right now."

"I don't get it, Rick. I know you, you'll be bored out of your mind." She paused as if considering how much to say, "I miss you. I miss us. It's lonely and the bed's so cold."

He couldn't agree more. He missed sex and it had only been two days.

"I'll see how things are by the end of the week and probably come back for the weekend, how's that?"

Her voice went up an octave, "The weekend? Rick, that's ages away." There was a pause and he knew the cogs were turning around, "Do you want to me to come there to see you . . . you know, to give you a bit of support?"

"No." Bloody hell, if she saw how fit Eve was, she'd really give him a hard time. "Don't do that, Lu. This isn't the best place to be at the moment, the old man's too ill."

"I know he is, but you don't even like him, so I fail to see why you have to be there."

"It's not just about me. There's my sister to think of, she's very upset, and there's the kid here."

"What's he got to do with it? You've never been bothered about children. Look, I'm sure it must be hard for them. I could understand it more if he'd been a normal parent, but you haven't seen him in years. He's got Jo, so it's not as if he's on his own, and his wife," there was a short pause, "what's her name, I can't remember?"

No, you wouldn't as I've never discussed her with you.

"Someone's knocking on the door," he lied, "I'm going to have to go. I'll ring you tomorrow."

Her displeasure at being dismissed was evident by the huge sigh, "Okay, speak tomorrow then. But please, try and come home at the weekend."

"I will do. Speak later. Love you." He cut the call.

Why all of a sudden was he dismissive of her? He'd thought long and hard about asking her to marry him. He'd had a string of women over the years, but Louise was the only one who'd captured his heart and he didn't want to live without. No, that wasn't strictly true. There was someone else, but as soon as his back was turned, she'd married his father. Who would do that? A bitch after the main chance, that's who. Yet despite that, he still lusted after her. Maybe a quick fuck would get her out his system. He smiled to himself, *like she'd allow that.*

A hundred lengths of the pool seemed a good idea and might cool his arousal. Thinking about her again had well and truly kicked that into gear.

He pounded across the pool, enjoying the cool water and must have done fifty lengths when he became aware of someone at the side of the pool. He reached the edge and looked up to see Ollie with Gilly.

"Now then, matey, you coming in?"

"Yes, I've come to do my practice."

Rick ran his fingers through his hair to stop the water running in his eyes. "Practice? For the school competition?"

"Yeah. Remember I told you the county selectors will be there."

"That's right, you did. Come on then, we'd better see how fast you are. Jump in and we'll have a race."

Ollie fished his goggles out of his pocket, "You'll be much faster than me," he grinned.

Rick smiled. He liked the kid and his innocence. "Have you won any competitions?"

"I used to but not since Danny Pritchard joined our school, he's faster than me."

"Well, we'll have to make sure that you beat Danny Pritchard, won't we. Come on then."

Ollie took off his robe and tossed it onto the lounger.

"He's okay with me Gil if you want to leave him," Rick said to Gilly.

She hesitated, "Mrs Forrest asked me to watch him while he practiced. She's with your dad."

"I'll watch him, don't worry. I'm sure you've got other stuff to do."

"She doesn't like him to swim for more than thirty minutes. She thinks that's long enough."

"Does she . . . right," he nodded. "Thirty minutes it is then. We wouldn't want him to catch cold, would we?"

She widened her eyes, "You'll have Mrs Forrest to answer to if you keep him in too long."

"You're scaring me, Gil," he playfully pretended to bite his nails. "Go on, you get off," he winked at Ollie, "we men have training to do."

"Thirty minutes I'm telling you," she reminded him, "and don't you forget."

He grinned, "I daren't do any other," and turned to Ollie as he climbed in the pool, "come on then, show me what you've got."

14

Eve dismissed the nurse, "Why don't you take a break now, Sarah?"

"Thank you, I will. I've been trying to encourage Mr Forrest to sit in a chair near the window again, but he doesn't want to today."

"Not to worry, I'll sit and keep him company," Eve smiled, sitting down next to the big brass bed.

Sarah left the room. The agency nurses had been a godsend. She couldn't have looked after Chester. His illness was advancing now, and while she felt guilty as the only thing she was doing was sitting with him, she couldn't have done any more. It would have been entirely different if their marriage had been a love match, but it wasn't.

Chester had lost so much weight and his eyes had sunken further into their sockets. He'd been such a vibrant man; it was becoming increasingly more difficult to watch his daily deterioration.

"How's the pain?" she asked gently.

"Painful," he answered without opening his eyes.

"Sarah's given you an injection so that should kick in shortly. Is there anything I can get you?"

"No," he must have realised his abruptness as he opened his eyes and added, "thank you."

He looked strangely at her as if he wasn't sure about saying something.

"What is it?"

"I've been dreaming a lot about Ann. She's been dead almost fifteen . . . or maybe longer, I can't remember. I rarely think about her, yet now she's constantly on my mind."

"She was a huge part of your life. You were married for years and had children together; you can't just wipe that out. I would think because you're unwell, you'll be remembering her illness and when she died. It'll all be flooding back."

"I wasn't a good husband to her," he said, and Eve detected genuine sadness in his voice.

He never spoke about Ann so the conversation was unexpected. "I'm sure you weren't that bad. Maybe try to focus on the positives, there must have been many happy years."

If there were, he didn't acknowledge it.

"Rick loved her so much. He was inconsolable when she died. I don't think he's ever got over it. He worshipped her," he exhaled a breath, "yet hated me."

What could she say? Rick did hate him. There was no point in denying it.

"Yes, but he's here now . . . at least he came back."

"Yeah," he drifted off for a few seconds, and then opened his eyes again. "I see so much of myself in Rick. He'll deny he's anything like me," his abdomen moved and she suspected breathing was becoming more difficult, "but he's a chip off the old block. He's driven, and doesn't always do things by the book. He'd have ended up in prison if he'd stayed round here so I was right to send him away. He doesn't see it that way though, that's why he'll never forgive me."

He coughed and became quiet and still. Was he asleep? She sat quietly, watching his breathing, not quite sure.

"He knew I didn't love her you see . . . knew I didn't love his mother."

"Don't do this, Chester," she soothed, "it's all in the past. Leave it there, eh."

His eyes closed again, a few more breaths, "I never should have married her," he appeared to drift off, his breathing deepened, but his eyes flickered open again, "when I loved someone else."

"Shush, rest now. Try and think of something else. I'll sit here for a while with you."

Chester eventually drifted into a deep sleep. Eve walked towards the window that overlooked the swimming pool and saw Oliver on the diving board with Rick in the water. He was repeatedly diving off the board, swimming to the edge and doing the same thing over and over again.

He'll end up with a headache diving in and out like that.

As soon as the nurse returned, Eve furiously made her way to the pool. "Oliver, come out now."

"Aw, Mum, no. Rick's been showing me how to dive in at the beginning of the race. That's where I'm losing time."

She ignored his plea, but softened her voice. "You've been in long enough. It's time to get out now."

"Can I show you? I'm much quicker now."

She glared at Rick. He was so bloody infuriating.

"Quickly then," she conceded.

Rick said nothing, just looked his usual smug self. "Come on then buddy; let's show your mum what you can do. This time, when you dive, swim the length. Fast, until you touch at the other end."

She watched Oliver stand on the edge of the board.

"Right, lean forward. Remember, shut out the noise. Ignore everything around you. You're going in the water, fast. When I shout go, dive. You ready?"

"Yep."

"Get set. . . Go!"

She watched Oliver dive on the word go, and unless she was very much mistaken, he swam the length much quicker. She hated to admit it, but a male role model was good for him. He was always around her, Jo, and Gilly, which he loved, but she worried about him not having any masculine input in his young life. Niall was nice to him, but he was staff so couldn't really be counted. Chester was barely there before his illness, and he was hardly what she'd call a role model as he always seemed to be chiselling away at Oliver about something insignificant.

Oliver reached the end of the pool and whipped off his goggles, "Did you see how much faster I am? Rick says I can beat anyone if I put my mind to it."

Did he now? He would do, Rick Forrest was a born winner.

I bet he's never lost at anything.

"You did brilliantly, darling. Come on now, though, it's time to get out and showered."

He climbed out of the pool and she grabbed the big white fluffy towel from the chair and wrapped him in it, but her eyes were distracted by Rick emerging from the pool. He looked like some sort of Adonis with water dripping off his torso. His muscular pecs gave a great big nudge to her libido; he really needed to wrap a towel around himself. It was doing her no good at all looking at his half naked body with those rippling muscles. She tried to concentrate on towel-drying Oliver's hair, trying not to look at Rick's biceps as he lifted first one arm, and then the other to dry his armpits.

God, that six-pack.

She was getting used to her pussy fluttering when he was around, but seeing him half naked, it positively throbbed. Did he know the effect his body was having on her? Most probably judging by that stupid sexy grin of his.

"Do you like what you see, Eve?"

What on earth was he doing talking like that in front of Oliver? She gave him her best *I hate you* glare which made him laugh, and he raised his eyebrows, "Watching Ollie improve his speed."

He didn't mean that at all, he was playing with her and it was best to ignore him.

He wrapped the towel around his neck and pulled it back and forth like a loofa brush. There were still some droplets of water on his torso causing her heart to race much faster than usual.

"When is the race, buddy?" he asked Oliver.

"Saturday."

"Good, we need to do a few more practices before then."

"Won't you be gone before Saturday?" she frowned.

He shook his head, "Not now I've got a reason to stay."

He really needs to cover himself up.

"Don't you have anyone at home? Someone waiting for you?"

"Nothing that won't keep."

Ollie cheered, "Yay."

She wasn't giving up, "What about work, surely you have to be back for that."

He shook his head again, grinning at her obvious displeasure that he wasn't leaving immediately. He slowly towelled his torso before wrapping the towel around his waist and securing it. Every sinew of his toned body glistened. Her skin prickled. He was so sexy, but the trouble with him was, he knew it.

She tried for an uninterested face. "Okay, maybe after school tomorrow then. Half an hour's practice won't hurt."

"No, it'll be better in a morning," he insisted, "what time do you leave for school, mate?"

"Not *before* school," she said firmly, "he'll be tired out all day."

"He's eleven years old. Half an hour's exercise before school won't hurt him."

"It won't Mum," Oliver interjected and smiled eagerly at him, "I get up at half past seven."

"What do you say then, mate. You get up at seven and that'll give us half an hour."

"Yeah," Oliver answered excitedly, "I can do that."

How had he managed to out manoeuvre her as a parent?

"Just this once then and we'll see how you go."

She tried hard not to look at him. She tried so hard. But her eyes had a will of their own and were drawn to his huge defined muscles, his abdomen with a delightful six-pack, and those hairs jutting above his towel. God . . . he really was so hot.

"Do you fancy anything, Eve? Maybe a swim . . . to cool off?"

"No, I don't. Not right now. Come on, Oliver, let's get you inside."

Did that arrogant devil just whisper, 'chicken'?

15

Jo twisted a cluster of hair in the heated curling wand and held it for a few seconds before letting it drop. After a shaky start a couple of days ago and a few burned fingers, she was getting the hang of styling her thick brown hair. For years she hadn't bothered; there seemed little point when all her spare time was spent in the library researching and writing. It was easier to scoop it into a ponytail.

She lifted the last section of hair and repeated the curling action. With both hands, she fingered the curls to spread them, and the end result was much more volume to her normally straight hair.

A different woman looked back at her in the full-length mirror. Usually she saw casual Jo Forrest, sister and author in her ordinary jeans and top with a kind yet insignificant face, but tonight she'd scrubbed up well and she inwardly chastised herself for neglecting her appearance for as long as she had done.

The dress she'd dug out of the back of her wardrobe was one she'd previously worn at a book launch her publisher had organised. She'd remembered looking at the photographs afterwards and thinking the pretty pink colour was quite flattering. It wasn't flashy or anything, but it did nip in at the waist and sit nicely above her knee, and she was pleased with the strappy white sandals she'd had to dust off as they hadn't been worn for so long. The heel was just the right size to somehow elongate her legs.

An excited smile added to the new look Jo Forrest. She couldn't help it, she was happier than she had been in a long time. There was one reason for the transformation and very shortly, she was going to be having dinner with him - and whatever else that entailed. That very thought ignited a fidgety, giddy feeling inside her chest. She couldn't remember the last time she had felt so energized. And it was all down to gorgeous Niall.

She glanced at her watch. Fifteen more minutes and she'd be with him. She was going to fake a headache this evening to get out of dinner, but if she was seen leaving the house all dressed up, it would look rather stupid. At the last minute, she decided to tell Eve a fib. She'd gone for Rachael, a friend from school who had married and moved to Newcastle, who was back in Edinburgh visiting her mother and she was meeting her for a quick drink in town.

The only shadow on her excitement was her father. She'd sat with him earlier and was able to have bit of a conversation with him but he was sleeping more and more each day, yet there was so much she still wanted to say. Tears threatened, but she sniffed to try and avert them as she didn't want to spoil her newly made-up eyes. She wished for her dad's sake he could just go to sleep and not wake up. Anything was better than watching him slowly decline bit by bit.

Rick disappointed her. As far as she was aware, he'd only been to see their dad once since he'd returned. She'd questioned both of them. Rick said one visit had been one too many, and her father had asked when he was going home, adding *the sooner the better.*

It was a mystery why Rick was still around. He had a demanding job in London and admitted Louise was giving him a hard time for being at Chanjori, yet he didn't seem in a rush to leave. As always he was evasive, giving vague answers when she questioned him about how long he was staying.

Oliver loved him being here though. The only light in all the gloom was watching their relationship develop. They were half-brothers after all so she was hoping Rick would be more prominent in his life now. It was going to be hard on them all when their dad died, but Oliver had a lot of years ahead without a male figurehead guiding him, and she hoped that now Rick had come into his life, he'd remain in it. Certainly when she visited Rick and Louise in London, she could take Oliver along with her. She secretly hoped he'd hang onto Chanjori House and not sell it, as it was their home, but Rick hated it since their mother died so that seemed unlikely. She'd made up her mind to talk to Rick again when the time came though, because if he and Louise had children, he could pass the house on. It was the family heritage after all.

One thing she was absolutely certain about was, Rick would only do what he wanted and would not be influenced by anything she said to him. She'd been watching him carefully since his return and something odd was going on with Rick towards Eve, which puzzled her. She'd seen the way he looked at her, and had asked him outright if he found her attractive, which he'd quickly dismissed and almost convinced her he didn't. But she wasn't stupid; she could tell he definitely had an eye for Eve. She'd caught him looking at her more than once in a way that would suggest he most definitely did find her attractive. And why wouldn't he, she was stunning. It wasn't appropriate, of course, and she knew categorically Eve wouldn't do anything to hurt her dad, but she could tell there was an underlying connection between the two of them when they were in the same room.

She glanced again at her watch. It was time to take her car down the drive to Niall's cottage and hide it in the garage so it wasn't visible from the house. The last thing she wanted was for Eve or Rick to suspect anything. Eve would be okay, but Rick wouldn't. He'd be exactly like her dad. He'd see Niall very much as an employee. She felt bad enough even thinking as she did about Niall with her father being so ill, but she couldn't help it. Their flirting and kissing was going to move to another level tonight. Her tummy flipped again.

She closed her bedroom door quietly and quickly made her way downstairs and through the kitchen to the back of the house where she'd parked her car earlier.

As she made her way down the drive in her car, she daydreamed about the day when Niall had first kissed her. They'd been driving back from a book signing in the city and were behind a car indicating it was turning right, and as it did so, it smashed straight into the side of an oncoming vehicle. Niall pulled in and they rushed to assist the drivers. The lone female driver of one of the cars was badly shaken but it didn't appear anything was broken, so Jo helped her out of her vehicle and got her to sit in the Mercedes while Niall called an ambulance. The chap in the other car was only young, and Niall stayed with him.

Fortunately, neither of them was badly hurt, but the woman was taken to hospital.

The whole episode had shaken her, and instead of taking her straight home, Niall took her to a secluded country pub and ordered her a brandy. Two brandies later, she was talking to him like an old friend. She found herself telling him about her life and the difficulties she'd encountered at the all-girl school she'd attended where she'd been excluded from lots of activities. She'd been the odd one out, which more than likely was largely down to her own shyness and low self-esteem.

She explained that when she'd gone to college, she'd met and fallen deeply in love with Tom Grundy. The brandy made her tongue loose, and she rambled on about how much she'd loved Tom and how his sudden disappearance had devastated her. As long as she lived, she'd never understand how he just upped and left. They were soul mates and had made so many plans for their future together. They'd even got names picked for their children. Talking about that time in her life still had the ability to upset her, but it wasn't just that, it was her father's terminal diagnoses also. She wasn't normally so open about her feelings but Niall seemed such a good listener, and once she started talking, whole miserable life seemed to spill out. She'd started to cry.

Niall was sitting at the side of her on an old-fashioned settle and put his arm around her as if it was the most natural thing in the world. She liked the comforting feel of his big strong hold and eagerly accepted the white handkerchief he gave her. She'd felt embarrassed breaking down as she had done.

It must have only been a few seconds before he pulled away and looked directly into her eyes as if to gauge her reaction at him consoling her. She wasn't cross at all, more surprised really. And then she was even more surprised as he leant forward and kissed her. Only gently, but nevertheless a nice kiss you would give someone you were familiar with. He did apologise afterwards, obviously concerned he'd overstepped the chauffeur client relationship, but she wasn't worried at all. It felt right.

He was so much like her really, lonely but with a big heart. His long-term relationship had broken up so he'd returned to Scotland to make a fresh start. She quickly developed a real affinity with him and would look forward to seeing him each day. He seemed to be the light in her secluded life; an escape from the darkness of Chanjori with death waiting in another room.

She pulled up to Niall's cottage. He'd texted her earlier and said he'd leave his own car out so that she could put her car in the garage and it wouldn't be seen. The garage door was open and she eased her Mini Cooper in and turned off the engine.

As she closed the garage door behind her, she saw him waiting in the doorway of his cottage. Her previously excited tummy churned with nervousness. What if she was rubbish at making love? What if her hip was a problem? It had been so long since she'd had sex and he must have been with loads of women.

"Hi," he smiled.

"Hi. I'm not too early, am I?" she asked nervously.

"Nope. Right on time."

"Good."

He took her jacket from her and must have sensed her anxiety as he leant forward and stroked her face, "You okay?"

His little tiny touch and the concern in his deep blue eyes calmed her racing heart. The same heart she'd given away once and had it crushed, he managed to smoothly steal with one small gesture.

16

Jo put her coffee cup down, "That was a lovely meal, Niall, thank you."

"You're welcome. Have you had enough to eat?"

"Yes, more than enough. It's so kind of you to cook for me."

Niall took a sip of his coffee, "Right, I'm going to come straight out with this."

Please don't tell me it's off. I couldn't bear it.

"It's been a nice evening talking about your writing, and my sister in America, and I've loved hearing about your childhood at Chanjori, but I think we've skirted around the issue long enough now. We both know I haven't invited you here tonight to try out my cooking," he smiled so cutely, "okay, so I can rustle up mediocre spaghetti bolognaise, but I'm not too bothered about whether or not you liked it."

Butterflies swooped inside. She'd enjoyed their conversation and had spent most of the evening imagining what it would be like to have sex with him, but now it actually came to it, she was panicky.

"I know why we're here, Niall, I'm not stupid. I just don't get it. I certainly wasn't at the front of the queue when they gave out looks, and then there's my limp. You're an attractive man, why aren't you with someone else. Why me?"

His eyes were kind. That's what she liked when she first started to notice him, his lovely gentle eyes. "I don't know why you. Why are people attracted to each other? I've liked you since I first came to work here, but it's only recently you've given me any indication that you might feel the same way about me." He smiled tenderly at her, "I've got it right, you do feel the same?"

"You know I do, but it's not that simple. All my life I've lived with disability and my father insisting nobody would really want me for myself, only for my money, so I'm cautious."

"Well your father's wrong. I'm not interested in your money. I want you. I don't see a limp when I look at you, I see you," he took her hand, "a lovely young woman. I want a relationship with you. I'm not promising the world, but I'd like for you to trust me so we can get to know each other."

"I do trust you. I know you're a decent man. And I do . . . you know . . . want the same."

"It's sex, Jo. It's what men and women do. Can't we go to the bedroom and enjoy each other . . . if you feel the same and it's what you want?"

"I do feel the same."

"I want you, Jo," his eyes softened, "I want to be with you. And I don't want to be hiding away either."

"I do want a . . . relationship with you Niall, but I can't just rush into something, especially now with Dad being so poorly."

"Rush into something? Jo, have you heard yourself. You're a young woman. You should be having relationships. He shook his head, "I think you've been locked away in Chanjori House for so long that you don't know any different. Have you ever thought making love with someone might be a good thing for you right now? That you might enjoy having someone caring for you and making you feel nice?"

She took a deep breath in, he was right. She needed this, she needed him.

"You're right, I know that but I want to take it slowly. I need to tell them. Currently they think I'm having dinner with a friend."

A gorgeous roguish smile spread across his face, "Well you are. I'm your friend, so let's just go for it, shall we? No more talking, eh?"

He stood and reached out his hand. She stood too and clasped it, "The thing is . . ."

His mouth interrupted her. Virile lips glided slowly over hers like honey, all soft and silky and warm. Every nerve ending came frighteningly alive, weakening any further resistance from her.

Once they moved into the bedroom, nerves kicked in again. Her heart was tense in her chest, thumping like a hard, tight drum. What would he think of her body, would she satisfy him? Would he want more after tonight? What if afterwards he decided it was just a one off? He was so gorgeous, why did he want her?

They stood by the bed and he cupped her head and brushed his thumbs across her cheeks. He brought his lips down on hers again and she tried to recall a time when a man's mouth felt as good. She couldn't. His tongue slid across her lips, tasting her, filling her. She wasn't hugely experienced, but his lips made her want so much more. She moaned softly.

"How about I'll just nip to the bathroom and you get into bed?" he said softly.

Her heart surged at his words and she felt his hardness as he was kissing her.

As he closed the bathroom door, she quickly removed her clothes and flung them on the chair. She slipped between the cool sheets before he came out of the bathroom. Weren't they supposed to be ripping each other's clothes off in the heat of passion? She hadn't imagined it quite this measured. Maybe he was being considerate with it being their first time and the clothes-ripping came later?

Thankfully there was only a small lamp on the dressing table so the room wasn't too bright. Hopefully the dim lights would be kind to her and he wouldn't see her hip scars.

She knew how fit he was, she'd admired his body for ages. And the back of his head, she knew that intimately from sitting behind him in the car. The blunt cut of his sandy-coloured hair, his thick rugby neck, which must have been groomed as it was smooth with no sign of straggly hairs.

The times she'd looked at him in the front when he was driving and fantasised about him. She made up fictitious trips just to be in the car with him. She'd get him to take her to town, to the library for research even though she had an extensive library at Chanjori, the hairdressers, when she didn't like having her hair done, and shopping, she'd never shopped so much in her life. The joy of the trips was him taking her, and then coming back for her.

Their conversations deepened on the journeys. He told her about America and how he'd enjoyed living there but yearned to come back to the UK for a pint of real ale and fish and chips, which had amused her. He liked her father which was a rarity. Not many people *liked* Chester Forrest, but Niall seemed to, and by all accounts her father liked him. Niall was everything she dreamed of in a man. He wasn't just good-looking; he had an infectious charm about him. You couldn't fail to like him.

Her tummy did a somersault as he came back into the bedroom wearing just his boxers. He tossed a packet on the bedside table before slipping his boxers off and climbing into bed. He pulled her into his arms. "Ah, just what I need, a good woman to warm me."

She giggled, "I'm not that warm myself."

"Then we need to do something about that," he grinned.

He was so sexy. Her pussy tingled in anticipation.

He supported himself on his elbow and stroked the side of her face. Her heart rate accelerated. "You okay with this?" he asked.

Was she okay? This gorgeous man was about to make love to her. She was more than okay.

"Mmmm, very okay," she smiled.

He began kissing her. Long, slow, mind-blowing kisses, seducing her beyond reason with his mouth; his tongue playing with hers.

How can you like the feel of a man's tongue?

She rested her palms on his chest, enjoying his hardness and the feel of her nipples pebbling against him. She felt him kiss the curve of her neck, and he drew his fingertips up through the valley between her breasts and then found what she wanted them to find. He circled her nipple with his thumb. She relished the feel of his big hands splayed over her breasts, gently tugging at her nipple, and as he moved onto the other breast, the feelings he was creating were so new and exciting. His hand felt huge around her breast. What she really wanted was for him to use his teeth and suck on them hard.

He took one of her hands and placed it on his cock. She grasped it and moved her hand up and down, enjoying his groan, and circled the top of his hardness. He felt good. A flash back to lovemaking with Tom came into her mind. Compared to Niall, he'd been just a boy. Niall's cock felt firm. Even his balls felt nice.

The thought of him spilling inside her caused the heat in her tummy to burn.

His head moved towards her breast and his mouth replaced his hands. The pleasure of his mouth on her nipple was amazing as he bit and sucked. Her tummy contracted.

She enjoyed looking at his head on her breast and watched as he brought one nipple to a peak and then moved to the other. His mouth was amazing, and she did fleetingly wonder what it would be like on her pussy, but as he started to move down her tummy, she chickened out and pulled him up towards her and started kissing him on his mouth again.

He broke the kiss, "You're alright?"

She nodded. He must have understood her nervousness as his hand reached down and began caressing her pussy. The pleasure was incredible. She could feel her wetness as his fingers glided, but nothing prepared her for him sliding one finger inside her, and then another. She closed her eyes, lost for the moment in the erotic sensations he was creating. His fingers moved faster, deeper, and pushed harder. It took her pleasure to a different level. He moved them in and out and she tilted her pelvis, begging for more.

"You're so lovely, Jo," he groaned, kissing and biting her neck while his fingers continued to work their magic deep inside her. And then his thumb found her clit. Round and round he circled it with just the right amount of pressure. Every nerve ending came alive. Her pussy throbbed. The delightful feelings he was creating were excruciating. She would have loved these new found sensations to continue but as much as she tried to make them last, she was too turned on.

"Come," he urged in a husky voice.

His inviting demand was all she needed. She was drowning in him as his fingers worked her and his sexy command brought her pleasure to a head. The inferno burst and waves of pleasure poured down her body. "Niall," she sobbed, and he held her as she cascaded into a million pieces.

She opened her eyes and he was watching her intensely. He put the fingers he'd had inside her to his lips. "Next time, I'll suck all of you." Her pussy clenched . . . next time she'd let him.

He reached for the condom and opened it. Anxiety drove though her like an express train as he reached for her pussy again, even though she was wet and well ready for him.

"You're lovely when you come, Jo."

She was hardly lovely, but he made her feel lovely. He made her feel good. He made her feel sexy. Excitement fizzled in her chest. *Hadn't he just said there was going to be a next time?*

Powerfully male above her, he positioned himself, and her thighs fell open naturally to accommodate him. His cock nudged gently before slowly pushing forward. "Yes," she breathed as her tender tissues expanded to accommodate him and he sank deep inside her. Their hips locked. She loved his gentleness and for taking things slowly, but she wanted more of him.

Her hips began to move of their own accord, and rhythmically they began to move together . . . it felt perfect. She wanted to preserve the memory of the intimacy between them but he began to move deeper and was driving her where they both wanted to be.

She dug her nails into his back as if she'd never let go. With each thrust, she found herself building again. He licked and sucked and bit with abandon. On her mouth, her neck, her shoulders, her breasts. She'd only just climaxed, yet she was climbing towards another with the heat his mouth was creating and the friction on her clit from the base of his cock.

She raised her good hip to give him greater access and wrapped her arms around him tightly. All of his weight was on her, yet he didn't feel heavy at all. His power excited her. She felt overwhelmingly female, with his face in her neck and her chin tucked in his shoulder.

Her pussy clenched his thick length as he pushed deeper and fucked her harder. A high-pitched cry escaped from the back of her throat as another orgasm rocked through her. Her whole body shuddered as wave after wave of quivering ecstasy surged through it, and still he carried on thrusting, shifting the pleasure deep inside her. He was like a man possessed. Again and again, pounding into her, until he jerked and groaned with a release so strong, she instinctively clenched herself around his throbbing cock until the waves finally stopped cresting.

Her heart thudded with nervous happiness as he rolled onto his side, taking her with him. She buried her face in his shoulder.

"You're so beautiful, Jo," he said.

And for the first time in twenty-eight years, she felt beautiful.

17

Eve was sat by Chester's bed listening to his deep breathing. In his sleep, he looked tormented even though the nurse had given him an injection for the pain. She thought about their conversation before he'd become agitated.

"When I've gone, I want you to promise me something. And don't look at me like that, I need this sorting."

"What," she frowned, "what needs sorting?"

"Rick gets the house as you know, but I've made generous provision for you in the will. There's enough for you to buy a place for yourself and Oliver. You can live comfortably for the rest of your life. I've asked Rick if he'll consider keeping the house and letting Josephine stay here, but he won't commit to anything."

"We'll have to sort that out when the time comes, Chester. I really don't think we can influence what Rick is going to do. He'll do exactly as he wants to."

"Did you know he's got a fiancée?"

"Yes, Jo said. He doesn't discuss anything with me."

"He doesn't with me, but I've been watching him for years."

"Watching him? What do you mean watching him?"

"Don't be acting all coy and innocent, you know what I mean."

"What? Are you saying you've had him followed?"

"Not exactly followed. I've contacts in London who keep me informed."

"But why?"

"Because I like to know what he's up to. You've heard of the saying keep your friends close and your enemies' closer?"

"Yes, but Rick's not your enemy, he's your son."

"He's his mother's son more like."

She shook her head, "You know what I mean."

He closed his eyes and drifted for a few seconds, before opening them again.

"You'll stay in touch with Josephine, won't you? You've been good for her. She's going to struggle with all of . . . you know, all of this."

"Of course I will. I love Jo, and Oliver does too. She'll always be part of our life."

"Good," he said as if he'd already known that but was just checking.

He closed his eyes for a few more minutes and Eve watched him carefully and considered her life without him. He'd dominated it for the last eleven years and he'd been kind to her and provided a home when she was desolate. The marriage might have been loveless, but she had nothing to complain about in terms of his benevolence towards her. She would miss him when the time came.

He opened his eyes, "I've made provision for your mother so you don't need to worry about that either."

"I am grateful, Chester . . ."

He raised a hand, "I need you to promise me something."

"Of course . . . anything."

"Whatever happens, you won't get involved with Rick again. You have money to build a new life for yourself and Oliver. Do it, but don't be dragged down by him."

Of all the things she anticipated he was about to say, she hadn't expected that. "Why are you so hostile towards him, I don't get it?"

"Answer me, Eve. Promise me you'll not get involved with him. You move away with the boy and let Rick make a life with his fiancée."

"I don't need to promise anything, Chester. Rick and I were teenagers before, we're adults now and don't share those feelings we once had. In fact, I barely like the man now if I'm honest."

Chester didn't appear to be listening, "He's unpredictable. He operates under the law. He might be a fancy lawyer with an inflated salary, but the type of people he represents are criminals, Eve. I can rest easier if I know you'll keep away from him."

She wiped his head with a cool flannel as he'd started to perspire.

"And remember. If he gets as much as a hint that Oliver is his, he'll try and take him from you. Don't forget that. He's ruthless and he'll do it, you mark my words."

"He's not going to find out. There's only you and I that know."

"Make sure you keep it that way. He'll stop at nothing to get him if he found out." She nodded, she didn't need telling that. She knew Rick. He would.

Chester cleared his throat. "Josephine says he's still here but doesn't know when he's going. Do you know?"

She shook her head, "I've no idea. I can't imagine he'll be here much longer though. He must have to go back to work, surely?" There was no sense in letting on she knew he would be here at least until Oliver's swimming race. Rick hadn't told her that, it was Oliver who was revved up about it.

"Before he leaves, I'll need to see him."

He started to cough again. She reached for the jug and poured him some water, "Here, have a drink of this."

Even though she didn't love him, she felt desperately sorry for him. Only a few months ago, he was larger than life, a dynamic oil entrepreneur with a vibrant personality, and now his hand was trembling so much that she had to hold the glass for him so he could sip the water through a straw.

"Is that better?"

He nodded and rested back against the pillows. "I don't want him to be part of your life. He'll wreck it."

"I hear everything you say," she reassured, "and I promise I won't be getting involved with Rick. Now please, try and get some rest. You're fighting the injection the nurse gave you."

He closed his eyes and continued to mutter, "He's trouble, Eve, big trouble."

His breathing seemed laboured.

She stood up and went to the window. The swimming pool was below and she could see Rick pounding from one end to the other. What had gone so wrong with their relationship that they hated each other so much? She just didn't get it.

18

Eve was in the hallway urging Oliver to get a move on tying his trainers. "I'd rather you came in the car with me, and Niall can take us. Rick can follow us if he wants to."

"Aw, mum, I want to go with Rick in his Audi. It's really fast, Rick says he sees Mercedes in his rear view mirror."

"I'm not arguing with you."

Rick came down the stairs, "What's the problem with him coming with me?" He looked at Oliver, "We need to talk strategy on the way don't we, mate?"

"He's an eleven year old boy," she reminded him, "I hardly think he needs to *talk strategy*. In fact, I think you're making far too much of this. It's a swimming competition. He doesn't have to win; it's the taking part that counts."

Rick gave her an insolent grin, "That's what you think. We're in it to win it, aren't we, buddy?" He ruffled Oliver's hair which he lapped up, "There's no such thing as second place, that's for wimps."

"Yeah," Oliver joined in, "that's for wimps."

"That's enough, Oliver. Where's your bag?"

"Upstairs."

She sighed. "What's it doing upstairs? Run and get it, quickly."

She waited until Oliver had reached the top of the staircase and was out of earshot. "I wish you wouldn't talk like that, he's going to be terribly disappointed if he doesn't win. One of the boys is much faster than him. He's never beaten him before."

"That's because he didn't have me before. Today, he's going to win."

"And if he doesn't?"

"He will. He's a Forrest. We don't lose at anything. Anyway," a playful grin spread across his face, "why are you so agitated about being in a car with me? You used to love it."

She felt her face turn flame-red. How was it she was composed in all aspects of her life, yet around him, she was like a love-sick teenager?

Rick raised an eyebrow as Oliver came down the stairs. "Ah, saved by the champ," he smirked. "So what is it? Are we going in my car so I can talk tactics with Ollie on the way, or is he going with you and the chauffeur so you can talk about the importance of *taking part*?"

Oliver's little face was willing her to say they could go with Rick. It was probably easier to do that than argue. The trouble was he was right. She didn't particularly want to be in the car with him. He unnerved her.

"Fine," she shrugged, "we'll come with you. I'll have to tell Niall as he'll be expecting to take us."

"No need. I saw him earlier and told him I'd be taking you."

She glared at him. He was so arrogant and conceited.

As much as she tried, she couldn't suppress her awareness of Rick on the journey. She liked the way his voice softened when he spoke to Oliver.

She looked at his huge hands casually placed on the steering wheel, and the slick way he manoeuvred the car until they were on the open road. The luxury cream leather interior of the car was a turn-on itself, particularly the speed he was driving.

Isn't he bothered about speed cameras?

Knowing him, he's probably got a get out of jail card if he's caught.

The leather seats seemed to envelop her bottom, and her pussy clenched as her eyes traced the hairs on the back of his hand. She remembered those years so long ago when he'd caressed her with his huge hands. Even as a young man, he had such a skill with those fingers, and that mouth of his. She'd never had any real experience of the male species before him. There'd been no place for sex in her world of music, but with him, she turned into some sort of nymphomaniac. She couldn't get enough of him. They'd had sex anywhere they could. Some nights, he'd climb onto the garage when her mother was in bed, and creep into her bedroom and fuck her senseless.

He'd been spot on earlier, implying she didn't want to be with him in a car. His first car had been a little MX5 sports car, courtesy of his mother's legacy he told her, and they couldn't travel anywhere without stopping for sex. He'd drive along, caressing her legs underneath her skirt until she was begging him for it. Any lay by would do. Time and time again he would make her climax. He was so unselfish, and his patience and stamina during sex was incredible. She remembered the filthy words he'd whisper in her ear as he urged her towards ecstasy.

Did he ever think how it had been between them?

God, this journey was not a good idea at all. She really didn't want to be thinking about sex with him, particularly with her son in the back of the car.

His voice brought her back to reality, "So, remind me what you're searching for when you're on the blocks, Ollie."

"The pretend circle I'm going to dive into."

"Good. And what are you thinking?"

"I'm going to win," Ollie answered.

"Louder."

"I'm going to win," he replied convincingly.

"What about when you hear, on your marks?"

"I'm counting, one."

"Get set?"

"Counting, two."

"And when you hear the whistle?"

"I'm diving in."

"You forgot two and a half, mate. Two and a half is the same time as the whistle. When you've counted that, you're going in. The whistle goes at two and a half. Remember that."

"I will."

"Then what are you going to do?"

"Swim like I'm in the Olympics and I'm going to get a gold medal."

"And when you turn at the far end?"

"I'm going to beat Danny Pritchard."

"Louder?"

"I'M   GOING   TO   BEAT   DANNY PRITCHARD."

"Don't you forget it. Now put your headphones on and relax until we get there."

Eve had heard enough now. "Really Rick, is this absolutely necessary? You're turning him into something he isn't. I think you're putting far too much pressure on him."

"No, I'm not. There's no place in life for coming second."

He swung the car into a parking space, cut the ignition and turned to her with a twinkle in his eye, which made him look far too sexy.

"We came here once, can you remember?" he raised an eyebrow.

She could. Every detail of being at the pool with him was etched on her mind. They'd gone there one evening when the pool was almost deserted and frolicked around in the diving area. The main part of the pool was watched by a lifeguard who didn't seem too concerned about the deep end. She wasn't a good swimmer and Rick had carried her into the deep end, away from prying eyes. His expert fingers had slipped inside her bikinis bottoms and he'd made her climax in the water.

There was no way she was going to tell him she remembered though. Those days were in the past. She shook her head, "Not really."

"Liar," he whispered, and turned to Oliver in the back. "Come on then, champ, we've got a race to win."

19

They made their way to the entrance of the Olympic-sized pool. She tried to hug Oliver before he left to go to the changing room, but he was having none of it, "Muuum, don't." He pulled away.

Rick made a fist and Oliver copied and they knocked them together.

"Knock 'em dead, Ollie."

"I'll try."

"You'll do it," he winked, "see you soon."

They both watched him walk towards the changing room.

I wonder how he'd feel if he knew it was his son?

Rick took her arm, "Which way?"

"There," she pointed.

They made their way to the spectator area. It was a new experience having someone with her for Oliver's race; she normally came on her own. Jo had come with her a couple of times, but Chester never did. He was too busy working. Having Rick there gave her a warm, sort of comfortable feeling. She liked the sensation of his arm on hers. She was so used to doing everything on her own.

Rick led her towards the seating area as if he attended every week. She looked up to the graduated seating, deciding where to sit.

"We're along here," he indicated to two seats with reserved signs attached to them on the front row. These particular seats would normally be occupied by parents who arrived at an unearthly hour to get them, so how had he managed to secure two? He moved aside to let her in the row before him.

Rosemary Pritchard, the mum of Oliver's close rival Danny, was sitting further down the row with Danny's grandparents.

As they edged along to their seats, Rosemary gave her a lukewarm smile, "Hello, Eve. How's Chester?" Her heavily made-up eyes were looking straight past her at Rick.

"Very poorly I'm afraid. Jo's with him this afternoon . . . we're trying to keep things as normal as possible for Oliver."

"Yes, I'm sure it's the right thing to do."

She had to introduce Rick, it would have been awkward not to, "You'll remember Rick, Chester's son." She would do of course, they'd all gone to school together. Rosemary was one of those firmly ensconced at the back of the school bus, joining in with the ridiculous boys chanting, *Evie, Evie, Lemon squeezy.*

"Yes of course. Hello Rick, nice to see you back. I'm so sorry about your father."

"Thank you, Rosemary."

"How long has it been since you visited?"

"Too many years to count," he smiled politely. "Ollie tells me your boy's quite a swimmer."

"He is. We're hoping he'll be selected to swim for the county today. The touts are here so he needs to win today to stand a chance."

"Let's hope he does well then."

"Oh, I'm sure he will do. He practices every day in the pool and has managed this last week to knock a second off his timing."

Rick nodded, "That's really good."

"Anyway, how long are you here for? You must call on David and I, you'd be most welcome. You remember David my husband, David Pritchard?"

"Yes, I do. How is he?"

"He's fine. Busy running his own company specialising in hot tubs and Jacuzzis of all things actually," she smiled flirtatiously.

"Really?"

"It would be lovely if we could all meet up while you're here, you know, to reminisce about old times."

"It would but I'm afraid I'm leaving shortly." He gave a regretful smile, which Eve knew was fake. "Do send him my regards."

"Oh, that is a shame, of course I will. But if you do find a window before you go, then please drop by. Eve has our address," she smiled seductively, "no appointment necessary."

Rick nodded. "Nice to see you again Rosemary, and best of luck to your son."

"Thank you," she smiled, "that's very kind of you."

Eve couldn't believe the way Rosemary had been fawning over Rick like some sort of long lost relative. "She was flirting with you?" she whispered through gritted teeth as they took their seats.

"Was she?" he shrugged, "I didn't notice."

"Yes, you did. And she wasn't asking you to call on her *and David*. She was asking you to call on *her*, and it wasn't for afternoon tea either."

"Is that right?"

"You know it is. And why are you creaming around her as if you want Danny to win?"

"Because I know he won't. Ollie will."

"I really wish you wouldn't keep calling him Ollie," she sighed, "his name is Oliver."

"Yeah, well, that's stuffy for a kid his age. Ollie suits him better. And he likes it."

The tannoy announced the first race. Oliver used to race in this group, but he'd been too quick for them so had moved up to the older group. How would he do today with Rick around? A role model was good for him. Although Eve didn't always approve of things Rick did, she had to admit it was lovely to see Oliver happy. It had only been a couple of days since Rick arrived, yet he'd developed a real affinity with him.

If only things had been different. They could have been married. Oliver would have known Rick as his dad, and they may have had more children together. That would have been so much better for her son. She'd hated him being an only child and would have loved a sibling for Oliver if circumstances had been different. Would Rick be having children in the future? He'd be a good dad and he'd definitely won Oliver over, that was for sure. There was something about watching a man with a child she found attractive. She always liked images of masculine men holding tiny little babies. If he'd never left Chanjori, they might have had babies together. Oliver would be the eldest, but he could have little brothers and sisters. She felt all warm and excited at the thought of more children but it was a daydream she'd learned to stifle over the years.

It was distracting having Rick sitting next to her. Particularly as he was so close and their legs were almost touching. His aftershave was seriously intoxicating. She'd caught a whiff of it in the car a couple of times and it certainly gave her libido a kick, but now it was saturating her senses.

She crossed one leg over the other.

Everything about him was such a turn-on. His masculinity, his toned body, and his dark two-day growth, which on some men would look scruffy and unkempt, but on him, it just coated his angular jawline and made him look hot. His lips were slightly apart and her eyes traced the outline. His top lip was generous, but not pouty. It was just right, and she could remember with absolute clarity how exquisitely he could use his lips and tongue.

Phew. It was turning really warm.

She reached in her bag for her bottle of water and took a generous mouthful. She was about to screw the top back on when Rick reached his hand out, "Yes please."

He can't be serious.

"She looked at the bottle of water in her hand before passing it to him. There was no way she was going to drink after him. No way.

His lips wrapped around the bottle and he threw his head back as he glugged. She couldn't help her eyes being drawn to his throat as the water glided past his Adam's apple. If her pussy was wet from fantasising about his mouth minutes before, then it was positively soaking now watching him drink.

He handed the bottle back, "Here, you finish it."

"No, I'm fine," her voice had suddenly gone higher, "you have it, if you want to."

He gave her that stupid sexy grin of his, as if he knew exactly what she was thinking.

"You never used to have a problem drinking after me?"

"I haven't now," she lied, "I'm just not thirsty."

He widened his eyes, "Really?"

"Yes really. Stop messing about, Rick. Just drink it and I can get rid of the bottle."

"Nah, I'm okay." He handed the bottle back to her, "you might fancy it later."

She snatched it from him just as the boys were filing in for the second race. Oliver was amongst them.

His little eyes quickly moved towards the seating area until he spotted them. Her heart filled with love for her son as he gave them the most beautiful smile before he approached the blocks where the race would begin.

She watched as he started shaking his hands and leaning on one leg and shaking first one foot and then the other.

"Oh, dear, I wonder if he's got cramp or something? He doesn't usually do that."

Rick looked sideways at her and gave her a scornful glance, "It's not cramp," he dismissed, "I've taught him to do it. It loosens him up before he gets in the water."

"Oh, right."

It was probably best to keep quiet and out of the macho thing they had going on. They were both going to be disappointed anyway, there was no way Oliver was going to beat Danny Pritchard. The last time they'd raced, Danny won easily. Shame, as it would have been nice to knock that supercilious grin off Rosemary's face.

Eve glanced around the seating area. "How come we're sitting on the front row? I've never had seats this close to the pool before."

He was watching the boys getting ready for the race and didn't turn. "Because I rang up and booked them."

"You can't book seats for a swimming race," she frowned, "you just grab what's available."

"You'd never get the best seats if you relied on that."

She didn't believe him. "So, you just rang and asked them to reserve two seats on the front row and they agreed?"

"Yep. He wrinkled his nose, "Well, not at first. I had to tell a little white lie."

"Oh, I bet," she replied sarcastically, "what white lie would that be?"

"I told them you had a height phobia and couldn't sit on the graduated seats."

He was staring ahead at the boys taking their lane positions.

"Please tell me you're making that up?"

He didn't answer.

"Rick," she nudged him. "You haven't really said that, have you?"

He patted her leg with his usual stupid, sexy, infuriating grin of his. "Relax. We've got a race to win. Ollie will do better if we're close by."

He wouldn't have, surely?

The announcement came over the loud speaker, "The next race is the 200 metres freestyle for the under twelve's." Her tummy plummeted with nerves for Oliver. She wished Rick hadn't revved him up with all this winning stuff. She wasn't bothered if he won or not.

Was she?

Her eyes surveyed the blue tint of the water with all the lanes carefully segregated with ropes, and she smiled supportively at her son. It was quite an achievement to even be in the race. It was hard to tell once he'd put his goggles on where he was looking, even though his head was facing their direction, but she sensed he was maybe focussing on Rick rather than her. Their bonding had made her see that Oliver needed a father figure in his life. Chester was nice to him, but not particularly the role model he needed.

She watched Rick nod back at Oliver. What good was a nod? It wouldn't have been that hard to have given him a thumbs-up or something to encourage him. *Honestly, men.*

All the boys got into position and Oliver looked down towards his feet and wrapped his toes around the edge of the block before tucking his head between his arms. He reminded her of a spring, ready to explode.

"On your marks."

He'd be counting now, as Rick had told him.

"Get set," her tummy twisted for him.

The starting gun blasted and Oliver was off. Was it her imagination or was he off his block before any of them? It must be okay as they weren't pulled back for a false start.

Oliver pounded down the length of the pool. He'd always been quick, but no match for Danny who was already in front. Oliver was keeping up though. He clawed his way through the water, one, two, three, four strokes, and then came up for air. One, two, three, four and more air. He pounded down his lane and his feet were splashing furiously.

They approached the far end and would need to turn. Oliver disappeared under the water and must have taken the turn better than Danny as he popped up a millisecond before him. They were both ahead of the others, but it was neck and neck.

She'd watched every race Oliver had ever been in, and not once had he beaten Danny. She always encouraged him and said one day, but in her heart she knew he was no match for the bigger boy. But today, as she watched Oliver thumping the water with every bit of strength he had, she felt a great surge of hope. His speed was blistering, and he wasn't far now from the finish, surely his young muscles would let him down. He couldn't keep this pace up, *could he?*

She was on her feet, "Go Oliver, go!" she screamed. He couldn't hear her, but it didn't matter. Tears filled her eyes as she willed him on with every fibre of her body. He was clawing at the water now, pulling it with his little arms, and throwing them back across his head. Every fourth stroke his head came up for air.

Do, it Oliver. If you never do it again, just this once, do it.

He pounded forward for the last few metres and as he got close to the wall, he stretched his fingertips to touch before Danny. The official put his hand in the air, which only meant one thing. Her precious boy had won. Her sensitive son had beaten them all.

He pumped his little fist in the air.

Rick was on his feet as well, fist pumping, and Oliver looked across and gave them both an *I did it* grin.

Rick turned and smiled at her. She was so thrilled, she wanted to throw her arms around him and hug him for helping Oliver, but she didn't dare.

"I told you he'd win," he said with that supercilious smile of his.

Yes, he had. And the win was largely down to him. Guilt washed over her. It had been wrong of her to keep the truth from Rick all these years. It was too late now though. She daren't risk him finding out. Too much was at stake. What if he and his new wife wanted Oliver? He was a slick lawyer, and if it was true what Chester had said about him not playing by the rules, she couldn't risk a battle that might end up with joint access between the two of them. Her son was her life; she couldn't live with having to share him.

Oliver jumped out of the pool and while all his classmates were congratulating him, she watched

Danny leave the pool area. She turned in her seat and saw his mother had slipped out the other end of the row. It must be hard. They weren't used to losing.

20

Jo pulled away from Niall, "What's the matter?" he frowned.

"Nothing. It just feels a bit odd being here with you in the house, that's all."

"Come to the cottage then," he said, taking a step away from her.

"I can't right this minute. I'm waiting for a conference call with my agent and publisher." She widened her eyes cheekily with her new found confidence, "I can in about an hour though, how does that sound?"

"Better," he smiled, "I've missed you."

A warm glow flooded through her. He'd been so patient and the sex was amazing.

"It's only been two days," she grinned, loving that he wanted to see more of her.

"Two days too long," he pulled a face, "how I'm going to manage when I have to go to the States, I don't know. I'm seriously thinking of only staying a week now."

An ache twisted in her heart. She was going to miss him so much. "You'll not get any arguments from me if you come back early."

His eyes showed her how much she was beginning to mean to him. You couldn't fake that, surely?

"I hate all this hiding away," she sighed. "Do you think we should say something about us . . . you know, about the fact we're together now? Like you said, it is perfectly normal for two people who are attracted to each other to be in a relationship."

She didn't like the way he scowled. It spoiled his handsome features. "I'm not sure," he dismissed, "going public feels awkward with your dad being ill. Maybe now's not the right time."

She loved him for caring so much, but was disappointed. She wanted to shout from the rooftops that she was with him.

"I know," she agreed, "it's just that I'd love to tell him about you . . . about us, but he's asleep most of the day now." Tears threatened. They seemed to be a daily occurrence now. "I don't think it's going to be long, that's what the nurse said anyway."

Niall wrapped his arms around her and held her. Thank goodness she had him. He made her feel safe, as if there was a future after her dad died.

He pulled away and took her hand, "I'm worried about upsetting your father, especially as he's not got long. If he's angry about you being with the hired help, it will only hurt you. Don't look like that. We both know he won't be happy about you being with me."

"I don't care what he thinks, and please don't talk about yourself that way. I shouldn't have to hide our relationship away."

"It's only for the time being. It won't always be like this."

"Yes, but I want everyone to know I'm with you. I thought you'd want that too," her tummy tightened, "or is it you're ashamed . . ."

"Stop that," he said sternly, "you know that isn't true. I'm just enjoying the two of us right now. How about we discuss this later? It doesn't feel right when I'm supposed to be working." He glanced at his watch, "I'd better get off and clean the cars or do something before Gilly catches me in here."

"Don't worry, I've got it covered," she smiled, loving him for his thoughtfulness. "I told Eve you came to speak to me about extending your US trip and she bought it."

"Yeah, well she's got a lot on her mind at the moment. Gilly's a completely different kettle of fish. Not much gets past her."

She rolled her eyes, "You're right there," and walked with him towards the door.

"I'll see you later, then," she whispered, loving the fact that within the next hour or so, he'd be making love to her.

She opened the door and raised her voice for the benefit of anyone in the hallway.

"Okay, Niall, that all sounds fine. I'm sure it'll be lovely in San Francisco this time of year."

He nodded and winked as he went out of the door.

Jo caught sight of the familiar figure of Gilly surreptitiously dusting the hall table. "Ah, just the person."

*

Eve quietly closed Chester's door and made her way to the staircase. She spotted the back of Niall leaving the house.

Jo was talking to Gilly in the hallway as she came downstairs and smiled as she approached them. "Ah, Eve, I was saying I'm not in for lunch. Do you want any?"

"Erm . . . it's a bit hot today for much," she replied, "Maybe some fruit and yoghurt outside by the pool might be nice?"

"Of course, Mrs Forrest. I'll get on with that now."

"You'll have to excuse me," Jo said, turning towards the library door, "I'm waiting for a conference call and don't want to miss it."

Eve followed her as she made her way into the library. "Have you got time for a dip in the Jacuzzi when you're finished, it's gorgeous out there?"

Jo moved towards the settee and checked her phone resting on the arm as she sat down.

"No, sorry. I'm nipping out after the call. How's Dad?"

"Asleep. It takes ages for the pain relief to kick in, I think he fights it."

"Oh, he does. I'm so pleased we've got the nurses, I don't think we could have managed on our own."

"Me neither. Your dad wouldn't take any notice of you and I, that's for sure."

That was putting it mildly. Chester Forrest never took notice of *anyone* but himself.

"What was Niall doing in the house again," Eve smiled knowingly, "confirming his travel arrangements?"

Jo flushed, and put her head to one side. The penny must have dropped. "You know, don't you?"

Eve grinned. "I saw the two of you together the other day and it looked very much as if he'd progressed from being the chauffeur." She sat down on the sofa next to Jo.

Jo was blushing furiously. "I can't believe this is happening. I really, like him. You know what I mean . . . really, really like him."

"Well that's good, isn't it . . . to really, really like someone?" Eve teased.

"Yes, but I'm scared." She puffed out her cheeks, "Scared about it all to be honest."

"What's there to be scared about?"

"I don't know," Jo shrugged, "maybe that it isn't real. He's so gorgeous looking, and could have anyone he wanted. Why would he be with me . . . and my hip," a wave of sadness passed across her face, "and everything else? I'm scared he'll leave me like Tom did."

Eve would hardly call Niall gorgeous looking . . . not like Rick was gorgeous looking.

"Hey," she reached for Jo's hand, "you're a lovely person, Jo. Why not you? I think you're over analysing things?"

"Maybe." Jo nodded. "I just can't believe he wants me. I'm fine when I'm with him, but when I'm not, I start to have doubts."

"You need to enjoy him and what you have for now," Eve reassured. "Life isn't very pleasant right now for any of us, so you should grab any chance of happiness while you can. That other boy that left you was only young. Niall's a man, and I'm sure he won't be making promises he can't keep."

A huge smile lit up Jo's face, as if she'd been given approval to be happy, "You're such a kind person, Eve. Thank God Dad brought you here. It would be such a sad life without you in it, and Oliver, of course."

Eve hugged her, "And thank God you were here when I came."

"Right," Eve stood up. "I'm going for a dip in the Jacuzzi."

Where was Rick? She didn't want to bang into him while she was in her swimsuit.

"Rick's not around, is he?"

"No, he's gone out. He didn't say where though, only he'd be back later."

"Okay, I'll leave you to it then. Don't work too hard."

21

Jo crept into the cottage at the entrance to Chanjori and clicked the lock behind her. "Niall, I'm here." She couldn't see him but could hear the shower running so made her way towards the bathroom.

She opened the door and paused. His gorgeous naked body was visible through the screen. His skin was a delightful bronze colour, but it was his white bits that made her pussy clench.

"You really shouldn't leave your front door unlocked when you're in the shower you know. Anyone could come in."

The shower door opened slightly, and a wet smile greeted her, "Here's hoping." He beckoned with his head, "You joining me?"

Her gaze was drawn to his semi erection. Why not? He made her forget everything except the overwhelming desire for him to make love to her.

She quickly unzipped her sundress and slipped off her bra and panties and left them in a heap on the floor, eager to join him.

As she stepped into the shower, his huge hand grasped her neck and he pulled her towards him. He really did know how to kiss. She loved the feel of his mouth telling her how much he wanted her. He smelt so male, of musk and shower gel. There was something so sexy about a man's body soaking wet from the shower. She still couldn't believe a man as gorgeous as Niall would want her.

He pulled away, "What took you so long?"

She giggled, "Work."

He reached for the shower gel and filled his hands. The onslaught on her breasts was divine as he massaged them until her nipples pebbled.

He found her clit with his fingers and rubbed it. She moaned for him as her pussy buzzed with need.

"Let me taste you, Jo. I really want to."

With her heart racing, she nodded, loving him for his patience with her. He'd wanted to go down on her a couple of times, but she'd resisted. Much as she wanted to experience it, she lacked the confidence. It seemed so intimate. But the last few days since their first time together, their lovemaking had intensified. He'd started off slowly with her, which only added to his attraction. She'd explained to him about the life she'd lived, rich girl in the ivory tower. A Billy-no-mates. Who'd be interested in a cripple who'd only ever had one sexual partner which she now knew had been immature and rushed? Yet Niall had been so patient with her, showing her how beautiful lovemaking could be.

He knelt down in front of her and parted her legs. She found it erotic enough gazing at his lithe body, but nothing prepared her for the feel of his mouth latching onto her clit. This was a new experience for her, and as he licked her, the pleasure was so intense; she had to lean against the tiles as her legs wouldn't hold her up. They were cold on her back, but she didn't care. "Oh God, that's so good," she groaned.

The difference between his mouth opposed to his fingers was incredible. Her breasts constricted as sparks of pleasure bounced through them with the sensation of his mouth sucking greedily, his tongue probing and flicking.

Her hands went to his hair and she groaned out loud as the pleasure intensified. Her pussy was on fire with his delicious mouth and his beard scratching her skin. Her clit throbbed and pulsed and the ache inside continued to grow until she felt as if she was about to explode. Within seconds she did, bucking against him with a force that took her breath. "I'm coming," she screamed, shuddering and gasping as waves of pleasure cascaded through her body as Niall held onto her hips and continued licking her clit until she begged him to stop.

He gently dried her and himself and then lifted her up and took her into the bedroom. No towel could dry her pussy completely, and when he lay down on the bed on top of her, she opened her legs eagerly to accept him.

"Jo," he groaned as he entered her.

What was it about this man saying her name in the throes of sex? She loved how it made her feel all feminine and sexy.

She held him tightly, enjoying her body giving him pleasure. After her own incredible orgasm, she wanted him to experience the same.

His thrusts were hard and fast, and his huge hand cupped her breast firmly. He bit and sucked her neck so hard, a fleeting thought was his teeth might leave a mark.

He was more forceful than usual, but not rough at all. His cock filled her, pulling out and filling her again, slamming deep and withdrawing in a frenzied rhythm and she moaned for him the whole time, tilting her hips higher to meet each thrust.

He felt so good deep inside her as he lifted her ass off the bed and pushed himself in to the hilt. His mouth devoured hers until he pulled back and even though his eyes were closed, she loved watching his face as he pushed himself deep and spurted into her. She held him tightly while he spilled into the condom. One day she hoped his seed might be giving more than just pleasure.

She had an overwhelming urge to tell him how much he meant to her, but it seemed far too soon for that. Instead she lay sated and wrapped in his arms.

The oral sex had been incredible. She must learn how to do that to him. He'd been patient with her inexperience and had started to show her sexual positions she'd had no idea about. He was so caring, always making sure that she was comfortable with her hip as he effortlessly moved her around the bed, or settee as they'd used the previous time.

She particularly liked riding him, even though it hurt her hip with them flexed across his hips. The look on his face as she moved on top of him was worth a bit of discomfort. For the first time in her life, she felt quite powerful when he'd come with her on top of him. His pleasure was her pleasure.

Her feelings for him weren't just about the sex though, she'd known for a few days she was in love with him. Although he hadn't indicated he was in love with her, she desperately hoped he felt the same way. When she was with him like this, she was much more relaxed, but alone she would question what he saw in her.

She kept her head on his shoulder, enjoying their intimacy but at the same time avoiding looking directly at him. Casually she muttered, "You know tonight it's the gala for Dad's achievement award?"

"Mmmm." His eyes stayed closed. Of course he'd know, he had a rota and would be taking her and Eve.

Would he come if she asked him? Would he want to be seen out in public with her?

"I wondered if you'd like to come as my guest?"

She felt him stiffen before turning his head towards her, "I'm not sure about that," he pulled his brows together, "I don't think that's the right place for us to be going public."

"Why? What difference does it make where it is?"

"It doesn't really, but this evening is all about your father and his award from the oil industry. It's not about us."

He seemed definite, so she needed a different tack. "I know it is, but Eve and I will be going alone, so it'll be nice to have a male escort."

He rested his head back on the pillow and scratched his eyebrows with his thumb, "Isn't Rick going?"

"No. I've asked him, but he won't. He reckons it will be hypocritical of him to turn up at Dad's award night when he hasn't had anything to do with him all these years."

"He's here now though and from what you've told me, he's the bigger man for doing so. He must care about your father to have come back before . . . you know . . . before the end."

"Bless you for saying that," she kissed him gently on his cheek. "I wish it was true, but I don't think he does. I don't know why he came back and to be honest, I'm not sure he does either. But people round here have long memories and he's right, they are unforgiving."

"From what I've seen of Rick, he doesn't look the sort to be troubled by any gossip."

"He's not, but he still won't come with us tonight. Rick's . . . how can I put it . . . different from the rest of us."

"In what way?"

She took a deep breath in, "Dad always says he's a rule-breaker. He qualifies that by saying Rick doesn't actually break the law, only that he operates just under it."

"But he's a lawyer. Surely that's a bit of a risky approach?"

Jo widened her eyes, "I think risky is Rick's middle name. That's why Dad sent him away. He was getting into too much trouble, mixing with some local lads who were not the type you'd want your kids to hang around with. Dad felt he was more than likely going to end up behind bars. Rick would never have been anything if Dad hadn't sent him to Uncle Norman in Australia. That's where he started studying and gained all his qualifications."

"Shame then that he can't stand up and thank your father publicly tonight. It sounds to me as if your dad's responsible for the man he is today."

"You're right about that, but Rick would never admit it. He definitely won't be coming tonight, so it'll be down to Eve to accept the award on Dad's behalf and give a bit of a thank-you speech."

"Would you have liked to have done it?" he asked, running his warm hand down her arm.

"God, no. I couldn't walk up on that stage with everyone focussing on my limp."

"Jo, you have to stop this," he chastised kissing her head, "you're a beautiful young woman. Nobody notices your limp."

She kissed him back, "You are such a good man. Thank you for saying that, but I'm still not doing it. I'm too self-conscious to deliver a speech to an audience of that size. My book launch events are a significant challenge for me when I have to say a few words in public. No, Eve will be brilliant, which you'll see yourself if you come with us."

"I don't know," he frowned, "what would your father make of it if he knew?"

"I really don't care, Niall. I haven't told him about us as he's not really coherent for much of the day. Nobody is going to tell him anyway, but if they do, then so be it. As you keep telling me, I've got to be myself. I'm not going to hide you away."

She noticed his face looked almost pained, which was stupid, it was only a night out she was talking about. "What?"

"You said earlier Eve didn't know about us?"

"I didn't realise she did then, but it seems she spotted us together the other day at the garage and put two and two together. She's pleased for us so don't look so worried."

"Does she know you want to take me tonight?"

"No, not yet, but she'll be fine."

"I don't know. I feel uncomfortable about the whole thing. I should drive you and pick you both up afterwards. It is why I'm employed here."

"Don't say that. I want you there with me. It'll be a lovely evening," she paused for a moment, knowing he wouldn't like the next thing she had to say, "it's a dinner suit do, though, so I'd need your measurements to get you one delivered."

"Hey, hang on a bit. I've got a dinner suit," he pushed the end of his nose in the air, "so I'm perfectly prepared for a swanky date."

She smiled at his gesture, "Date?" she supported herself on her elbow, "does that mean you're coming?"

He rolled his eyes, "It sounds like it. And before you even think it, I can afford to buy drinks tonight."

"Good," she laughed, but you won't need to. This swanky date won't cost you a penny. Everything is free at the Petroleum functions, so you just need to bring yourself."

"Is that right?" He stroked the side of her face, his expression more serious, "Promise you'll run this by Eve first, I don't want her uncomfortable in any way."

"I will." She leant forward and meant to kiss him gently, but he deepened the kiss.

"I've got to go, Niall," she breathed.

His hand found her pussy, "So go."

22

Eve stared at the laptop and self consciously read her speech out loud.

"Firstly, I'd like to say thank you to you all for this wonderful honour you have bestowed on Chester, I'm only sorry he can't be here this evening to receive it. As you'll all be aware, he is very ill and unable to attend in person, but he has asked me to convey his sincere appreciation. I don't think anyone could doubt his commitment over the years to the Institute of Petroleum."

She glanced at the script again. "I wish I could pass on encouraging news about Chester's health . . ."

A slow clap from the doorway made her turn around quickly.

"What are you doing, Rick? You've no business eavesdropping on me."

"I'm not *eavesdropping*, you left the door open. I take it that's your speech for tonight then, singing the praises of the great Chester Forrest."

"Yes, it is." She widened her eyes enquiringly, "Unless of course you'd like to come and say a few words."

"Yeah, sure. I can tell them what a bastard he really is."

"That's enough. I would have thought even you could at least say something nice considering he's been given an award. It is expected."

"Forget it. There isn't anything *nice* to say about him."

"Fine, then let me get on with it. I can't believe you're not even trying to support Jo. Even Niall is more encouraging than you."

"Niall? Niall the chauffeur," he frowned, "what's he got to do with anything?"

Blast, she shouldn't have said anything, but it was out now.

"Niall and Jo have been seeing each other."

"Seeing each other? What the fuck's that supposed to mean?"

"Do you mind not using that sort of language? Oliver could be around."

"What, like he's never heard that at school?"

"It's a good school he goes to, so I'm quite sure the boys are educated enough not to use it. They can find replacement words for swearing."

"Yeah, right, course they do." He shook his head, "Sometimes, I think you still live in that ivory tower with that over-protective mother of yours."

She didn't answer as his remark didn't warrant one.

"Anyway, what you on about, Jo's been seeing the chauffeur. Define *seeing,* do you mean he's screwing her?"

"Oh, for goodness' sake, do you have to be so crude? They are beginning a relationship together and he is escorting us both tonight."

"I can see the pound signs in his eyes already," he sneered.

"Don't be ridiculous. It's all very new and she's happy, so don't you dare spoil things for her."

"Spoil things? Get real, Eve. He'll be hanging around Jo knowing when the old man pops his clogs, she's going to be the richest dolly in town."

"You really are coarse, and I *am not* listening to anymore of this."

"And I am not listening to anymore of your crap either."

Crikey, was he heading over to Niall's cottage?

"Where are you going?"

"To hire a suit."

"What for? You're not coming now, are you?"

"I'll have to. Someone's got to keep an eye on get-rich-quick chauffeur boy, because you two lovesick bloody teenagers clearly can't."

Eve sighed, "You should have come to my hairdressers with me Jo, she'd have put your hair up for you."

"I know, but I hadn't thought I'd be wearing it up until now. I tried my dress on again and realised it would look better up. You don't mind, do you?"

"Of course I don't mind. It's just that someone paid to do this for a living would be far better than me at it."

"Nonsense, you're a whiz with those curling tongs."

Eve continued to twist each curl and secure it with a pin on top of Jo's head. Jo was right, her hair was looking better up.

Jo looked at Eve through the dressing table mirror, "I'm a bit nervous about tonight with it being the first time Niall and I have been out together."

"Yes, I bet. I must say, as far as first dates go, I think this is a bit much. Couldn't you have gone for dinner with him or something? I feel a bit sorry for him. I bet he's dreading it."

"You're right, I know," Jo agreed, "it's just when I thought about it and asked him to come, it was almost like a test. You know, if he really wants me, then he'll come. It was daft really, but I want people to know we're together."

"I understand that, of course you do. He makes you happy, and there's nothing wrong with wanting to show him off. As long as he's okay about coming?"

"He's not overjoyed or anything, but he said he'll come, and I do really want him there."

Eve noticed Jo's loved-up expression. She used to have it too, many years ago.

"Let's hope it doesn't put him off altogether then," Eve smiled, "we're hardly a conventional family, are we?"

"No, but it's only you and I tonight and he likes you, so it'll be fine I'm sure."

Oh, dear!

Eve gave a clearing of the throat cough.

Jo frowned, "What?"

"I hate to tell you this, but your delightful brother's joining us."

Jo's expression said everything, "No, surely not?"

"I'm afraid so."

"But he said he wasn't going when I asked him?"

"I know. I'm sorry, I think it was my fault. I mentioned that you'd be bringing Niall and he sort of invited himself."

"Oh, God . . . if he starts."

"He won't, I'm sure. You know what he's like. He's just being all macho trying to protect you."

"From what? I'm twenty-eight years old. I hardly need protecting, least of all from him. He's not been around for years so he needn't start trying to play the father figure with me. I've already got one of those."

"Don't get upset, it'll be fine. We can hardly stop him coming."

Jo let out a breath, "You're right, but he is being hypocritical. Please don't tell me he's going to do the acceptance speech?"

"No, of course he isn't."

"Thank God. That really would have been too much."

Eve reached for the hand mirror to show Jo the back of her hair, "What do you think?"

Jo's face lit up as she stared at her reflection and her brother was suddenly forgotten. "It looks beautiful, thank you. I can't wait to see Niall's face when he sees me all dressed up."

Eve felt a pang of envy. She'd never known what it was like to dress up to please a man, even though personal grooming was part of her everyday life. She always dressed well, Chester expected it. To be his wife meant looking good. Tonight, she was going to make an extra special effort with her appearance. Even though Chester most probably would be asleep, she wouldn't want to let him down. That was the only reason, *wasn't it?*

Eve felt awkward in the library with Niall having pre-dinner drinks with him and Jo. She wasn't sure if it was the situation of now seeing the chauffeur as Jo's boyfriend, or the fact she was worrying over how Rick was going to react. Gilly certainly didn't help. She was distinctively frosty as she mixed their drinks, no doubt perturbed by the sudden elevation of Niall's status.

Where was Rick?
Will he think I look nice?

"When is your sister's wedding, Niall?" Eve asked politely.

"The fourteenth. I'm flying over on the tenth though to have a bit of a wander around."

"What part of the States does she live in?"

"San Francisco."

"Oh, lovely, it'll be nice and warm then."

"Yes. Just as well because it's going to be a beachfront wedding."

Jo smiled lovingly at Niall, "I bet your sister will be thrilled to have you there."

His affectionate smile back was so nice to see. Eve had never had anyone smile at her like that. Well, maybe once, a long time ago.

Eve glanced at her watch, "I wish Rick would hurry up, I can't imagine what's keeping him."

"Can't you?" Jo replied. Eve knew what she was implying. Rick wouldn't want to spend any time having social drinks with Niall.

As if he'd heard them, the door opened.

Handsome didn't even come close to Rick Forrest wearing a dinner suit. A fidgety, giddy feeling erupted in Eve's chest as her eyes soaked in his wide shoulders and narrow hips filling out the tailored lines in all the right places. It was difficult to tear her eyes from his muscular shoulders, and his pristine white shirt wrapped comfortably around his thick smooth neck. She was used to seeing men in bespoke evening dress, but very few filled them quite as well as he did.

Does he have any idea how hot he looks?
Probably, knowing him.

"I've brought the car round to the front when you're ready," he said, looking at her as if to say, *why are you staring?*

Niall jumped up from his chair, embarrassment written all over his face.

"Er . . . Rick, I've arranged a driver for us tonight," he looked at Eve, "Jo didn't want me to drive, so I've organised a driver from the local company we use. I'm sorry, I should have said."

Rick gave him a stern look. "He arrived but I sent him away. I'll drive us."

Anger surfaced inside Eve at him taking over, and she could see Jo wasn't happy.

"I don't think there was any need to do that."
She chose her words carefully, "You're on a social
night out too. You can't have a drink if you're driving."

"I don't need a drink," he answered abruptly.
"Shall we get a move on?"

Jo interjected, "Rick, you're being really mean
and making Niall feel uncomfortable. Please remember,
he's *my* guest. There's absolutely no reason for you to
drive other than you wanting to embarrass Niall and I."

Rick glared arrogantly at them, "Are you
ready?"

Jo snapped, "I don't know who you think you
are Rick, carrying on as if you own the place. You
remind me of Dad."

*I wish you hadn't said that, Jo . . . he will own
it shortly, and he'll hate being likened to his father.*

Rick moved towards the door, "I'll wait in the
car."

Eve was cross for Jo and Niall. It was their first
date and they both had looked so happy together.

"Take no notice," she reassured them both,
"just ignore him. If he wants to prance around like
some sort of head of the family, let him. The main thing
is you two enjoying yourselves tonight." She looked
deliberately at Jo, "We've got a lot ahead of us in the
next few weeks so there won't be much time for
partying."

Jo smiled lovingly at her, "Thanks, Eve. I know
he's my brother but he can be a real pain in the ass
sometimes."

"Exactly. Come on, we'll ignore him. With a
bit of luck there'll be some woman that might take a
fancy to him and keep him occupied all night."

Jo laughed as they made their way to the front
door, "I think his fiancée might have something to say

about that. Remember, he's getting married next month."

Eve's stomach clenched, which was completely ridiculous as she knew he was engaged. An image of him waiting at the altar for his bride flashed before her, which she tried to push out of her mind. What difference did it make to her that he was getting married?

23

Rick watched her chatting to the man on her left. Evie Henshaw was still the most beautiful woman he'd ever known. She was gorgeous as a teenager, but time had been good to her. She was stunning and he knew he wasn't the only one noticing that. She'd turned heads when she arrived.

The dress she wore was black, which could look drab on some women, but not on her. There wasn't a gaping neckline, no, that wasn't Eve's style. She was much too subtle for that. The lace shoulders of the dress giving him a glimpse of her flesh turned him on. Christ how he'd like to take her home and rip that dress off her. His dick twitched in his pants. He'd love to fuck her senseless like they used to, and try as he might, he couldn't stop wanting to. She'd given him no encouragement whatsoever, but he knew she remembered how it was between them. He could almost make her come just by kissing her.

How often had the old man fucked her?

That initially had been a massive turn off, but now it wasn't. Although he hated the thought of the two of them together, his desire for her overrode that.

He sipped his mineral water. Coming back to Chanjori had been a mistake. All the feelings he ever had about her were still simmering away inside of him. He looked at her throwing her head back as she laughed exposing her beautiful long neck. His fingers ached to pull that hair out of the pins holding it firmly in place. It was sacrilege to tie up that thick mane of hers. It should be draped around her shoulders, preferably skimming her tits as she was riding him.

Jesus, if only he could get her out of his system. Maybe a fuck for old times' sake would do it?

Then he could clear off and as soon as the old sod died, and she'd have to leave the house. An image of Ollie flashed before his eyes. He didn't really want to evict him though. It was his home.

Even if he kept Chanjori, he'd have to force her to leave. There was no way she could continue to live there. Louise would go mad if she knew about their past, and if she had any idea about the way his thoughts were going right now, there'd be no wedding.

He'd purposely not enlightened Louise when she'd asked about Eve, and it was unlikely Jo would have said much. She rarely discussed anything to do with Chanjori House on the occasions they met up in London. So, Louise's assumption that Eve was his father's age suited him. What was the point in telling her anything different? It would only make her jealous and he really didn't want the grief.

His thoughts drifted to Chanjori and his overwhelming desire to get rid of it. Doubts kicked in though when he thought about his mother. She loved to tell him when he was younger that he'd be able to pass it on to his eldest child when he eventually had children. If he had them. He couldn't quite imagine Louise wanting to be pregnant. That might be a step too far for her, playing havoc with her almost perfect figure. An image of a naked Louise sprung to mind. Strange how his cock didn't twitch thinking about that, yet one look at Eve with her body covered by a dress, and he felt the ache in his balls.

Rather than make any hasty decisions, maybe he should wait and encourage Jo to continue living at the house. That was a good option, having someone there all the time to look after the place. Then he and Louise could come up for long weekends and holidays. But then again, looking across at Jo, she was obviously smitten, so fuck knows what was going to happen there once the old man had gone.

One thing he *was* certain about, the old man would share his view the chauffeur was a money-grabbling loser. Poor Jo. She certainly wasn't at the front of the queue in the looks department, and her leg deformity, which no amount of surgery had ever been able to rectify, had given her a massive complex. She was giggling right now, at something chauffeur boy had whispered to her. Yep, she was loved-up, so it was obvious he was sorting her. But that predator wouldn't want Jo for herself, Rick was sure of that. Men like him were only after one thing, and it wasn't good sex. Money would be his driving force, and it was obvious she'd be his way to get it. And his sweet sister was totally oblivious.

The band was playing a song he liked and he had a sudden urge to hold Eve. He walked around to her seat, "Would you like to dance?"

She looked stunned. "Err . . . no thank you. I'm just chatting to Hugh. He's in the middle of telling me about his recent holiday to the Far East."

Rick painted an exaggerated wounded expression on his face for Hugh's benefit. "Can you believe she's turned me down after I've plucked up the courage to ask her to dance?"

The old geezer smiled, "Go and dance, my dear, lighten things up a bit. It must be a very difficult evening for you."

A glance at Eve's face told him she wasn't happy. Accomplished as she was at social etiquette, he knew everything there was to know about her. She had nowhere to hide and being the lady she was, she wouldn't want to draw any attention to herself by refusing again.

"Very well then, that would be nice, Rick, thank you."

He pulled her chair out for her and trailed his arm along her lower back as he led her towards the dance floor. Pleasure curled in his chest at the thought of holding her.

He needed to remember what she'd done.

They reached the dance floor and stood facing each other. Even the touch of his arm around her waist sent his senses into overdrive. He linked his hand with hers. She felt soft and amenable, although she kept a respectful distance from him as they started moving to the music. She was so tense. He could feel her stiff body and she purposely wasn't speaking to him.

"Relax, Evie," he whispered, "all this sexual tension isn't good for you."

She pulled back, "Do you mind, speaking to me like that," she snapped, "I think you're forgetting who I'm married to."

"I'm not forgetting anything; I know exactly who you're married to." His voice softened, "But I know he can't give you what you need right now, whereas I can."

She went to move away but he'd anticipated it and pulled her closer, moving their bodies to the music. She was so feminine and smelled fresh and sensual. He savoured the softness and curves of her alluring body as they moved rhythmically to the music. God, he wanted her.

"What are you protesting for? You feel the pull between us, Evie." He whispered in her ear, "You want me as much as I want you. And tonight, all you have to do is say the word and we can relieve all that stress you're carrying around."

"That's enough, Rick. Let go of me. Have some respect, will you."

He threw back his head and laughed as if she'd told him a joke.

"Respect? Are you kidding me? How could I possibly respect you after what you did? Actually, I've just realised why you like chauffeur boy, it's because you have so much in common. You're both after the star prize."

"How dare you. Keep your comments and your dirty mind to yourself."

This time she got away and he didn't try to stop her. Now he was really up for her. Tomorrow, he was going to leave, but before he did, he was going to have her begging for him. It was going to happen. He was going to fuck her one more time. Then he could leave her behind, leave the old man behind, and Chanjori House. He'd forget the whole depressing lot and get on with his life in London.

24

Rick's eyes were still on her as she walked gracefully toward the stage to receive the award for the old man. She didn't just walk, she glided. Her poised movements no doubt due to some sort of deportment training. That would be down to her mother pushing her into ballet, tap, and singing lessons as a child; reliving her failed life through her daughter.

He could tell Eve was anxious. She hid it well, but he knew her. The bloke giving out the award kissed her on both cheeks . . . and lingered there far too long for his liking.

Eve leant toward the microphone, and cleared her throat. She was clutching the award in one hand and holding a prepared speech in the other. But she didn't need it really. Eve was a performer and was able to articulately deliver a thank-you speech to rival any great orator.

She referred to his father, *her husband,* explaining that he was too ill to collect the award himself but had asked her to say a few words on his behalf.

She looked stunning under the bright lights of the stage. That gorgeous long hair of hers pinned up on top of her head, shining as if she'd just stepped out of a salon. It exposed her beautiful long neck and simple pearl earrings and matching necklace.

Her breasts were high and firm. Not like a woman that had given birth at all. And that flat stomach of hers, even Louise, who hadn't had children didn't have a stomach as flat as Eve's. Was she wearing that dress to tempt every man in the room? It was almost as if she'd sewn herself into it, the way it clung to every contour of her body causing his blood to rush hot and fast southward. Good job he was sitting down. He looked around the table and reached for her glass of red wine and took a long slug, eventually finishing it.

His eyes drifted towards his sister sitting with chauffeur boy. They were holding hands while they listened to Eve's speech. Jo glanced lovingly at him and he lifted her hand to his lips and kissed her fingers. Judging by the look on Jo's face, she'd got it really bad. But he could see the pound signs in chauffeur boy's eyes. There was no way he was in love with Jo. Rick had met his type before. He'd found a way of elevating his status, and stupid bloody Jo was sucked in by it all. He'd no doubt ask her to marry him when the old man died. Jo would be grieving and say yes, and bingo, he would have a millionaire for a wife. He'd only need to stay with her a couple of years at the most, and then he'd be made. A quick divorce and a huge settlement.

Poor, poor Jo. As a teenager, she'd never really had a boyfriend. It wasn't just her disability, Jo didn't have the confidence. She didn't have the looks that the other girls had. She was a plain girl and concentrated on studying rather than trying to make the best of herself. She was academically able, but that was because education was all she had.

At college, she met no-mark Tom Grundy. He had no prospects whatsoever, studying one of those Mickey Mouse degrees in media. Jo thought she was in love with him, but the old man had seen him off. The spotty twenty-year-old had accepted a large amount of money to go to university across the other side of the country and have no further contact with his sister. Jo was devastated at the time, but soon came to believe he didn't really care for her. She still had no idea he was paid to leave her.

What would it take to get rid of chauffeur boy? He needed to think. There was no way he was going to allow him to marry his sister.

25

Eve sat next to Rick in the front of the car on the way home. It was a better option than Niall sitting next to him. She sensed all evening the tension simmering away inside of Rick towards Niall.

Jo and Niall whispered together in the back as lovers do, and it felt almost as if she was alone in the car with Rick. She was aware of him surreptitiously glancing at her legs. The dress she was wearing wasn't helping. It was elegant enough, but she hadn't counted on a sitting position and it riding up far too high on her thighs. She attempted again to pull it by the hem but it hardly shifted.

She needed to detract from the tension in the car, "I think the evening went as well as can be expected. So many people asked about Chester, they were really concerned."

Jo spoke from the back of the car, "You did a great speech, Eve, well done. Dad would have been so proud of you. Don't you think, Rick?"

"What?"

"I was just saying about Eve's speech, wasn't it good?"

"It was, yes."

"Oh, don't hold back on the enthusiasm will you," Jo said sarcastically, "we think she did brilliantly, don't we Niall?"

It was obvious Niall didn't want to be involved in the conversation. Eve could sense it. But he did give a fitting reply.

"Yes, you did really well. It's not easy speaking in public."

"Like you'd know," Rick replied cynically.

"That's enough, Rick," Eve chastised.

He shrugged, "I was only meaning that I wouldn't have thought a chauffeur would have experience of speaking publicly."

"Well he can generalise, can't he? There's no need to be so sarcastic."

She gave Jo one of those let's just get home looks, and put the car radio on. For the rest of the journey nobody spoke. It wasn't far, but it felt like miles until they turned onto the drive at Chanjori.

Rick accelerated past Niall's cottage.

"Hey," Jo said, "we want to get out there."

Rick speeded up.

"Rick. Take us back," Jo told him assertively, "we want to go to Niall's."

He carried on down the drive until he pulled up at the main house. Whether that was his way of making Niall walk home to his house, Eve wasn't sure. She was fairly certain though after a night out with plenty of alcohol, Jo and Niall would want to spend the night together. Whatever Rick's plan was, it clearly backfired by the new assertive Jo. As soon as they stopped, she opened the car door and stepped out and Niall followed her.

"Right Niall, I wasn't going to suggest you stayed at Chanjori with me just yet, but maybe it's time you did. Come on, we'll have a night cap before we go up."

Rick was out of the car in a second. "He's not staying here."

"Yes, he is. You don't own the house yet, Rick. This is still Dad's house."

"Yeah," he sneered, "and I don't think he's going to be happy about the chauffeur shagging the rich heiress in it, do you?"

Niall delivered a sharp unexpected punch, smack into Rick's face. He'd taken them all completely by surprise. Rick stumbled backwards onto the gravel, catching the side of his head on one of the huge stones marking the driveway.

He was back on his feet in no time, and Eve anticipated what would happen next. She threw herself in front of Niall.

"Get out the fucking way," Rick barked at her.

"No. Stop this. Have some respect . . . both of you."

Still standing in front of Niall, Eve turned towards Jo, "Please Jo, go to the cottage," she didn't want to bar them from the house, but tonight wasn't the right night for Niall to stay. "Just for tonight."

Jo hesitated.

"Please," she begged, "No more tonight. Think of your dad."

Fury was written all over Jo's face but she turned, and without another word, looped her arm in Niall's and started walking towards the cottage."

Rick's eyes were black with anger and Eve matched his stare.

"We'd better get you inside and look at your head," she said, breaking the eye-lock between them.

The warmth of the house was inviting as they entered, but Eve felt cold and a little nauseous from the red wine she'd had. Rick was behaving like a total prick.

"You'd better go in the library and get a drink," she told him, "I'll check with the nurse on your father, and bring the first-aid kit. Here," she opened her clutch bag and handed him a wad of tissues, "that looks nasty, use this against your head so you don't get blood everywhere."

Chester was sleeping peacefully.

"Hello, Mrs Forrest, have you had a nice evening?" the nurse whispered.

"Yes, thank you. How has he been?"

"Very sleepy now. He's been reminiscing with your housekeeper and I think that tired him out."

Eve smiled. She'd asked Gilly to sit with Chester and she'd been eager to help.

"Oh, he'll have enjoyed that. Gilly's been with this family for much of her adult working life. Mr Forrest is very fond of her."

"Yes, it appears that way," the nurse smiled, "she was making him laugh with tales about things that happened when the children were little."

"That's nice." She looked across at Chester. He looked settled. "I'll leave you to it then. Goodnight."

"Goodnight, Mrs Forrest."

How sad. We're all going about our daily lives while he's slipping away.

Eve returned to the library with the first-aid kit and a small bowl. Rick was sitting on the sofa with a large whisky in one hand, and pressing the tissues to his head with the other. She widened her eyes at the measure in the glass.

"You're sure you've got enough to drink?" she said sarcastically.

"It's medicinal," he replied with a glint in his eye, "and unlike you all, I've not been drinking this evening."

"Yes, and you've nobody but yourself to blame for that. You should have let the agency driver take us."

He took another drink of his whisky, to avoid replying no doubt.

She sat next to him and poured Savlon into the small bowl she'd rested on the coffee table. Rick was still pressing the tissues to his head.

"Here, let me see."

A deep gash was prominent from the side of his head to his forehead.

It must hurt.

Her tummy knotted, which was stupid; he'd brought it on himself. The cut would benefit from a hospital visit, but she knew he wouldn't go. Men like Rick and his father saw anything requiring medical treatment as a weakness.

She soaked some cotton wool and leant towards him and applied it to the cut. It would sting like mad and anyone else would have flinched, but not Rick. He was far too tough to be affected by a little smarting.

She tried to ignore his closeness and focus on cleaning the wound but his face was so near she could feel his breath on her cheeks as he exhaled. And he seemed to be exhaling rather a lot.

"I've got some steristrips left over from when Oliver cut his leg. That will hold the cut so it can heal. Hopefully it's not deep enough to scar."

"I wouldn't worry too much about scaring, I've had worse than that from a woman's nails."

An image of her hands raking down his naked body sent tingles through her clit.

She needed to focus on the injury, but the only thing she could sense were their knees touching. Was it deliberate? She wouldn't put it past him. He'd implied earlier that she only had to say the word and he'd have sex with her.

"Anyway," he stared at her, "what's this caring approach all about? I hadn't got you down as a regular nurse."

"No, and I hadn't got you down as regular thug either. Why were you goading Niall like that? It was obvious he was going to react." She dabbed his cut with some clean cotton wool, "Press on that a minute."

"Because he's after only one thing, that's why. He sees Jo as his ticket out of the crap life he has."

"That's not fair. Can't you be happy for her? She's going to lose her dad soon, and she'll need someone to lean on. She loves him."

"Yeah, right."

"Why are you so cynical? You're engaged to be married. You must be in love?" She started to pull the cut together with a steristrip.

"Ah, love. I find that subjective depending on what sex you are," he mocked.

"What do you mean what sex you are?"

A smirk found his lips. "Take men for instance. They fall in lust, but women sugar-coat it and call it love."

She applied the last steristrip. The cut had stopped bleeding. Why she was even having this conversation with him she didn't know.

"I have no idea what you're talking about, Rick."

"I'm talking about when a female snares a bloke because they want a husband, a home and children, and to them that's love. They spend the next ten years trying to mould him into something he isn't, and eventually when they can't, they divorce him and screw him in the courts."

He sniggered, "Whereas the male species, all they really want to do is fuck regularly without hassle. So they get married, and then do you know what happens?" He didn't wait for her to answer, "As soon as the woman gets a ring on her finger, she gets altitude sickness."

She frowned.

"Oh, come on," he said sarcastically, "don't say you've never had a headache going upstairs to avoid sex."

She scooped up the bloody dressings and put them in a plastic bag. "You're being ridiculous and I feel sorry for your fiancée. I don't know what's made you so cynical?"

"Don't you?" He arched an eyebrow, "Maybe it's got something to do with a young girl who couldn't get enough of me and told me over and over again how much she loved me, but saw pound signs and married my old man instead. What sort of love is that, eh, you tell me?"

She really didn't want to go there. "That was a long time ago," she dismissed.

"Do you love him?"

She didn't answer. His voice become guttural, "Do you scream his name like you screamed mine when you're coming? Has he ever fucked you until you could barely stand up?"

He grabbed her arm and their faces were centimetres apart. She remembered. Calling his name every time she climaxed with his fingers, his mouth, his cock. She'd only ever screamed for Rick.

His eyes flickered dark and dangerously.

She could have pulled away, she *should* have pulled away, but she didn't. She wanted him to kiss her.

Energy pulsed through her as his mouth found hers. His lips were firm, hers were pliant. There was no softness, no holding back.

His possessive mouth seduced her. Caressing. Nipping. Inviting. Taking. It had been so long, yet it felt like only yesterday.

"I want you," he breathed, "and you want me, Evie."

She did. She wanted to feel him again. She wanted him to fuck her like he had all those years ago.

"Say it!" he rasped.

Liquid heat oozed through her body. Everything felt throbbing and swollen, especially between her legs.

His hand reached behind her and as he released her zip, the blood rushed down to her core. "Say it," he repeated as his lips trailed down her neck.

"Yes," she breathed, "yes."

Her dress was around her waist and she eased it from her. She didn't want to pause from the kissing, it felt so good. The dress was in a heap on the floor and he released her bra, and seeing his pupils darken as his eyes devoured her breasts, thrilled her. She knew how much he used to love her firm breasts.

His mouth gorged on one while his fingers played with the other. The feeling was sensational. He sucked hard on her nipple before drawing it into his mouth. Her pussy was flooding and her clit throbbed as he sucked one nipple and rolled the other. Jolts of pleasure ricocheted through her.

"Your tits are beautiful," he moaned.

He pulled away from her and ripped off his shirt. A glimpse of his rock-hard pecs travelled to her pussy, making her ache with need. He undid his trousers. He wasn't even wearing underpants. Every nerve in her body quivered at his heavily veined shaft. Forget any foreplay, she wanted him deep inside her.

He didn't disappoint. He ripped off her pants, and slid his hand between her wet mound, inserting one finger inside her, and then two. She moaned for him, clenching her inner muscles around them as he circled her clit with his thumb.

He looked into her eyes, "You want this, Eve, as much as I do."

He manoeuvred himself, holding his huge dick, and she wrapped her arms around his neck pushing herself against him, feeling her nipples against his chest. Her entire body was crying out to be fucked by him.

One thrust and he was deep inside her. He felt amazing. For a second his eyes met hers and they were still. She wasn't sure who moved first, but very quickly, their rhythm began. He slammed into her and withdrew in a frenzied pace, grinding against her swollen clit. He pulled out and pushed back in, his dick filling and stretching her while his balls slapped against her ass.

"You're so fucking wet," he breathed.

It had been years since she'd had sex, and the excitement was quickly mounting. He plunged relentlessly in and out, taking her so close.

His thrusts became harder and faster, "Mine Eve, you're fucking mine. You belong to me."

She tangled her hands in his hair as the pressure was peaking, the tingles intensifying.

"Come for me, Eve."

A rocketing surge of heat and ecstasy clasped her belly as her skin tightened. An explosion burst deep within her, "Oh God, yes, Rick," she screamed as she writhed, with every nerve twitching and quivering as she desperately rode her orgasm.

He eased one of her legs over his shoulder and pounded into her, faster, and then faster still. The pace was melting and unrelenting.

"Your cunt's so fucking tight," he groaned. She kissed the sweat off his brow and felt his thickness deep within her as he jerked and thumped his seed high with brutal force.

Their breathing subsided. What had they done? Her husband was dying upstairs and they were having sex downstairs. Could they have got any lower?

Neither of them spoke.

He moved away from her to retrieve his trousers, and passed her dress to her.

She couldn't look at him as she quickly slipped it on, minus her underwear. There wasn't time to mess about putting that on.

She looked at him and shook her head. "God, Rick, what have we done?"

His expression hardened. Gone was the man who'd just given her the most incredible orgasm from the only sex she'd had in years.

"It was sex, Eve, that's all," he shrugged, "it was long overdue."

"But . . . what happens now?"

"What do you mean, what happens now? Nothing. We fucked," he raised an eyebrow, "and nice as it was, it doesn't change a thing. You're still the woman that married my father for money, and when he pops his clogs, you'll still be out of this house. A quick shag isn't going to change that. I'm sorry if you thought it would."

Sadness flooded through her. How could he be so cold after what they'd just shared? While it was quick and lustful sex as opposed to making love slowly, she didn't deserve his contempt.

"Get out, Rick," she hissed, "get out of this house. I never want to see you again."

She hated the casual way he picked up his dinner jacket, as if he couldn't care less about her feelings.

The heated desire in his eyes that had thrilled her minutes earlier had now been replaced with distaste. It was painful to see.

"You might be married to Chester Forrest and think that gives you airs and graces, but to me, you'll always be Evie Henshaw. You've just proven that the way you dropped your knickers. So, you can cut all the high and mighty lady of the manor crap and stop ordering me around." He widened his eyes, "And let's not forget who'll own this house soon."

She walked towards the door, trying to hold on to some dignity. She reached for the handle. "Well, right this minute, my husband owns it. So, *let's not forget* that." She wrenched the door open, "And you're no longer welcome. I want you gone by the morning."

She held her head high. He didn't need to see exactly how cheap he'd made her feel. But he had. She was appalled at herself. What woman has opportunistic sex while her husband is dying a few feet away?

He walked towards her, smirking with his jacket flung over his shoulder and held casually in place by his hand.

He paused at the doorway. "Great trip down memory lane," he winked, "happy house-hunting."

Despite an urge to slam the door on him, she didn't. She closed it quietly after him. But once it was closed, she sank down to sit on the floor with her back against it. Then the flood gates opened.

She cried for her dying husband she'd betrayed. She cried for her mother who could no longer give her a hug and reassure her everything would be okay, and she cried for her son who she was going to have to uproot from the only home he'd ever known. But most of all she cried because for a few blissful minutes, she'd forgotten the pain and forgotten her responsibilities, she'd been happy. And he'd managed to crush that by implying she was nothing more than a slut.

26

Rick sat by his father's bed. He'd seen him when he first arrived at Chanjori but since then he'd kept away from his room. Listening to Jo going on about him was more than enough without having to see his miserable face. Looking at him today though, it was obvious he hadn't got long. He was grey around the gills, and thin with an odd aura about him. Today would be the last time he'd see him alive.

But he wasn't sad . . . it was indifference he felt.

The nurse was fussing around the old git, positioning the pillow behind his head and then smearing Vaseline on his lips with a tissue.

"Enough, now," his father pulled away, "can you leave us? We need to talk in private."

"Of course, Mr Forrest. I'll go and get myself a cup of tea. Would you like one bringing back?"

"Not right now."

"Okay, long as you're sure."

"I am."

The nurse walked towards the door and smiled invitingly at Rick. He was used to females trying to catch his eye, but this morning, Eve's unique smell was still on him despite showering to rid himself of her.

How was it she was the only woman that ever left a mark on him? He'd fucked endless women but it was her that lingered. Yet another reason for him to get the hell out of there.

Rick waited until the nurse closed the door and he was alone with his father. "I'm leaving today."

The old bastard's face showed no emotion. "I'm surprised you stayed as long as you have."

"Yeah, me too, but I'm going now. Jo didn't want me to leave without saying goodbye."

"Bye then."

He couldn't keep the hate from his voice, "You really are a piece of shit, you know."

"Yep, that's me."

"You're not even bothered what I think of you, are you?"

"No."

"So why . . ." he shook his head, "why send for me in the first place?"

"I told you. I want to make sure that Josephine will be looked after. She'll be a wealthy young woman and I don't want some bloody gigolo coming along and benefitting from my money."

"Your money? Without my mother, you wouldn't have half as much as you have. You always seem to forget that."

"I don't forget anything. And you of all people should know things are not always as black and white as they seem."

"Oh, spare me the details. I know you married my mother for her money. She knew it too. She knew everything about you . . . even the whores you paid for."

"You know nothing," he spat. "People often marry for money and have done for centuries. If you honestly think the woman you're marrying is doing it because she's madly in love with you, then you're a bloody fool. Do you think she'd be interested if you were Rick Forrest the plumber? No," he dismissed, "you know damn well she wouldn't be. She's interested in exactly what she can get out of a union with you."

Rick walked over to the window and looked out at the pool. Ollie was practicing his diving. He was a good kid and suddenly he realised why he had such an effect on him. It was because Ollie reminded him of himself at that age.

His chest seemed to tighten. He needed to leave now before he got any more attached to him . . . and his slut of a mother.

"Anyway," the old man interrupted his thoughts, "pleasant as it is to have this father and son chat, you haven't answered my question. Will you look after Josephine?" The sly bastard played his ace card, "It's what your mother would have wanted."

Rick turned and focussed on the withered-up man in front of him. "Yeah, I'll look after Jo's affairs, but not because you're asking. I'll do it for my mother." He couldn't stop himself, he loathed him so much, "And one other thing before I go, just so you know. You were the worst husband and father anyone could ever have, and I hope where you're going it'll be bloody hot."

The git never even flinched. It wasn't until much later Rick realised why. He was waiting to deliver his sucker punch he'd kept in his back pocket for years.

His evil grey eyes suddenly seemed to have some light back in them. It wasn't happiness, but it was close to excitement. "There's something *you* need to know."

Rick stopped him. "I'm through with all this family shit. I've had your number for years. You've always hated me, even as a kid, you never had any praise for me, never attended any parents' evenings or sport events. You were only ever interested in Jo. You even married Eve to get back at me. But why the hell she'd marry an old fart like you, God knows. It could only be for money."

He almost smiled. "That's the trouble with you, Rick, you might be a hot shot lawyer, but you'll always be that pathetic mummy's boy. Only someone with an ego as big as yours would think I married her to get back at you."

"I know that's what you did," he sneered.

"Well you're wrong. I married her to keep her *away* from you."

Rick needed to leave. He didn't want to talk anymore about her. "Like I said, I've not got time for this mumbo jumbo family crap. I'm not interested in anything you have to say. I'll do what you asked and oversee Jo's estate." He moved towards the foot of the bed and took one last look at the old git's eyes, which he didn't know then, would be etched on his mind as he delivered his final blow.

"Before you go," the ugly bastard smirked, "you need to hear this."

Jo woke up and found the other side of the bed empty. She hadn't heard Niall get up, but they'd been late getting to sleep. She grabbed his discarded white formal shirt and buttoned it up. A smile played on her lips remembering how he'd ripped it off as they'd fallen into bed and made love after the ball. His dinner suit was in a heap, so she quickly put the trousers and jacket on a hanger.

Rick had been awful last night. She was furious with him. She'd never been one for confrontation but she was determined to have it out with him when she went back to the main house. He had no business talking to Niall the way he had. She abhorred violence of any kind, but her heart had given a little leap at the way Niall had defended her and thumped Rick. He deserved it.

Since she'd been with Niall, she'd become a different person. It was like she'd been a closed bud for all these years, but finally the bud had opened and she was flowering. The thought of him leaving for America, tore her apart. She feared that once he left, their cosy bubble might burst.

She found him in the kitchen, chopping up some tomatoes and bacon. He turned to her as she stood in the doorway, "Now then, sleepyhead, you've spoiled the surprise. I'm cooking you a Niall special."

She widened her eyes, "And what exactly is a Niall special?"

He began cracking eggs into a bowl. "My Spanish omelette, which I can assure you is renowned in many parts of the world."

"Sounds delicious. I can't wait."

He walked over to her and wrapped her in his arms. "Last night was lovely," he kissed her gently, "you were lovely."

She kissed him back; he would be leaving that evening and she was going to miss him so much. Clutching the nape of his neck, she pressed herself against him and deepened the kiss. It had only been a few hours since they'd made love, but she wanted him again. She couldn't get enough of him. All the years she'd lived without sex, and now with him, she wanted it all the time.

He groaned and pulled away, "Any more of that and we'll not be having my special, well not the Spanish omelette anyway," he grinned and hoisted her up. He walked a couple of steps to the kitchen table and sat her down on it, pulling up a chair for her to rest her legs on.

"You sit there and watch the master in action."

He reached into the cupboard for salt and pepper and sprinkled some in the omelette mixture. She didn't want to spoil their breakfast but she was anxious to talk about how the previous evening had ended.

"I'm so sorry about Rick's behaviour last night. Maybe I shouldn't have taken you to the ball. I honestly didn't know he was coming when I asked you."

"Don't you worry about it," he shrugged, "I can understand he's looking out for you. I'd be the same if you were my sister."

"You're too generous. I'm going to have it out with him when I get back to the house. He's got no business talking to you that way. It's my life and I'll see who I want to without any interference from him."

"You don't need to on my account." He made a face, "I think it was probably a step too far suggesting we slept at the house though."

She smiled at him. How come he was so wise and she wasn't?

"You're probably right. Still, his behaviour was unforgivable and I'm going to speak to him about that, but not until I've sampled your delicious breakfast. Remind me, what time's your flight?"

"Eight thirty. I've got to take Eve and Oliver to the pool today; apparently, it's the swimming final. I'll leave about five for the airport."

Jo glanced at the clock on the wall. "Yes, I'm sitting with Dad, otherwise I'd have gone with them."

It hit her again he was going away from her. They'd only just started their relationship; she didn't want it to stop, even if it was for only a couple of weeks. Tears pricked her eyes.

"What's the matter?" he frowned.

There was a thickness in her throat, "I'm going to miss you, that's all."

He moved the chair away with his foot and positioned himself between her legs. Their heads were almost level.

"Hey," he wiped the tear that had escaped and rolled down her cheek with his thumb, "the time will fly by, you'll see, I'll be back before you know it."

"When you come back," she sniffed, "maybe we could spend some time together. Perhaps you could come to London with me to visit my publisher? I usually go on my own but I'd love to take you and visit some sights together."

Was she rushing the relationship, asking him to spend a weekend away with her? He didn't look gushing, maybe she was pushing too much? "If you want to, that is, you don't have to."

"Of course I want to come." He leaned in for another kiss.

Who'd have believed she'd ever find such happiness?

He started to undo the buttons on his shirt she was wearing, "As nice as I think you look in my shirt," he breathed, "I think it's got to go."

Heat churned within her belly, sending a shooting fiery sensation between her thighs as he removed the shirt from her shoulders. There was something rather decadent about being naked on the kitchen table, while he was still in a tee shirt and shorts. Her nipples tightened, stung to life by the desire in his blue eyes.

His gaze slid down and paused at the valley between her breasts, before he reached to stroke the hard nipple and roll it between his fingers.

He thrust his tongue in her mouth as he kissed her hungrily. She felt him pull her towards the edge of the table.

The kissing assault continued. Pleasure burst down her body as his fingertips moved from one nipple to the next. "Has anyone ever told you, you have gorgeous breasts?"

She breathed into his mouth, "not lately."

He pulled away, eased her back onto the huge table and hitched her ass towards the edge.

Slowly he slid two fingers deep inside her, "You're so ready for me."

She was always ready for him.

"I can't wait," he breathed, taking a condom from his pocket and easing his shorts down. "I need to be inside you." Seconds later, he was, in one long, smooth motion. Pure feminine delight fizzled through her at the fullness of him, and it was thrilling to see him stood between her legs while she lay naked and exposed.

He pulled out almost all the way, and then thrust into her, filling her to the hilt again and again. She loved his guttural groan each time he pushed in.

The table was uncomfortable and her hip ached from the position, but nothing was going to get in the way of the sensations the friction of his cock was creating against her clit. In and out, the pleasure was mounting. She moaned as his fingers found her clit. He rubbed hard as he rammed into her again and again, faster, deeper, harder.

She placed her elbows on the table to steady herself. It felt like she was hanging from the edge of a cliff and ready to drop. Her pussy clenched around him as his thick length drove into her with increasing speed, shifting the pleasure as she instinctively tried to drive him deeper.

The first spasm hit her, "Niall, Niall," she screamed as a seizing, clenching orgasm burst deep within her, "Oh, God, Niall."

Seconds later he gave his own ragged cry and she felt the throb of his dick as he came deep inside her.

It took a few moments for their breathing to settle. He moved away from her and pulled up his shorts before helping her into a sitting position.

"You didn't fancy my Spanish omelette, then?"

"I do now," she laughed, "I'm starving. Have I got time for a quick shower . . . or do you fancy a bath? Both of us I mean."

"Sounds good to me. And then we have to eat. I need sustenance."

"Pity we aren't at the house, we'd get fed there."

"Well we aren't, so you'll have to get used to my cooking if you're stopping with me."

Stopping with him . . . Does that mean he wants a permanent relationship?

Jo lay between his legs with her back to him in the bath. It was cramped but she didn't care. She was with him and that's all that mattered. Her tummy tightened at the thought of him leaving. Her fear was it would break the magic they had between them.

She wanted to know everything there was to know about him. "All this cooking you like to do. Who taught you, your mother?"

"No. She can cook but it's very basic. I was married once upon a time to a chef."

"Really. How long ago was that?"

"Ages ago. We were both young and it didn't last long."

"Were there any children?"

"Good God, no. Lucy wasn't interested in children. Not then anyway, she was only twenty three."

"Aw, that's sad. You'd make a great dad."

Did he want children in the future? She knew so little about him, but she didn't want to come across as clingy and wanting to settle down, when they'd only just got together.

It was almost as if he knew the way her mind was racing ahead.

"I like kids, but they're a long way off in my life. What about you, do you want kids?"

"Yes, eventually," she purposely kept her voice light, "but not right now. I'm like you; it's something in the future."

Was he relieved?

"Your brother's a great kid. I like him."

"I know I'm biased," she smiled, "but he is rather special."

"What's going to happen when I'm away? Will Eve use an agency driver to take him to school?"

"She's thinking of letting him go on the bus. He's been on about it for ages, so she's going to give it a try. Don't say anything to Oliver though, in case she changes her mind."

"Good for her, he's always going on about the bus to me. He's growing up now so she's going to have to let him sooner or later. The bus will stop outside the gates anyway so she doesn't need to worry."

"That's what I've said. But if she does let him while you're away, he'll not want to go back to being chauffeured when you get back," she laughed.

"You're right," he kissed her neck and his beard tickled her chin.

"Have you always had a beard?"

"I've had this for," he paused, "about seven years now I think. I shave it off as and when."

"As and when?"

"It's my disguise. If I rob a bank, I can shave it all off and then look nothing like the CCTV pictures. That way the police can't find me."

She loved this playful side of him.

"So, you rob a lot of banks, do you?"

"Only when funds get low."

She turned her head and looked up at him. "I'm going to miss you so much, you know."

He leant forward and kissed her, "Not half as much as I'm going to miss you."

28

Eve sat in the back of the car with Oliver on the journey to the swimming pool. It was the final swimming gala and she'd asked Niall to stop at a pharmacy on the way.

He pulled into a space outside a row of shops. "There's a pharmacy there on the corner," he said. Oliver unbuckled his seat belt to go with her.

"You stay here, I'll only be a minute," Eve told him.

"Can't you go later," he groaned, "we don't want to miss the start?"

"We won't. I'll only be five minutes. You tell Niall your tactics while I'm gone."

Eve got out of the car and headed for the pharmacy. Oliver was right, it would have been better going later, but time was of the essence. She needed emergency contraception.

It was unlikely she could get pregnant so soon after her last period, but it wasn't worth the risk. Unprotected sex was exactly that, and the consequences didn't bear thinking about.

Twenty minutes later she made her way back to the car irritated at having to endure the pharmacist firmly explaining that she needed to access a permanent form of contraception rather than relying on an emergency one. She knew that. Sex with Rick Forrest wasn't likely to happen again. It was a one off that she bitterly regretted.

The whole morning had started badly. Her head was beginning to ache, which wasn't helping. Plus, Rick leaving had unsettled Oliver. She would do anything to prevent her little boy being sad. Even though it was her that had told Rick to go, she didn't realise how it would affect Oliver.

She got back into the car. "Sorry, sweetie there was a queue at the pharmacy." She nodded at Niall to go and glanced at her watch, "Don't worry, there's plenty of time."

Oliver pulled a face, "I wish Rick was here to see me in the final."

"I know you do," she sympathised, "but he must have had work to go back to in London. He's stayed longer than he should have anyway."

"Is he going to come back?"

"I'm really not sure. Jo will know."

"I wanted to win it for him, 'cause he's helped me."

"Yes, but I've told you before," even as she was saying it, Rick's insolent smirk flashed before her eyes, "it doesn't matter if you don't. It's the taking part that counts."

"No, it isn't. Rick said fairies talk like that."

A firm talk to her son was in order, but right now wasn't the time. She'd wait until after the race.

"I think that's quite enough about Rick for today."

Oliver took no notice. "If I win, can we ring him after the race?"

Maybe it was a good thing Rick had left when he did. Oliver was getting far too attached to him.

"We'll see. Oh, look, we're here."

He wasn't going to be distracted. "I'm going to ask Jo if we can Skype him.

Eve felt the tension in her neck being back at the pool watching Oliver. She tried to ease it by rubbing it. She couldn't stop thinking back to the semi-final when Rick had sat alongside her. Daft as it was, she missed him. It had been a lovely day. She still couldn't believe Oliver had beaten Danny and wasn't sure at all he would be able to repeat that again in the final. It was probably a one off.

She looked around the seating area and could see Rosemary sat nearer the front with the usual entourage. No doubt she'd be on edge, not wanting her son to lose again to Oliver.

Minutes later, the boys filed out for the race. The seating area was full to capacity and the crowd cheered. She gave Oliver a thumbs-up as he looked at her before putting his goggles on.

Her tummy fluttered with nerves. Although she'd repeated the mantra of taking part being the most important thing, she still wanted him to win. She hated the turmoil her little boy must be going through with Chester being so ill, and she wanted him to experience a bit of joy amongst all the gloom.

The adjudicator interrupted her thoughts. "On your marks . . . get set . . . go!"

The boys dived in. Oliver entered the water marginally before the others and Eve's heart thumped as he pounded relentlessly down the pool. It was evident he was much faster now. Rick had not only coached him, he'd given him confidence in his own ability.

Totally oblivious to anyone around her, she was on her feet shouting and willing him on with every stroke. He turned first, but Danny caught up with him. It was neck and neck along the last few metres, but Oliver found strength from somewhere to touch before him. Eve's heart was bursting. He'd done it again. This time all on his own.

She watched Oliver on the rostrum with the other boys receiving his medal. She was so proud and wished Rick could have been there. A decent male role model had been lacking in his young life. That's why he'd taken to Rick. She knew she was a little overprotective, but she'd had to be a mother and father to him all these years. What a different life it would have been had Rick been in it from the beginning. He'd gone now though, so they needed to forget about him, but that was easier said than done.

The sex between her and Rick was still on her mind. It wasn't easy to block it out. He still had the ability to make her feel she was the only woman he wanted when he made love to her. He'd dismissed her so casually afterwards, yet despite that, there had been a magnetic pull between them. A sort of compelling dance of power and compliance. Was he like that with his fiancée? Did she make him feel that intense?

Oliver came running over to the seating area. His little face was beaming, "I did it Mum, I did it."

"You did, my darling." She gave him a hug, and for once he let her. Only for a second though. "I was bursting watching you get your medal. Let me see it."

It was still around his neck as she lifted it and examined it. "I knew you could do it," she said with more conviction than she'd actually felt.

"Did you see I touched at the same time as Danny? I thought he'd beaten me."

"I did too. But he didn't." She rested his medal on his chest, "You've done brilliantly and I'm so proud of you."

"The county selectors are here again and Mr Fell thinks they'll pick me as I won the semi's and the final."

"That'll be fabulous, darling. I hope they do."

She felt sad that they couldn't go out to celebrate his win. If only they were a normal family and could sit in a restaurant and enjoy his achievement.

"We'll have to get home to Dad. Do you fancy a McDonald's on the way home? We can get Niall to stop off."

"Yeah. Are you going to have one?"

"Definitely," she grinned. He wasn't to know how queasy she felt after her antics with Rick the previous evening and that junk food was the last thing on her mind.

"Have you got everything?"

He glanced at his bag on his shoulder, "Yeah."

"Come on then, let's get to the car and then you can ring Jo. She'll be over the moon for you."

"I wish she'd been here to see me."

"Me too, but someone had to stay with Dad."

As they left the pool area and made their way to the exit, she was poised waiting for him to ask again if he could ring Rick. She was so delighted by his achievement that she was going to give in and let him.

"Rick will be thrilled for you too. All the training he did with you on the diving in paid off."

"Yeah, he said I was a champion and he knew that from the first time he saw me swim. I wish he could have stayed though."

"Yes, but like I said, he has to work. I'm sure he was willing you on today."

His face crumpled into a frown, "I meant I wish he could have stayed for the medal ceremony. He was here watching the race."

"Here? When? I didn't see him."

"He was over the other side," he indicated with his head. "He said he'd dashed here to watch me, but then had to go straight after the race. He came to the changing room to see me. He couldn't get a seat near you so stood at the back."

Rick was actually here? How had she missed him?

"It was really crowded everywhere, sweetie, I didn't realise he was here."

"I wish he could have stayed. I like having him here."

"Yes, but he has a life in London and he's going to be getting married soon, so I don't think we'll be seeing a lot of him."

Her phone was ringing as she opened the car door. Jo's name was on the screen. "You get in, Oliver and show Niall your medal while I take this."

She pressed answer, "Hello Jo."

"Eve, you need to come home. Dad's much worse and the nurse has suggested I get you back here quickly."

Her tummy plummeted. She had mentally prepared herself, but the reality was very different from thinking about it. Chester hadn't woken when she checked on him first thing, but she hadn't thought anything was imminent. She wouldn't have left if she had.

"I'm on my way."

29

Eve held her husband's hand, while Jo clung to the other. They watched Chester slip peacefully away that evening. The nurse and Bruce were on hand but discretely kept their distance. Although expected, his death was still painful. Possibly the intravenous drugs had assisted him, Eve wasn't sure, but she was pleased for Jo that the end was peaceful. She'd expected Chester to fight for every last breath, but that didn't happen.

Eve hugged Jo and told her how much Chester loved her, and made comforting noises about him caring in his own way for Rick, which wasn't true, but it seemed the right thing to do. Jo had called Rick during the day and told him their father had deteriorated and it appeared his passing was imminent, but he hadn't come.

The hardest part was telling Oliver. She'd let him into the room in the afternoon for a short while to see Chester, but sent him to bed as normal in the evening. It wasn't a place for an eleven year old boy.

Eve was in Oliver's room when he woke up the following morning. As he wiped the sleep out of his eyes, it registered why she was sat at the side of his bed.

"Has he died?"

"Yes, darling, I'm afraid so."

Her beautiful little boy's eyes filled with tears and she wrapped her arms around him and held him tightly. This was his first experience of death.

"It's okay. He's not in any pain now. He just drifted off to sleep."

Oliver wept silently for a few minutes and then pulled away, "Is he still in his room?"

"No, sweetheart."

"Where is he?"

"He's been taken to a chapel of rest until the funeral."

"When's that?"

"I'm not sure yet, we'll know more today."

"Are you sad?"

"Yes, I am. Very sad. But he was suffering and I didn't like to see that. He was a strong man and was rarely ill, so it was hard for him coming to terms with being poorly."

"Do you think he's gone to heaven?"

"I hope so. Heaven sounds a nice place to be."

"Why, what's in heaven?"

"Flowers, music, calmness. A sort of tranquil place for people who have suffered like your dad."

"I heard Rick saying that Dad was going to hell. What's it like there?"

"Rick's being silly talking like that. Dad will be in heaven I promise you. Now then, I think it's best to stay off school today, I'll give them a ring and explain everything."

"Rick said hell was hot. Is it?"

"Let's not talk about things Rick said. He's always teasing, so it's best to take no notice. Are you okay to get showered or do you want me to stay a while?"

"I'm okay. Can I go in the pool?"

"Maybe not today, sweetie. We'll just have a quiet day. There's a lot to sort out."

"Is Rick coming back?"

"I'm not sure."

He didn't come back yesterday so he's hardly likely to come today.

"I hope he does. I like Rick, he's good fun."

"Well don't be setting your heart on him coming, he's a busy man so might not be able to get away."

"He'll come for the funeral though, won't he?"

"Maybe, we'll have to see."

The funeral was an elaborate affair attended by many. The crematorium was packed to capacity with work colleagues and distant family, but the one person that should have been there, and whose absence was noticed, didn't come. Rick Forrest stayed away. Eve felt terribly sad for Jo. Surely he could have made an effort for her; it was their father after all.

Eve mourned the loss of Chester. He'd been a very hard man all his life, and she was sure he didn't play by the rules. He had a private side to him she wasn't privy to, but that suited her. She had a wonderful lifestyle because of him. He could be rude and obnoxious, but she really had no reason to complain. He had never tried to be intimate with her, which was a huge relief. Quite what she would have done if he'd made advances towards her she didn't know. Thankfully, he never did. She guessed he went elsewhere for sexual gratification, but wherever or whenever that had been, she'd not heard as much as a whisper.

The eulogy was very fitting and the vicar talked about the hard working man Chester had been all his life. Nobody could argue with that. He lived and breathed oil until his illness.

Eve sat clutching Oliver's hand, worried about the impact of a funeral on her son, but he appeared to be fine. She did have to tap him a couple of times as he kept turning to look at the door. She knew exactly who he was looking for. She'd willed Rick to come also.

A huge framed photograph of Chester was prominently placed on his coffin. Jo had insisted on it. It was a photo that must have been taken about seven years ago. Chester had been such a vibrant charismatic man and the photo showed him laughing, which was a rarity. He wasn't a man to laugh very much, he'd been quite serious really. Jo must have taken the photo as she wasn't familiar with it. It must have been on one of those rare days he was relaxing and not working. The background was the beautiful grounds at Chanjori. Looking at his face staring back at her, she was struck for the first time about Rick's likeness to him. She'd never noticed it before, but now she wondered how she'd ever missed it.

The wake was held at Chanjori in the marquee that had been erected. Eve played her part thanking individuals for attending and listening to endless stories about her husband. Oliver was restless with never-ending men ruffling his hair, telling him he was *just like his dad,* and if he followed in his footsteps, he wouldn't go far wrong.

"Can I go to my room now?" Oliver asked.

She didn't blame him; she wished *she* could go to her room.

"If you want to. Will you be okay on your own?"

"If I can play on the computer."

"Go on then. I'll come up shortly. I think people are starting to make a move." She kissed his head, "You're sure you're okay?"

"I'm fine," he smiled reassuringly, "honestly Mum."

She proudly watched as he made his way to the house.

She was lucky to have him. She loved him so much.

It was an eternity before the last guest left and Eve and Jo were alone in the snug. They'd flopped on the sofas, both clutching a glass of red. Eve breathed a sigh of relief it was finally all over.

"I think it's been a wonderful send-off, don't you?" Jo said, almost reading Eve's mind.

"Yes, it has. Your father was certainly well-respected by his colleagues."

"He was. Oil's been his life really, even when he was married to Mum, he was never here. She brought us up really, not him. We were those children that were *seen and not heard*. When he came home from work, we usually had to make ourselves scarce. He certainly wasn't a father like the other kids had, taking them out for the day, trips to the cinema, attending parents' evenings. Dad didn't do any of that."

"No, but he did love you Jo, very much. He told me that often."

"I know he did," Jo nodded. "It's always been hard though as he favoured me over Rick. You'd think I would have enjoyed being the favourite over my horrible older brother, but it never pleased me, even as a young child. I wanted Dad to love us both equally."

"I thought his dislike of Rick came about when he became a teenager. I hadn't realised it stretched back to when you were children."

"Yeah, I'm afraid so," Jo sipped her wine, "I can't remember him ever being nice to Rick. It's so sad really."

"Maybe we need to cut Rick a bit of slack not being here today then, although there is part of me that thinks he should have come."

Jo shook her head, "I knew he wouldn't come. I'm surprised he came when he found out Dad was dying, to be honest."

They sat silently for a few minutes.

"Have you heard from Niall. Does he know?"

"Yes. I rang but it was his answer phone, so I emailed him. A text seemed a bit crass."

Eve sipped her wine. "That's fine then. As long as he knows."

"Bless him, he rang me and offered to come back, but I said not to."

"Really? How lovely is that? He obviously thinks a lot about you. It sounds very serious to me."

"God, I hope so." Jo's eyes filled up, "I love him, Eve."

"I guessed you did. Does he feel the same?"

"I don't know. He hasn't said as much, but the way he is with me makes me think he feels the same."

"I'm sure he does. It's still new and you've only just got together. Men are a bit slower than us women about their feelings."

"I know. Maybe I'm rushing things. I've already got myself married to him with two children."

Eve smiled. "There's nothing wrong with that. Why shouldn't you be married with children, you'd make a brilliant mum."

"Aw, thank you Eve. You must promise me, whatever happens, we'll always be this close. I can't imagine a future without you and Oliver in it." A wave of sadness passed across her face, "It's bad enough getting used to Dad not being here."

"Listen, I promise you, I'm not moving far away from here." Eve took a sip of her wine, "Anyway, changing the subject slightly, do you think Rick will sell Chanjori?"

"I don't know. He's told me to stay here and not do anything. But of course, when Niall comes back, there'll be no job for him so he'll be moving on. I'm hoping that includes me."

"I'm certain it will do. Niall strikes me as a man that will take his time. I'm sure whatever plans he has, you'll feature in them. I've seen the way he looks at you, he won't be walking away and leaving you behind."

"I hope not. I can't see a future without him in it." Jo drained her glass and placed it on the coffee table. "I hope one day in the future you meet someone too. You're only young and I'm sure with your looks, you're not destined to be on your own forever."

Eve smiled at her kindness. "Nice as your lovely words are, I'll not be on the lookout for anyone. All I want is to make a cosy home for Oliver. But not too far away as I don't want him to have to move schools, so somewhere in the village would be nice."

"You'll miss Chanjori though?"

"Yes, and Oliver certainly will. That's the hardest part, dragging him away."

"I really don't want you to go. Maybe I can speak to Rick and he'll let us all stay on."

"No, don't do that," Eve dismissed, "it would be awkward with his new wife coming here if I'm still in residence. However nice she is, she'll not like that, I'm sure."

"Mmm, I guess you're right." Jo checked her phone again and sighed. "I'll be glad when Niall does get back, as one thing him going away has taught me, he's not brilliant with communication. I would have thought today of all days, he'd have messaged me to say he's thinking about me. But there's nothing."

"There's the time difference, remember."

"Yes, maybe it's that. It's daft I know, but when I don't hear from him, all the doubts come rushing back. I start to think maybe he doesn't really want me and all of this is a ploy."

"A ploy for what?"

"Oh, I don't know. I'm just being silly. It's been a long day. I'd better go up before I drink any more wine and completely expose my paranoia."

Eve hugged Jo tightly, "Sleep tight, honey. Your dad would have been proud of you today. He loved you so much, and I do too. Don't worry about anything, you just get some sleep."

"Thank you, Eve, I love you too. Night, night."

30

Eve was sat in her car at the gates of Chanjori waiting for Oliver to be dropped off. It was day four of him going to school on the bus with the other boys. She'd reluctantly agreed, more so because it was easier while Niall was away. They used a driver from the agency if they needed one, but there didn't seem much point when Eve could wait at the gates of Chanjori for Oliver, then drive him to the house.

Oliver loved the freedom of travelling on the bus with his peers. She'd feel much better if he was driven each day to and from school, but it was unlikely when Niall returned, Oliver would want to go back to being taken by the chauffeur.

He was growing up and she knew she had to accept that. She couldn't wrap him in cotton wool forever. But he was all she'd got, and she couldn't help worrying about him. He'd been so grown up about Chester's death and wanting to get straight back to school. She'd have preferred him to stay off a bit longer. She was expecting an out pouring of grief from him, but it didn't happen. Apart from the tears he'd shed when she first told him, there hadn't been anything further, not that she'd seen anyway. Maybe he had a little tear at night in bed when she wasn't around? She'd spoken to Jo about him wanting to go straight back to school and she thought it best he should get back to his normal routine.

Eve checked her watch. Five more minutes and the bus would be here. She thought back to her bus journeys and how she hated them until that fateful day with Rick. Once he'd become her friend, she lived for them. Each morning she would get up early to apply eye make-up and blow-dry her hair. Anything that would make him find her appealing.

Rick Forrest. However hard she tried, he constantly invaded her thoughts. It was stupid, he didn't want her, but that didn't stop her wanting him. Maybe when he was married and totally out of bounds, she would think of him less. She hoped so. Her goal now was to move forward with her life. The Forrest family had dominated it so far, but now she needed to build a life for her and Oliver away from Chanjori. She'd toyed with the idea of informing Rick he was Oliver's father, but she was still scared that with his legal background he might take Oliver from her. She couldn't bear that. Even the thought of Oliver being a weekend child upset her and that would surely happen when Rick had his own children. She didn't want Oliver visiting Rick and his new family, and him feeling cheated on the periphery.

However hard she tried though to justify not telling the truth, she felt guilty. Rick was his genetic father. She'd managed to block that out for years with everyone thinking Chester was his father, which was deceitful, but she justified that as it was Chester's wish and part of their marriage agreement. She'd promised that she wouldn't divulge to anyone that Oliver wasn't Chester's son. But now she'd seen Oliver with Rick, the deceit was hitting her hard.

Thinking about it all gave her a headache. There was nothing to be gained in telling Oliver or Rick. She shrugged it off as the bus approached.

She loved it when Oliver first came home from school although he wasn't as communicative these days as he used to be. He used to tell her all sorts of stories about his day, but he was growing up now and a little less willing to discuss anything.

As the bus was level with the gates, she stared in amazement as it continued down the road.

What the hell is Oliver doing?

He's been distracted by somebody and not got off.

She put the car into gear and pulled out of the drive to follow the bus. She'd have to hope Oliver had seen her and would get off at the next stop. It would be too far for him to walk. She drove purposely behind the bus looking up at the back seat, but she couldn't see him looking out for her.

Blast. Where is he?

She indicated and overtook the bus and pulled up further down the road. She waited until the bus slowed down at the stop and exited her car. She rushed forward as a couple of kids were getting off.

"Hi," she said to the bus driver, "you missed the last stop, Chanjori House. My son should have got off there."

The driver shook his head, "Sorry, love, your lad's not on the bus."

Eve frowned, "What do you mean he isn't on the bus?" She stepped up onto the bus and looked down the back. There weren't more than a dozen kids sitting, but she couldn't see Oliver.

"Has anyone seen Oliver? Oliver Forrest. His stop is the one previous."

"He didn't get on," one of the girls replied.

Eve felt a sinking sensation in her chest. *Where is he?* She stepped down from the bus.

"Maybe he's got a lift with someone," the driver offered.

"Yes, probably. Thank you."

Eve went back to her car and telephoned the school.

"Good afternoon. Sir Michael Frodingham School."

"Hello, it's Eve Forrest. My son, Oliver Forrest hasn't come home on the bus. Is there any way you could find out if he's still in school please?"

"I'll ring the resource room, Mrs Forrest. That's where the stragglers congregate when they're waiting for a lift home. It might take a minute or two for someone to answer. Do you want to hold or I can call you back when I've located him?"

"I think I'll come straight to the school. When you've found him, can you tell him I'm on my way please?"

31

Rick reached for his phone vibrating on the bedside table.

"Leave it," Louise groaned sleepily.

He couldn't. It was his sister Jo and she wouldn't normally ring at 1 a.m., so something had to be wrong. It couldn't be the old man now though. Fuck.

"Hi Jo, you okay?"

He heard a sob, "Rick, it's Oliver . . ."

"Ollie? What's happened?"

"He's . . . someone's taken him . . . he's been kidnapped."

His voice went up an octave, "Kidnapped? What are you talking about?"

"He didn't come home from school. Someone took him. The police are all over the place. We're waiting for a call . . . from whoever has him . . . you know for a ransom or whatever."

"Jesus Christ. Are you sure? He hasn't just gone home with a friend or something?"

"Of course I'm sure," she snapped, "he's been taken, Rick. We've had to call the police. We haven't heard anything but the police insist there'll be a call."

Rick couldn't believe what he was hearing. Despite what had gone on between him and Eve, he knew how much she loved Ollie, and Jo did too. What bastard had done this?

Louise was sitting up, "What's happened?"

He put his fingers to his lips to shush her.

The news was a shock, but as the police were involved there wasn't anything he could do to help. Poor Ollie, he was such a good kid. He must be terrified.

"God, Jo, I can't believe it, I'm so sorry." He massaged his throbbing temple from too much alcohol with dinner. He had to dig deep for some words to reassure her. "I'm sure the police will be doing everything they can. They'll be doing stuff behind the scenes you won't know about. They have insider intelligence that they'll be linking into. They'll find him I'm sure."

There was a pause. He wasn't naive enough to think his comments would reassure Jo totally. His fear was that she'd want more from him. And he was right.

"Can you come, Rick? Can you come to the house?" she sniffed, "We need you."

We? Christ. He couldn't be anywhere near Eve now, if ever. The old man had made sure of that. But Jo's words *we need you* caused a sinking feeling in his gut.

He breathed in deeply. How do you explain to your sister you can't go back?

"There's nothing I can do, Jo. I wish there was." He'd have to lie about the inept police that he hated, "I'm sure the police will have everything covered."

Even though the line went quiet, he could hear her breathing.

"Hang on, Rick, Eve wants to say something."

God no. Not her. He didn't want to hear her voice. The reason he'd left the house was so he wouldn't have to ever again.

"Rick, it's Eve."

What the hell was he supposed to say? How do you comfort a person whose son has been kidnapped?

"This is terrible, Eve, I'm so sorry. I was just saying to Jo . . ."

"I heard," she answered in a clipped voice, "you're on speaker-phone."

"Right. Like I said, it's probably some amateurish individuals who've left a huge trail behind them, which the police will pick up."

The line went quiet and he wondered if she'd hung up. A glance at the screen indicated she hadn't.

"You still there, Eve?"

"Yes," her voice quivered and he felt her pain.

"Just hang on in there," he soothed, "Ollie's a tough kid." With as much bluff as he could muster he added, "The police will have him back in no time, you'll see."

"Rick," he could barely hear her voice, "You need to come. Oliver's yours . . . he's your son."

32

You didn't just knock on Saul Boylen's door, you had to set up a meeting. Rick knew he would see him though, as soon as he made the call. He also knew that if Saul Boylen could find out information about the kidnapping, he would want payment in return. He wasn't the type of man to do favours.

He'd called Saul Boylen on the mobile number he'd got from a previous call and left a message asking to be contacted urgently. Within fifteen minutes his call was returned, and a voice he wasn't familiar with instructed him to sit outside the tower block building which was now in front of him. He had been told to wait. Frustration was kicking in as he'd been waiting for what seemed like forever, but it was probably only ten minutes.

Would Saul be able to help? He knew he originated from Edinburgh and still had a house there which apparently his brother resided in. Neither brother was averse to bending the law either. They were two of a kind. Outwardly respectable business men, inwardly, law breakers.

He rooted round his glove compartment and found some chewing gum. Until yesterday when Eve had dropped the bombshell, he'd no idea at all that Ollie was his son. He was rarely shocked, so to hear Eve telling him that he was Oliver's father caused a churning feeling deep within him that he couldn't explain. He'd thought often enough about his future, and having kids featured in it somewhere down the line, but it wasn't something he'd been desperate for. Yet one phone call and the most important thing in his life right now was to get his son, his own flesh and blood, back.

The kid would be scared shitless. What fucking animals would do this? Please God, don't let it be perverted cunts that have taken him. Not that. He was a good kid, mollycoddled by his overprotective mother, but that was her. The old git wouldn't be any sort of role model that was for sure. Christ, if social services knew about how brutal he could be, they'd have removed Ollie from under his roof the night he was born.

Eve had no fucking right to keep Ollie from him all these years. Okay, so she couldn't contact him when he was in Australia, but he'd been back in London five years, she must have known that. He was always in the press and media regarding the lowlifes he represented, so unless she'd been in the outback of Mongolia, which she hadn't, then she couldn't have failed to know he was there. Yet not once had she ever tried to make contact. And Jo was no better. Did she know? She would have said something if she did, surely. The old man certainly knew he was in London. He remembered his ugly face during the court case when the greedy bastard had tried to legally get Chanjori back. That was never going to happen, he made sure of it. It was his mother's house and her parents before that, so there was no way that fucked-up shit of a father was ever getting it.

Rain pounded down on the car, and his thoughts drifted back to when his father had sent him away as a teenager. He hadn't wanted to leave Eve, but as the old man pointed out, if he didn't leave the country then, he'd end up in jail. He'd been stupid getting involved in criminal activities. He suspected it was a form of rebellion against the old man. Whatever it was, he would have been convicted as it was his car, the second one he'd bought with some money from his mother's inheritance that the gang had used as a getaway. It would have done no good protesting his innocence and trying to tell the police he was blotto at the time, having been high in the back of the car. He's been there during the robbery, so had been complicit.

That evening, he'd been bundled out of the country to his father's brother in Australia. It was a move that had shaped his life. He'd never been one for academia, but his uncle changed all of that. He was his role model, something he'd never had, and it was because of his patience and encouragement, he became the successful lawyer he was today. He'd always been bright, but owed his uncle and aunt a great debt for guiding him in the right direction. They were so proud of his achievements, unlike his father. Not once in his childhood had the old man told him he'd done well. He was good at sport and would come home with medals and certificates, but the old man was never interested. It was his mother who stood at the poolside urging him on at the swimming galas. When he was selected to swim for the county, his father told him swimming was for nancies.

A tap on the window jolted him. One of Saul's heavies stood by the car, a huge man with an ugly face. Judging by the shape of his nose and the scar running along his cheek, it was obvious he'd been in a fight or two.

The bloke indicated with the jerk of his head he was to follow him. There was no small talk on the way into the building, which suited Rick. He wasn't in the mood to engage in polite conversation. He was there for one thing only . . . to get his son back. He would have to pay, not in monetary terms, he knew that, but right now he was prepared for anything. All that mattered was getting Ollie back.

They travelled in the lift in silence until they reached the seventh floor and he was escorted into a chintzy apartment. Seated before him, behind a huge mahogany desk, was Saul Boylen. He'd met him at social events, and more recently he'd been visible in the court case where he'd managed to get Diffey acquitted. Looking at him now, the years hadn't been kind. He must be about mid-fifties, but looked ten years older.

He approached the desk and held out his hand which Saul took and shook firmly with a grip like a vice. Maybe that was intentional, a sort of, anyone messes with me is gonna get hurt.

"At last the elusive Rick Forrest." A glint of humour danced in his eyes, "Are you here to finally take me up on my offer?"

"Not exactly," Rick replied, "I'm here to ask for your help."

Saul widened his eyes, "Really?"

He gave him a cynical smile, "Yeah, really."

"You'd better sit down. I'm all ears."

Rick sat down reminding himself who he was dealing with. No need to disclose too much about Ollie being his. "My eleven year old half-brother in Edinburgh's been kidnapped."

Saul couldn't have known as there was a media blackout, yet he didn't look surprised.

"Kidnapped?" He grimaced, "Have they asked for a ransom?"

"Not yet, but I'm certain they're going to."

Saul opened an ornate box on the desk and offered him a cigarette. Rick needed something. This was the only way he knew to get Ollie back, he certainly didn't trust the cops to. In his experience, the police were useless fucking buffoons. There were no exceptions. He hated them all.

Saul reached across and lit his cigarette before sitting back and lighting his own. Rick dragged in deeply, enjoying the rush of nicotine to his head.

"Can the family pay?" Saul asked.

"Yeah, but they're not paying the bastards a penny. My sister and my father's wife," he clarified, "the kid's mother, understandably want to."

Saul nodded, "So what can *I* do for you?"

"Help me get the kid back."

His beady eyes widened, "And how do you think I can do that?"

Rick stared directly into his grey eyes, one of them being noticeably smaller than the other, "You've got contacts in Edinburgh, I know your brother lives there . . ." he needed to be careful not to insult Saul as he needed him, "I'm hoping you can find something out. Anything that'll help find the kid."

"What if I do have these . . . contacts you're referring to, why would I want to help? What's in it for me?"

Rick took a deep breath in. *This was so fucking hard.*

"Anything you want if you get him back."

"I see." Saul dragged on his cigarette. His silence was irritating Rick, time was precious. God only knew what sort of conditions they were keeping Ollie in.

"Look, Saul," he used his name as if he was a friend, "you've asked me repeatedly the last year or so to come and work for you and I've always said no. You get the kid back, and I'll help you."

"Ah, right . . . yes, that's true," another drag on his cigarette, "but that was then. I've got a lawyer working for me, a good one, so there's no vacancy right now. So, to use your phrase, it's *thanks, but no thanks.*"

"You've got Liam Jenner. He's good, but he's not as good as me."

Rick guessed what was coming next. Currently a huge name in the criminal fraternity, Kane Godfrey was locked up with a massive case against him for smuggling drugs in and out of the country. Rick knew it would take a miracle to get him off. The best they could hope for would be some sort of deal. And he knew without ever meeting Kane Godfrey, he wouldn't go for that. Prison would be the better option than grassing anyone up. You certainly wouldn't live long to enjoy any freedom you might get by betraying the mastermind of any plan. The world the likes of Saul Boylen operated in was not worth thinking about. He wouldn't be here now if he wasn't so desperate.

Saul cleared his throat, "Okay, this is how it's gonna go. If we find the kid, and there are no guarantees we will," Rick took a last drag on his half smoked cigarette and crushed it in the onyx ashtray, all the time listening. "If we find the kid and bring him back, I want you to represent Kane Godfrey. He's currently banged up . . ."

Rick interrupted, "I know what he's banged up for. You find the kid, and we've got a deal."

Saul relaxed back in his chair. "So it's as easy as that to get you to work for me," he smirked, which caused a kick inside of Rick.

Fuck, don't tell me this outfit is responsible for the kidnapping.

No, that's too farfetched . . . isn't it?

Saul crushed his cigarette and exhaled smoke into the air. "If we find the kid, what do you reckon would happen to the bastards that took him? You're the legal, what sentence would the great British justice system dish out for kidnapping?"

Rick knew it would be pathetic, especially if Ollie was unharmed. Kidnapping carried a life sentence, but in his experience, a slick lawyer could get that greatly reduced.

"Nowhere near what the cunts deserve."

Saul pursed his lips and nodded in agreement, playing his game a little longer.

"Probably walk in less than eight years, do you reckon?"

"Yep, about that."

Saul kept on nodding. It was really getting on his nerves.

"You know when I was this high," Saul gestured with the palm of his hand to about three feet off the ground, "I was playing on the green at the front of our house and I jumped into some dog shit. It was all over my new fucking school shoes. When I got home, my mother leathered me for being so careless. She ran them under the outside tap to try and get all the crap off. But you know what, it never came off. Every time I wore those shoes, I could smell that shit."

Rick watched Saul. For something fairly innocuous that happened to most kids, it was clearly a momentous event for him. Saul Boylen wasn't blessed with looks, but his expression turned even uglier as he continued.

"That's the trouble with shit, it sticks."

Saul paused, and his eyes told Rick he was reliving that time many years ago.

"I'd watch the lazy git from next door come home from his crappy job on the dustbins and let his dog out on the green. He never took it out for a walk, he just let it out where the kids played. I realised that the shit more than likely came from that dog, so you know what," Rick had an idea what was coming next as his expression went from ugly to evil, "he had to go. I emptied my pocket money jar and bought a great big juicy steak from the butchers. I cooked it on the barbecue and then injected it with anti-freeze. I can still see the greedy bastard of a dog salivating as he gobbled it up."

His expression relaxed, "Since then, I've never liked dogs. I hate them and their shit."

"You see my point, Rick? Whoever took the kid is responsible for the shit."

Although it was a question, Saul didn't wait for a response.

"So, like the dog, they've got to go, especially if they kill the kid."

Rick couldn't consider Ollie being killed. It thumped his gut big-time. He'd only just found out he had a son, he couldn't comprehend him dying. It was hard enough imagining what Ollie must be going through right now. The bastards had taken his son and caused God knows how much suffering to him at his age. He could be scarred for life.

He took a deep breath in. He had no idea about the analogy between Saul getting dog crap on his shoes to killing the neighbour's dog, but he wouldn't be stupid enough to say that. He needed him right now, so it was better to humour him.

"I hate dog shit. I'd have killed the fucking dog too."

"So, if we find the kid, and eliminate the shit, then I would say you would owe us, wouldn't you?"

Ollie was the most important thing in his life right now. Not Eve, not Louise, not Jo. He had to get him back. He'd worry about the price he'd pay later.

"It would be a debt, yes, but like I said, I'd be willing to represent Kane Godfrey. I'll get him the best deal I can. You have my word on it."

Saul was nodding again, "I'm sure you will, but the stakes have suddenly got higher looking at the . . . erm . . . excess shit. So, if we deliver on our part of the deal, I want you to work exclusively for me." Saul stared at Rick. He had the ace card and knew it.

Saul gave an evil smile, "Oh, come on, it won't be that bad. You might even like working for me. That's the only deal on the table right now so the choice is yours."

There was no choice. Nothing else mattered. The fact he hadn't been part of Ollie's life didn't matter. He was his own flesh and blood. He wanted to be the one who explained that he hadn't known about him, and if he had, he'd never have left his mother. He didn't care about anything else but a future with his son in it.

"You find the kid, and we've got a deal."

33

"Here, Eve, drink this." Jo pushed a brandy glass towards her with a generous amount of brandy in it. The last thing Eve wanted was alcohol, but if it helped ease the pain for only a minute, it would be worth it.

"Before you ask," Jo shook her head, "I'm really sorry, there's no news."

Eve moved to get up from her chair.

"Don't get up. There's nothing to be gained from coming downstairs, it's swarming with people."

Hilary, the liaison officer, stood up. "I'll just be downstairs if you need me."

"Thank you, Hilary," Jo replied.

Eve was going crazy staring at the four walls of her room. To think she used to love the tranquillity of her bedroom, now she felt like a prisoner especially with Hilary sitting alongside her. She was nice enough but she didn't really want to be talking to her. She just wanted her son back.

"I can't sit here a moment longer, Jo. I'm going out of my mind. I keep imagining they'll hurt him, or worse still . . ."

"Stop that, Eve. We mustn't think that way. We have to stay strong."

"I can't," she shook her head, "I'd rather die myself than this."

"Well that won't do any good now, will it? Come on, have a sip of the brandy."

Eve swallowed a huge mouthful, which burned her throat, causing her to cough . . . "Sorry."

"You okay now," Jo paused, "finish it. It'll make you feel better."

Feel better. She'd never feel better until her precious son was home.

"Oh, God, why haven't they found him?" she pleaded. "What are they doing? And what's Peter doing about the ransom money? He's overseeing Chester's estate, why isn't he coming up with the money? We have to pay it, Jo," she emphasised, "we have to."

"Everyone's doing their best, and Rick's on his way. I'll feel better when he's here."

More tears filled Eve's eyes and rolled down her cheeks. "He's going to be furious with me for keeping Oliver from him."

"He is furious. But I'm sure he won't be holding that against you at the moment. Like us all, he just wants Oliver back."

"When is he coming?"

"Soon. He's on his way."

"I can't cope with him cross-examining me, Jo, not right now. Please don't let him do that."

"Hey, he's my brother and subtlety is hardly his middle name, but even he isn't going to bombard you with questions. He just wants Oliver back, like we all do. In the short time he's known Oliver he's grown quite fond of him. And when he's back," she reassured, "he'll be getting to know him even better."

Eve smiled at Jo through watery eyes. She loved her step-daughter so much.

Jo looked at her as if she wanted to say something, but wasn't sure if she should.

"What?"

"I know it's not the right time to talk about this, but I keep going over and over in my mind why you kept Oliver from Rick all these years. I'm sure you had your reasons, but it really doesn't seem right, for either of them, Rick or Oliver."

"I know, but please don't judge me. I was only eighteen."

"Did Dad know Oliver wasn't his?"

Eve really didn't want to be having any discussions at all right now, but she owed it to Jo to at least share the truth. When she'd blurted out to Rick on the phone that he was Oliver's father, she saw Jo's face turn ashen. She hadn't meant to, but she could tell he wasn't coming back to Chanjori despite Jo pleading with him, and she needed him to know Oliver was his.

"Yes, your dad knew. He made me promise to keep it quiet though. That was the condition of our marriage, that people believed Oliver was his son. I promised not to divulge he wasn't," she shook her head, "but I wanted Rick to know . . . in case. . . you know . . ."

Jo reached for her hand, "It's okay, Eve. I'm not blaming you. It's just hard to get my head around it all. The little boy I thought for eleven years was my brother, is actually my nephew. It's such a lot to take in."

"I know, and I'm so sorry. Please say you forgive me?"

"Of course I forgive you. I'm not sure Rick will though. He really is angry. Did you go out with him, or was it just one of those casual things?"

"We were together for a couple of years as teenagers, but it wasn't an open relationship. My mother would never let me have a boyfriend, but her health was deteriorating, so I met Rick in secret. It ended between us when your dad sent him away. He didn't know I was pregnant."

Eve thought back to that fateful night when Chester had offered her a way out of her problems as if it was yesterday. No need to hide anything now, Chester was dead. She continued, "My father had just died and my mother was becoming increasingly erratic with her dementia. Your father had been to see my mother in the care home she was in for respite care."

She looked at Jo, "You know they went to school together?"

Jo nodded.

"I've thought about this a lot, and I reckon they probably were more than friends as teenagers themselves, or else why would he visit her? There was no reason to. It's only recently that I've come to that conclusion. Anyway, your Dad offered me a way out of my predicament. He initially offered to pay for mum's care, which is so odd when you think about it, why would he? But I wasn't thinking, I was only interested in Rick, and begged your Dad to tell me where he'd gone. But he wouldn't. All he would say was he wasn't coming back.

He offered marriage and gave me time to consider. Once I found out I was pregnant with Rick's baby, I honestly thought he'd renege on his offer, but he didn't. The only condition was that Oliver was brought up as his."

"You could have said no. Why would you marry a man so much older than you?"

"I had no choice. My mother required care, and even if the state would have funded that, where would I have lived? The house was going to be repossessed. I had a baby to think about. Your dad offered me a way out, and I took it. Not initially, but in the end it was easier to say yes than to do any other."

"That's awful, Eve. I knew you and Dad weren't a great love match, but even so, that wasn't right."

"Wasn't it? I thought that initially, but after a while, I realised it probably had been the right thing to do. Oliver and I had a lovely home, your father was happy, and I got to be with you. Even though he sent Rick away, your dad was always kind to me. I've never wanted for anything and neither has Oliver. Your dad has always had my respect for taking care of us."

"But what about Rick? Have you got feelings for him still? You know he's getting married soon?"

Eve started to cry again. "I can't think of anything right now Jo. I just want Oliver back," she sobbed.

Jo held her tightly, smoothing her hair down as though she was a child herself. Eve found Jo's secure arms comforting.

Minutes later, Jo pulled away. "We need to pray. That's all we have. Let's give it a try."

They held hands and closed their eyes.

Eve wasn't a religious person, but she'd prayed once before when she was desperate. And that was the day fate brought Chester Forrest to her.

Right now, she'd do anything if it meant getting Oliver back.

"Dear God, please don't let anyone hurt Oliver. I beg you," she pleaded, "bring him home . . . please bring him home. If it means me taking his place, then I'd gladly die if I could just see my son one more time."

34

Rick chartered a plane to take him back to Scotland and had a hire car waiting. With the little time he had, he could only get a basic Nissan and the journey from the local airport was fraught. The car had chugged along like a bloody lawnmower.

He opened the front door of Chanjori, and while he wasn't surprised to see people milling about, he hadn't reckoned on so many.

A young male uniformed officer in the hallway approached him. "Good evening, sir."

Rick knew they'd be checking callers in and out and judging by the look on his face, he didn't know who he was.

"I'm Rick Forrest, Jo Forrest is my sister," and almost as if he needed to explain further, he added, "Eve Forrest is my father's widow."

"Thank you, sir."

Jo's voice interrupted them, "Rick . . . oh Rick, thank God you're here." She flew into his arms and he held her for a few moments, before breaking away.

Jo never carried much colour, but she was worryingly pale. Her eyes looked bloodshot and sore.

"You holding up?" he asked.

"Only just," she replied. "Come on through," she led him to the main lounge.

Rick looked around at the makeshift desks, computers, printers, phones and industrious bodies. It resembled a productive working office.

"Rick, this is Daniel Hurst who's in charge," she turned towards him, "This is my brother Rick . . . Rick Forrest."

Daniel Hurst shook his hand, "Mr Forrest," he nodded.

"Please, it's Rick."

He couldn't see Eve, but didn't want to ask immediately where she was.

"Any news?" he asked, knowing there wouldn't be anything they'd share with him.

He was asking Daniel, but Jo cut in, "Nothing Rick, Eve's beside herself," her shoulders started to shake, "we all are. Who would do such a thing?"

He placed his arm around his sister and looked directly at Daniel Hurst, "Have you heard anything from the kidnappers."

"We have, yes, only in the last hour. And now we're waiting for another text."

Text? They'd be using cheap pay as you go phones and disposing of them.

"They're asking for money?"

"Yes, sir, they are. They haven't stipulated yet how much. We're waiting for further instructions and bank transfer details."

"Good, at least we know he's safe. Any clues who might be responsible?" Another question they wouldn't answer if they did. He knew exactly how they worked.

"Nothing tangible, but we are exploring leads. We have our contacts looking on the inside for any clues, you know, casual talk, that sort of thing."

Jo interrupted, "Isn't there something about loyalty amongst thieves? Surely they wouldn't sprag on whoever has Oliver if they knew?" She started to cry again, "This is hopeless. He'll be terrified, Rick."

"Shush," he kissed her head, "Everything's being done that can be, I'm sure."

"If you'll both excuse me, I'll update you when we have anything more." Daniel Hurst said.

Rick scanned the room, "Where's Eve?"

"In her room. The police have her phone. But Peter's here," she looked around, "I'm not sure where he's gone."

"Don't worry about him for now. I'll go up and see Eve."

"She's got someone with her, a liaison officer. She's not good at all Rick. Please don't tackle her about . . ." she stopped herself, "you know."

"I won't. I'm only going to let her know I'm here."

"Shall I come up with you? I don't know what to do. All this waiting around is killing me."

"I know and you're doing brilliantly. How about getting your brother some coffee, eh? Can you do that for me? I'll come back down for it after I've seen Eve."

He took the stairs two at a time, and tapped on her bedroom door. It was opened by a petite female.

"I'm Rick Forrest . . ."

"Let him in," Eve called, and he walked inside the room. His mother's room, it would always be that to him.

Eve was sitting in the window seat and looked like a porcelain doll with the light shining on her. She appeared almost translucent. She didn't stand and rush towards him as he'd expected.

"Thank you for coming, Rick."

His heart constricted. She didn't deserve this, nobody did. What bastard would take a kid from his home? And what words of comfort could he possibly offer? Fury didn't even come close to the anger he felt finding out he had a son, but to be dealing with that in circumstances like this was completely traumatic. This was unchartered territory for him. On the drive from the airport, all that kept going through his mind was would he get an opportunity to tell Ollie he was his dad?

He'd told himself on the journey to control his anger at her, for now. That would come later. When they got Ollie back he'd deal with her. How the hell had she thought it was acceptable to pass another man off as his dad?

He sat down on the chair beside her and took her hand, "I'm so sorry, Eve."

The liaison officer hovered, "Shall I go and get a drink, Mrs Forrest?"

"Yes, please do," Eve answered.

Why was she always so bloody courteous?

"Can I get you anything?" She turned to him, "Or you, Mr Forrest?"

"I think my sister's sorting drinks out," he answered and Eve shook her head.

As soon as the door closed he wrapped Eve in his arms. Okay, so they could never be together, the old man had well and truly seen to that, but she needed him right now.

He stroked her beautiful hair. It smelled fresh and citrusy. He had so many questions but now wasn't the time. He'd probably worked most of it out anyway. He knew why the old man had banished him to Australia, but he guessed the old bastard hadn't factored Eve being pregnant then. He needed to ask her about the letters. Did she ever get them, or had the old man intercepted them? The days he'd rushed to the mail box hoping for a letter from her, but none ever came. The telephone calls he'd made to her mobile number, but it was always switched off. That old git had well and truly sewn the whole thing up, and on his death bed, had delighted in telling him why.

She pulled away and blew her nose, "I'm so sorry, Rick . . . about everything. I wanted to tell you about Oliver, but your father didn't want me to."

"We'll talk about that later, Eve. We just need to concentrate on getting him back, that's what we have to focus on."

"I'm scared. I don't know anything about your father's estate and how to get my hands on any money. Can you help? Have you got money?" She started to cry again, "The police are saying there'll be no money changing hands, but we'll have to Rick. How will we get him back if we don't pay?" The tears turned to sobs.

"Shush, shush," he soothed, "I've got money. I'll speak to the police."

She looked at him with her huge doey eyes, almost as if she worshipped him. "Have you? Thank God, if we pay, maybe they'll bring him back." She clung to him again. "I can't bear this for much longer. What are they doing to him? I'm scared he's in the dark; he hates the dark. I'm going out of my mind, Rick," she cried, "I just want to die."

He held her in his arms and let her sob. Eventually, he eased her slightly away from him and with all his acting skills from the courtroom, he reassured her.

"Listen to me. We'll get him back, I promise you." He spoke with a confidence he didn't feel at all. "But for now, we have to listen to the police. They are used to dealing with these kinds of people, we have to trust them."

Tears streamed down her face, "I know, but the kidnappers said no police. I'm scared . . . they said no police," she shook her head, "Oh, God, Rick, what have I done?"

He stroked her hair again, "You've done everything right, Eve. Trust me on that."

"But what if . . ."

He put his finger on her lips, "There are no what if's. It's when. We have to stay positive."

"I've been praying and I've not prayed in years. I'm so sorry for everything Rick . . . I'm sorry you never knew about Oliver."

"Don't talk about that now. We can discuss that later when he's back with us."

"Can you stay . . . you know, until we hear something?"

"I'm not going anywhere." He smoothed her hair. "Now why don't you have a lie down and I'll go and get that cup of coffee Jo is making me."

"I'm coming with you. I don't want to be on my own."

"No, you don't need to be downstairs at the moment," he stood up and reached for her hand, "come on, lie down, even if it's just for a few minutes."

Surprisingly, she took his hand and he led her to the bed.

"Can you stay with me for a while?"

He climbed on next to her but stayed in a sitting position while she lay.

"Hold me, Rick," she whispered, and he did. He didn't want to, but he did. She needed that right now. But he couldn't hold onto her forever. The old bastard had seen to that.

35

Eve gazed around the lounge that now looked like a busy office and the occupants were smiling sympathetically at her.

There must have been seven or eight people in the lounge all talking as they waited for something from the kidnapper. Whatever shock was, she knew she was experiencing it. It felt almost as if she wasn't there. She could see their lips all moving, and she could hear sounds, but it was as if her ears were closed to it all. The thumping inside her head was the only thing that reminded her she wasn't dreaming.

She clutched Jo's hand as they sat huddled together on the sofa.

"Where's Rick?" she asked.

"He's gone to his room to make some calls. His fiancée, Louise, sends her love to us. She's praying for Oliver's safe return."

Eve willed her phone to ring or to hear the ping of a text message arriving. Any contact, however indirect with Oliver, she was desperate for. It scared her though. What if the next phone call was to say he was dead?

She relived her memories of him. Oliver taking his first steps . . . Oliver saying *mumee* . . .Oliver starting school, her brave little soldier waving at her . . . Oliver with chicken pox, lying in bed itching and hurting . . . Oliver feeding the donkeys at the farm she'd taken him to . . . Oliver winning his first swimming race when he was only seven. The memories flowed, causing a deep and agonising pain that could only be healed by getting him back. She blamed herself, maybe this was her punishment as she'd kept the truth from Rick all these years? She'd kept him ignorant of his own son. What sort of mother did that make her?

Who was everybody talking to on the phones? Did they have any information yet? Why weren't they out searching for Oliver instead of sitting inside the house?

An officer spoke to Jo, "Could we have a word, Miss Forrest please?"

Jo let go of her hand and followed him.

What did they want Jo for, and where the hell was Rick?

Eve stared at nothing. If Oliver died, she didn't want to live. She'd kill herself, that's what she'd do. A life without him in it wouldn't be worth living.

She heard Rick's voice outside of the room. What were they discussing? Please no, not that.

She stood up, "What going on," she called, "Rick . . . Jo, what's going on?"

They both came through the opened door and she looked directly into Rick's eyes with the unsaid question. Please, no, not that.

"He's alive."

Alive? Oliver was alive. Is that what Rick just said?

Jo rushed up and flung her arms around her, "He's safe, Eve, they've got him. Thank God."

Eve burst into tears, "Where . . . where is he?"

"He's at the station," Rick answered, "we're going straight to him now."

"Why haven't they brought him home? Is he alright? You're sure he's not been harmed?"

What were they keeping from her? How could he suddenly be okay?

"He's fine, Eve," he reassured, "now come on, he's at the station. We're going to see him now. Get some clothes for him."

"But why haven't they brought him straight home . . . where are his clothes?"

Why would someone take his clothes? Please God, not that. He's only a little boy.

"Hurry," Jo urged, "we can talk on the way. Grab some of Oliver's clothes. The police will want his for forensic tests, that's all."

"But how have they found him? Where has he been?" Eve's head was spinning.

"They got a tip off and raided a house," Rick explained, "we didn't tell you in case it came to nothing."

"You're sure he's okay? They haven't harmed him, have they?"

"He held onto her arms. "I promise you, Eve, he's okay."

And she believed him. Because he wouldn't lie.

"Come on," he urged, putting his arm around her, "let's go bring the little soldier home."

Eve clung onto Oliver as if she would never let him go. He held on to her just as tightly. Eventually, she did pull away. He was in a white boiler type suit with the cuffs and sleeves rolled up several times. It must have been an adult suit. She remembered Jo saying they'd have taken his clothes for forensic testing.

"Oh, God, Oliver," she sobbed squeezing him, "are you alright?"

"I'm okay Mum, they didn't hurt me."

"I've been out of my mind, sweetie, come here," she hugged him again.

Then it was Jo's turn to hug him. There was such a lovely bond between the two of them.

"Thank goodness you're safe, little man, we've been so worried." Jo kissed his head.

Rick didn't hug him, he just ruffled his hair. "You did good, matey."

Typical Oliver reached for the pile of toast on the table that someone must have made for him.

How could he eat?

The police had told them Oliver had been walking towards the bus stop after school, and he'd passed a van which they suspected the kidnappers were waiting in. One of the men had jumped out and grabbed Oliver. It sounded like they'd put something over his nose and mouth and he'd blacked out and woken up in a small bedroom. He wasn't able to tell them very much in terms of where he was held.

Eve smiled lovingly at him, "I know you've already spoken to the police, but they want to ask you some more questions. I've asked if it could wait until tomorrow, but they want to do it now. There's going to be someone in the room with you that will say when she thinks you've had enough questioning though, but you must say also if it becomes too much."

"I know, Mum, they told me what's going to happen. They don't want me to say much until I've had the interview. They've already got one of the men, but the other got away."

"Well, I hope they get him wherever he's hiding, putting you through all of this."

"I knew the police would come in the end," Oliver continued as if it was some sort of television programme, "I heard it all. There was a lot of banging about and someone shouting *get on the floor*, and then a few minutes later, one of the policemen opened my door." Oliver's eyes widened, "He had a gun and everything."

Eve shuddered. "You must have been so frightened, darling?"

"I was fine," he dismissed, "he's called Luke and he came to see me before you got here. I wanted to see his gun, but he's not allowed to have it indoors."

"Quite right, too. It's a shame he has to have it at all."

Was this her son, her little boy talking so casually? Maybe as Rick said, adrenaline will see him through the next few days and then it'll hit him.

Oliver finished his toast and glugged on the milk he'd been given.

"They don't seem keen to let me come in with you while you're interviewed," she told him, "but they've said Rick can if you want him to. It's because of his job," she quickly added, which was completely unnecessary as Oliver had no idea yet that Rick was his father. She'd asked if she could go into the interview room with Oliver, but the police had advised he may not be quite so open if she was there listening. He might hold some things back because of the risk of upsetting her.

"Yeah," Oliver answered excitedly, munching on the last of his toast, "let Rick come in. Then can we go home?"

Tears streamed down her face, "Yes my darling, then we can go home."

Oliver gave one of his 'mum's an embarrassment' looks. "Mum," he chastised, but she didn't care. Her son was safe, and by all accounts no pervert had touched him. They'd been incredibly lucky.

"You'll have to cut her a bit of slack, matey," Rick smiled, "she's your mum and she's been worried sick."

Oliver smiled so sweetly at him, causing a pang in her heart. She'd never stop loving Rick Forrest.

37

Eve had her precious son back and that's all that mattered. Her life was Oliver. What happens now though? Dare she hope that Rick could be in their lives? Was it worth asking? Was it fair to? He was getting married soon.

He'd gone from her life once, and she hadn't had an opportunity then to stop him. This time she had. Should she beg him to stay and make a life with her and Oliver in it? Would he want that? He definitely had feelings for her, she knew that from when they'd made love. Yes, he'd been dismissive afterwards, but for a few blissful moments, he'd felt the same way. She was sure of it.

This time she wasn't going to let him get away. She loved him and couldn't let him go again without telling him. There was no Chester Forrest to get in the way now.

She walked into the kitchen and found Gilly hovering over Rick as if he was still eleven himself. He was delving into a bowl of apple pie and custard, which no doubt she'd made him.

"Hi," Eve smiled at them both.

"Hello, Mrs Forrest, how's the little fellow?" Gilly asked.

"Crashed out. The police are going to speak to him again tomorrow along with a trained officer who apparently could extract information that he might have, but not consciously be aware of."

"They should bring back hanging, that's what I say. But even that's too good for them. Thank the Lord he's safe."

"I couldn't agree more. At least he wasn't hurt, so that's a blessing. It sounds like wherever they kept him, it was okay. He said there was an old television, and they'd given him some comics. I guess the most frightening thing for him was the masks they were wearing."

"Poor wee boy. I don't care how they kept him; they shouldn't have taken him in the first place. They're no more than animals. Rick says the police have got one of them?"

"Yes, apparently so, but the other one got away. Oliver said he only ever saw one of the men, but knew there was another as he heard muffled voices."

"Let's hope the police get him as well then. Thank goodness he wasn't harmed, we should be grateful for that if nothing else."

"Yes, that's a huge blessing. You know him though, he's putting on a brave face as if it's all been a big adventure, but I'm sure he must have been frightened."

"I bet. And maybe it'll not show at first. It'll probably kick in later."

"I'm sure you're right. One thing's for certain, he'll be going to school in the car from now on. No more buses.

"I don't blame you."

"Niall's back at the weekend, isn't he?" Eve asked.

"Yes, the Sunday after Rick's wedding. There wasn't any sense in him rushing back after Chester . . . you know," her voice trailed off.

"Of course."

Eve knew Jo expected Niall would come straight back when her dad died so she'd had to reassure her that there was no point in him doing that. It wasn't as if he'd have a job to come back to. Even as she'd spoken the words though, she'd felt Jo's sadness. Surely if Niall had loved her he would have rushed back after his sister's wedding to comfort her. She had lost her father, after all.

All the talk of weddings caused a wrench in Eve's gut. The thought of Rick getting married was too painful.

Her eyes were drawn to him at the table, quietly spooning mouthfuls of pudding and custard.

"Can I get you anything, Mrs Forrest?" Gilly asked, "some tea perhaps?"

"No thank you. I just needed a quick word with Rick."

"I'll leave you to it then," Gilly answered and turned to Rick, "I'll see you when you're next back, and good luck with the wedding."

Rick stood and wrapped his arms around her in a friendly hug, "Thanks, Gil, you'll be meeting Louise soon enough. I'll bring her after all the shenanigans."

"Shenanigans my foot," Gilly laughed, "you'd not be saying that if she was stood behind you, that's for sure."

She chuckled and left the kitchen shaking her head.

Eve followed her to the door, making sure it was closed behind her so that her and Rick couldn't be overheard. The mention of Rick's wedding sliced her inside, but she was determined to say what she had to. She swallowed; it was going to be hard.

Eve moved towards the table. "I didn't want you to go without speaking to you first."

He didn't meet her eyes, "You'll need to be quick then as I'm about to get off." His demeanour was relaxed, but she knew he wasn't. He'd been there for her and Jo since the kidnap yet she could tell he didn't want to have a conversation with her. Their relationship had shifted now he knew he was Oliver's father and she needed a plan of how they would move forward.

"I wanted to ask about when you feel it's appropriate to tell Oliver about . . . you know, who you really are."

He nodded and then looked directly at her. "I think maybe after the wedding. He's been through enough for now."

"You're right," she agreed. "So when will you come back?"

"After my honeymoon, and then you and I can speak to him together and explain everything. I'll have Louise with me, so that'll give him a chance to get to know her."

The thought of Oliver getting to know Rick's new wife stung. "Yes, of course."

His voice turned authoritative, "Ollie seems okay right now, but he might not be further down the line. It's important I'm around to support him. I want him to know he can rely on me, especially as he's likely to have to give evidence in court."

"I'm sure you're right. He's euphoric now he's home, but it has been an awful ordeal for him . . . for us all," she added.

"Yes, it has." Although Rick went silent, Eve sensed there was more. She was right.

"I'd like Ollie to come to the wedding. Jo said she'd bring him."

Oliver spending time with Rick and his new wife hurt like hell. He must have mistaken her silence as a no.

"I want him there, Eve," he emphasised, "you've had him for eleven years, so I think it's legitimately my turn now, don't you?"

She nodded. Images of Rick living at Chanjori flashed in front of her. How she was ever going to come to terms with Oliver coming back to the house at weekends, she didn't know. It would be intolerable for her living over the other side of town. But that might not happen. He'd gone out of her life once before and she was going to do everything she could to make sure he didn't again. She'd beg if she had to.

She cleared her nervous throat. "What about us, Rick?"

"There is no us," he dismissed.

"Yes, there is." She sat down opposite him at the table, "you know there is. You left once before and my life was in tatters, and I don't want that to happen again. I know it's complicated and you're planning to get married, but will you answer one thing before you go?"

He stood up and took his bowl to the sink, "I'm not answering anything, so save your breath. I'm going when I've said goodbye to Jo. I *have* to go."

Why? Why did he *have* to go?

"Are you happy with Louise? Do you want to spend the rest of your life with her?"

He turned on the tap and ran some water into the bowl. "Yes."

"And can you walk away a second time and forget about the two of us?"

He reached for a washing-up brush and started to clean the bowl.

"Easily. In fact, there's nothing I want to do more than forget about you and I. I know we have Ollie to think about now, and I will be part of his life," he looked at her as if he was giving her some sort of warning in case she had other ideas.

"I've agreed he needs to be told the truth. But what about us? You can't deny there's something between us. I know you feel it too."

"I can deny it and you have to. It was a mistake coming back. You need to forget what happened between us and move on with your life. That's what I'm going to do. I'm marrying Louise, end of."

She stood and moved towards him. "I'm not sure I can, Rick. The thing is . . . I'm in love with you. I always have been. And I know you felt something when we made love. That's why you were hateful afterwards. You can deny it all you like, but I know you feel the pull between us. It's always been there."

It was important that he understood that she'd never been with anyone else but him. "There was never anything between your father and me; there's only ever been you. He never touched me, not once all the time we were together. I promise you."

*

Rick stared, almost looking through her. He needed to leave now, quickly. He couldn't stay in the house a minute longer . . . it was killing him. She deserved the truth and to know why he couldn't stay. Not now.

"Haven't you ever stopped to think why he never touched you?"

She shook her head. It was obvious she had no idea. The bastard had never told her.

"For fuck's sake, Eve, think about it!" He had to tell her, she needed to know so she could forget about them being together. "The morning I left, he gave me the last bit of information that he knew would tear me apart."

"I don't know what you're talking about," she frowned. "What did he say?"

"He told me the truth. There was no way that bastard was leaving this earth without sharing that little nugget. Why he'd sent me away all those years ago, and why he'd married you," he ran a hand through his hair, "I should have known."

Puzzlement was written all over her face. "Should have known what?"

He had no choice. He had to give her the piece of information that would put an end to them once and for all.

"That the late, great, Chester Forrest was not only mine and Jo's father, Eve, he was your fucking father as well."

38

Rick left Chanjori and Eve didn't try to stop him. What was the point?

Chester her father? That would mean he'd had an affair with her mother while she was married. If there was one thing she was absolutely certain about her mother, it was that she upheld the sanctity of marriage. Yes, she'd guessed that Chester and her mother had been in a relationship when they were teenagers, but they'd both gone on to marry others.

Eve thought about the man she'd been married to for eleven years. Could it be true? It might explain why he'd never touched her in their marriage. Not once. The only thing he'd ever done was kiss her cheek and that had been usually in public at a dinner or social event. Privately, he'd never done that. They'd travelled together when necessary, but never shared a bed. Chester would always book a suite with two bedrooms.

It would certainly explain why he'd married her once he found out about her and Rick. He would know Rick would never want her again after him.

A wave of nausea flooded her senses. No. The way she felt about Rick and how they'd made love, they couldn't be half-siblings. It was too preposterous.

Would Chester lie? Why had he waited until he was dying to say anything?

And what about her mother? Would she have had an affair while married to her father? It was possible, but however hard she tried, she couldn't see it. If only her mother's brain wasn't so scrambled, she could ask her.

Eve tossed and turned all night trying to think how she could find out categorically if Chester had been her genetic father.

By morning, she'd come up with a way.

Her mother's recall was much better about her earlier life, but even if by some miracle she did remember, would she share that she'd had an affair all those years ago while she was married to her father? And worse still, that her father could well be someone other than the man that had brought her up?

Eve couldn't accept she was Rick's sister. It was easier to believe Chester would lie to keep them apart.

What are you looking for, Mum?" Eve asked, taking a seat in her mother's room at the residential home.

Her mother was bent down, looking in the bottom drawer of a chest. "My diary. I'm sure I have a luncheon appointment with Mary at one o'clock, but I can't find it. Would you have a look for me please, dear," she asked, shaking her head from side to side, "maybe someone's picked it up by mistake?"

It was easier to play along with her mother's ramblings than to discredit her. She needed to keep her on an even keel, so she could delve into her past.

"It can't be today, Mum, Mary's away on holiday."

"Is she?" She frowned, fiddling with her oversized beads around her neck, "It must be next week then."

"Yes, it will be. Don't worry, I'll find your diary before I go. Come and sit down a minute, I want to talk to you."

Her mother sat down in the winged armchair. Eve placed the footstool near the chair and lifted her feet onto it. "Ah, that's better," her mother sighed, "I don't know why I thought it was today. Never mind, would you like some tea?"

"No thanks, I'm fine for now."

"It's a relief I'm not out for lunch if I'm honest. I can feel one of my headaches coming on. I'll have to lie down before the day's out, I just know I will."

Eve never knew if her mother did ever have a genuine headache because she said that every time she visited. Her scrambled mind didn't stay focussed for long, so she needed to get straight to the point.

"I wanted to ask you about Chester Forrest, Mum?"

Her mother's eyes flickered with recognition. "Ah, yes, dear Chester. He and I went to school together you know."

"Yes, I remember you telling me." *Hundreds of times.*

"Such a lovely man." She leant forward and lowered her voice as if she didn't want anyone else to hear, "He was the love of my life," her radiant smile lit up her confused face, "before your father, of course."

It was a good start. This was the complexity of Alzheimer's, how the mind could go back years and remember early memories, but anything current, such as asking her what she had for supper the previous evening, she'd be clueless about.

"Why didn't you marry, if you were so close?"

A wave of sadness erased her mother's joyful smile, "We were too young, and when Ann Fisher came along, he married her. I was devastated at the time though, I can tell you. Swore I'd never have another relationship again," she sighed, "and then I met Daddy, who swept me off my feet. I think I'll take my cardigan off, dear, it's warm in here. Are you warm?"

"I'm fine, Mum." She quickly helped her mother remove the cardigan, and sat facing her again.

"You still stayed friends with Chester, wasn't Daddy jealous with him being an old boyfriend?"

"Jealous? What was there to be jealous about?"

"I don't know, maybe the fact you'd been lovers?"

Eve stared intensely at her mother's face. Not as much as a flinch.

She'd never had conversations with her mother about sex and relationships. Those things weren't discussed at home, ever.

Her mother fiddled with a tissue in her hand. "Your father was always courteous with Chester and Ann on the occasions that our paths crossed."

Had the ill-advised financial decisions her father had made, put a strain on their marriage?

"Did you and Chester ever rekindle your love affair?"

Her mother very slowly closed her eyes and then opened them. As if it was painful to recall.

Please remember, please, Mum, just this once. It's so important.

Would her mother admit to an affair? Would she even remember?

Her mother looked towards the window and her eyes glazed as though she was remembering every detail of their relationship. "We did, but it was a mistake. I loved your father deeply and regretted it afterwards."

Were there tears in her mother's eyes? "I don't think poor Chester ever got over it."

Oh, my God.

She *could* be Chester's daughter. It didn't really matter how long the affair was for, it only took once, but she desperately wanted to know more. She had to be careful and not show any surprise or change the mood. She coaxed gently, "How do you know Chester never got over it?"

"Got over what?"

"Your affair."

"What affair?"

"You and Chester?"

"Chester? Who's Chester?"

The moment was gone. All she'd gleaned was that there was a possibility she was Chester Forrest's daughter.

No, no, no.

She'd spent eleven years without Rick and she still loved him. Until recently, she never quite appreciated how much. She wasn't his half-sister. She couldn't be.

39

Eve sat at the side of the pool, grateful for the parasol shading her from the blistering sun. The outdoors was preferable since Chester's death; inside the house seemed so oppressive. Rick hadn't said anything about ousting them just yet, but she would need to move soon.

A pile of house brochures were waiting to be looked at, but her heart wasn't in it. She really didn't want to uproot Oliver from the only home he'd ever known in his short life. He loved Chanjori, so it was going to be such a wrench to leave. It sounded like Jo would be staying on, but for how long? No doubt when Niall returned from America, they'd be making plans of their own.

She needed to speak to Jo. Gilly was getting twitchy because Niall had extended his US stay again. She said on more than one occasion he was taking a liberty. It hadn't bothered Eve as she'd got used to driving herself about, and they could call on the agency if they needed a chauffeur. Niall had been employed primarily for Chester anyway, so there wasn't really a job for him to come back to. Rick certainly wouldn't want to retain him.

"Mum," Oliver's voice from the edge of the pool interrupted her train of thought, "are you watching? Was the turn any quicker?"

Seemingly Rick had told Oliver he was too slow turning after the first length so he needed to practice.

"Yes, I think it was slightly quicker, darling."

Her thoughts invariably turned to Rick as they did every hour of the day. What was he doing right now? It was his wedding at the weekend in the swish

Devonia Hotel in London. The thought made her insides twist. Since he'd been back in her life, she thought about him constantly. It wouldn't be long before he'd be sitting in the same seat she currently was, overlooking the pool, alongside his new wife.

Gilly appeared with a tray. "Here you are Mrs Forrest, some cool lemonade for you and Oliver."

"Thank you, that's very welcome." Eve turned towards the pool, "Oliver, come out and have a drink. I think you've done enough now."

Gilly smiled, "He does love his swimming, doesn't he?"

"He does." Eve raised her eyebrows and smiled, "Too much."

"Yes, but after all he's been through, it's nice he has something to focus on."

"It is, and he received some good news yesterday. He's been selected to swim for the county."

"Oh, isn't that wonderful. I'm so pleased for him." She smiled and shook her head, "You'll never get him out of that pool now."

Eve nodded, but her statement hurt. Oliver would miss the pool so much.

Gilly moved to walk away, but hesitated.

"What is it?" Eve asked.

"I'm really sorry to have to bring this up, but I'm wondering what to do about Mr Forrest's belongings? Would you like me to look at somewhere purpose built for storage away from the house?" She must have looked puzzled, as Gilly continued, "I'm wondering if they should be moved before Rick and his wife come. They might want the out-buildings for their own storage?"

The staff had packed all of Chester's belongings after his death. Although Eve hadn't been in the depths of despair when he'd died, the staff didn't need to know that.

"I am grateful for your help with everything. I must remember to thank the girls too. Maybe I can give them a little bonus?"

"There's really no need," Gilly dismissed, "they're only doing their job."

"Yes, but packing up a deceased man's belongings can't have been very nice for them."

"I agree, but hold your horses about a bonus. I'd like to check just how well they did things. Knowing Charlotte, she won't have folded anything properly before packing it up. You see, it'll all be shoved in bags. That girl is a bit slap dash to say the least."

"Don't be too harsh on her, she's only young."

"Mmm. Well, I'll be happier when I've checked everything is stored properly. Then perhaps we can make a decision on what to do with it all?"

"Thank you, yes. I'd appreciate you overseeing things, and I'll check with Jo, but I think most of it needs to go to charity."

"It's so sad," Gilly muttered shaking her head, "but it comes to us all I suppose. All our personal items stored in bags, ready to be donated for someone else's benefit."

"Put like that," Eve agreed, "you're right."

Oliver finished his lemonade and placed the glass back on the tray.

Eve handed him his robe. "Right then young man, we should go inside. You must have some homework to do."

"I hate homework."

"So did I at your age, but it will pay dividends later in life if you concentrate on it now."

They walked inside the house together. "Are you going to your room where it's quiet, or the library?

"My room I think."

"Okay. I'll give you a knock before dinner. And make sure it's homework you're doing and not messing about on your Play Station."

He rolled his eyes and she watched him take the stairs two at a time. Funny, she'd watched Rick do exactly that while he was here. Had Oliver seen him and was copying, or was it innate in him?

Eve made her way to the snug which was the most comfortable room in the house and was surprised to see Jo slouched on the sofa.

"Hi Jo, I didn't realise you were back. How did you get on at the dentist?"

"Fine. He's filled the bit of tooth that's chipped off at the back."

"That's good. Are you okay, you look a bit pale?"

"I'm okay. It's still a bit numb that's all."

"Do you want a drink or anything?"

"Not right now thanks."

Eve sat down on the sofa next to Jo. "It's not like you, watching daytime television."

Jo blew a breath out. "Not much else to do."

"Are you sure you're okay? Have you heard from Niall?"

Jo's eyes filled. "Yes, he's back on Sunday. I'm dreading it though."

Eve frowned. "Dreading it? Why?"

"I feel he let me down not coming back after his sister's wedding. He knows I'm upset about Dad."

"It is all a bit odd, I have to agree. He's put off returning twice, now, hasn't he?"

"Yeah. I'm wondering if he's met someone else to be honest."

"When did you last hear from him?"

Jo picked up her phone and flicked through some texts. "Friday was the last text he sent. Even that was only brief. *Hope you're doing okay. I'll be back Sunday, can't wait to see you*, and a load of kisses." Jo flung her phone down, "What's that all about? I've hardly heard from him all the time he's been away, and now only a text. I've tried ringing him, but it goes straight to answer phone."

Eve shrugged. "His behaviour certainly seems a bit odd. The only thing is, he doesn't really have a job to come back to now. Peter is planning on giving him notice."

"I know, but it's not about the job, though, is it? It's about the two of us. If I meant something to him, then surely I'd be his priority."

Eve couldn't argue. Jo was right. She hated seeing her so upset though.

Jo sighed, "Still, he wouldn't have been welcome at Rick's wedding, and I'd have wanted him to come with me if he'd been here."

Eve's tummy somersaulted. Rick's wedding made her feel nauseous.

"Are you all set for it . . . the wedding, I mean?"

"I suppose so. It's hard to get excited when I just want to see Niall to find out where I am with him."

"Yes. You need to talk things through and see if your future's likely to be with him. It's a shame he had to go away when you'd just got together really. Maybe he just needs a bit of time to work out what he wants."

Jo didn't look convinced. "We'll see. Anyway, have you thought anymore about coming to the wedding?"

"I'd like to, if only to keep an eye on Oliver. I'm so nervous about letting him out of my sight."

"Come then."

"I can't. Rick doesn't really want me there."

"Well don't be worrying about Oliver. I'll guard him with my life, I promise you. Have you heard anymore from the police?"

"No, nothing."

"When are you and Rick going to speak to Oliver?"

"After the wedding. Rick says he'll come after his honeymoon with Louise and we can sit down and talk to him."

"I still think you should come to the wedding. Knickers to Rick. So what if you both had a relationship when you were younger. You're not together now. You're Oliver's mum so should be there."

"Your brother doesn't see it quite like that. He only wants Oliver there, and if I'm honest, I can understand that."

"Why don't you come and book in the hotel anyway? You don't have to be at the ceremony. You could relax and spend some time using the facilities."

"Mmmm, that sounds nice. I'll have to see."

"Do. It'll be much better travelling with you. I love Oliver to bits, but I'm not sure even I can stand a long train journey with him sat next to me with his headphones on. Even if they come off, his head will be stuck in his iPad."

Eve smiled in agreement. "It might be nice to be at the hotel and as you say, use the facilities. I would like to be around Oliver."

Jo stood up. "There you are then. It's sorted. Make sure you bring a nice outfit though just in case you do decide to go to the wedding. One more isn't going to make any difference, and Rick will be too busy with Louise to even notice you're there."

Cheers Jo.

"Where are you off to?" Eve asked.

"To take some Paracetamol and lie down." Jo looked at her watch, "Then I'll be ready for some supper."

"Okay. See you later."

Eve picked up the remote and flicked through the channels. She needed something to distract her from thinking about Rick. She stumbled across a family drama and smiled at the irony about a young man trying to prove he was the son of a wealthy business man that had died leaving a huge unclaimed estate.

I hope he has better luck than me about proving parenthood.

With one eye on the drama, her mind was still on Rick and his wedding. The thought of him on his honeymoon kissing someone else, or worse still making love to some else, crushed her. You wouldn't have those sorts of feelings if you were related, surely?

This time next week he'd be married to Louise.

That really stung.

As the television drama progressed, it started to hold her interest. By the time the credits rolled, she'd discovered there was a way she could prove once and for all if Chester was her father.

But was she too late?

40

Eve found Gilly in the kitchen. "You know we discussed Mr Forrest's belongings in storage, have you got the key to the room please?"

"Yes, but I'm afraid I've not got round to checking things yet. Would you rather I did that before you had a look through everything?"

"No, I'd rather nothing has been touched."

Gilly looked puzzled as she retrieved the key from a cabinet. "Shall I come with you?"

"No, thank you. I'm just going to look for something."

"There's an inventory with the clothes. As you know, all the valuables are in the safe in his room."

"Yes, thank you. It's not the valuables I'm after. Have you got a freezer bag or something clean?"

Gilly handed her a sealed freezer bag with a questioning look on her face, but there was no way she was about to explain. How could she?

"Are you sure I can't help?"

"Quite sure, thank you."

It took much longer than Eve anticipated searching through Chester's belongings. Each item of clothing was familiar, but not in a loving way. She just remembered him wearing a particular shirt or jumper. He had so many clothes and shoes. During the search, she made up her mind she was definitely going to have them wrapped and forwarded to charity. The recipients would be delighted as the garments all had high-end designer labels attached to them.

The bags of clothes didn't contain what she was after. Her eyes drifted around the room and she spotted a large chest. Maybe it would be in there?

She dragged the chest to the centre of the room, and opened the lid to peer inside.

There it was, lying on top of everything. Her heart accelerated as she reached inside and lifted Chester's leather soap bag out. She quickly unzipped it.

Please, she willed, *let me find it.*

There was his brass razor, electric toothbrush, and various other things that should have been thrown out such as dental floss and cotton buds. And then she spotted what she had prayed would be there.

Chester's comb.

She gently removed it and carefully held it up to the light.

Bingo.

It hadn't been cleaned properly. Attached to the stainless steel, was several fine grey hairs.

Thank God for slapdash Charlotte.

She carefully placed the comb into the clean freezer bag. The hair would contain Chester's DNA. It was all she needed to prove one way or another if he was indeed her genetic father.

41

It was the day of Rick's wedding, and Eve was stood in front of the mirror in the hotel room, trying to secure a pink fascinator onto her head.

Although she hadn't received a formal invitation to the wedding, Jo had managed to persuade her to come. She was still nervous about letting Oliver out of her sight especially as one of the kidnappers still hadn't been found. School was the only exception, and despite his protests, she was driving him there and back herself.

Quite what Rick would make of her being there she wasn't sure. And she wasn't sure either how she was even going to sit through the ceremony. The thought of him marrying another woman was too painful. But for some bizarre reason, she needed to be there.

Despite texting Rick yesterday with a *can we talk message,* he hadn't responded.

Her last hope had been Jo, who was having dinner with him that evening. She'd entrusted her with an envelope.

"You will see Rick gets it, won't you?" she'd asked.

"Yes of course," Jo frowned, "although I don't think he'll be bothered about anything to do with Dad's estate on the eve of his wedding. Can't it wait?"

Eve hadn't indicated the letter was anything to do with Chester's estate, but she'd let her think that. Jo didn't know anything that had gone on between her and Rick recently, only the disclosure that he was Oliver's father.

"No, it's urgent. Best to let him have a quick look so he can advise."

"Okay." Jo placed the letter in her handbag, "Are you sure you won't come out to dinner with us. I'm sure Rick won't mind."

"Yeah," Oliver piped up, "let's go to dinner with them, Mum, I want to see Rick."

"Not tonight darling. It's best that Rick and Jo have dinner together without us. It's a big thing getting married and it'll be nice for them to have some time together. Plus, they'll no doubt be very late getting in. You'll see him tomorrow."

All evening she'd willed Rick to come and knock on her hotel room door. Every time she heard the lift door open in the distance, or someone walking along the corridor, she'd held her breath praying it was him.

She woke in the early hours and checked her phone, but there were no messages. As the early morning light shone through the curtains, she'd resigned herself he wasn't coming. He was going to marry Louise and there was nothing more she could do. They'd been jinxed in the beginning, and they still were. He wasn't meant to be hers.

Butterflies fluttered around Eve's tummy. It was time.

"Oliver, put your iPad down please and put your jacket on."

"Where's Jo?" Oliver asked.

"I think she'll probably be downstairs already with Rick. I rang her room but there's no answer."

Oliver tugged at his collar, "I hate wearing a tie. It's like being at school."

"It's not for long and you do look very smart. You'll be able to take it off at the reception."

"I hate dressing up. I wish I could have stayed at home."

"Well you couldn't. It's important you are here, you're Rick's . . ." she hesitated. He wasn't Rick's brother but he didn't know that yet, "you're Rick's family so it'll be nice to see him married."

Oliver put his jacket on. Her breath caught in her throat as she stared at her little boy who in the blink of an eyelid, seemed all grown up, and so like Rick.

Her precious son who she'd almost lost. The pain of the kidnapping was still raw.

She wrapped her arms around him. "I love you so much, and I'm very proud of you." She swallowed the lump in her throat, "You know that, don't you?"

They were on their own so he hugged her back, "Course I do, Mum. I love you too."

For a few precious seconds she held him tightly, his head fitting nicely under her chin.

She pulled away, "Come on, we better get a move on, we don't want to be late." She reached for a comb off the dresser. "Here," she handed it to him, "run that through your hair again."

He moved towards the mirror and combed his hair. "Jo showed me a picture of Louise, she's really pretty."

"Is she?"

If you only knew how much that hurt, son.

"Yeah, she's got ever such long legs. She held a record when she was sixteen for having the longest legs in Britain."

Kids, how hurtful they could be. Knowing the length of Rick's fiancée's legs was like a knife in the gut.

Despite willing all night for Rick to come to her, he hadn't. So he must love long-legged Louise after all. Tears threatened. Not only for the loss of Rick, but for the handsome young man stood in front of her who she'd come so close to losing.

"Gosh, how handsome you look. Let me take a quick photo and we'll go downstairs for the ceremony."

Her cheerful smile hid the numbness she felt deep inside. She positioned her phone, "Say cheese."

Eve and Oliver made their way down the huge staircase and towards the room where the ceremony was going to be held.

The hotel was spectacular. She approached the double doors to the magnificently decorated room. It was stunning. The decorations were all cream, ivory, and gold, and the scent from the fresh flowers strategically placed around the room was beautiful.

Rick was a wealthy man so could well afford it, and he'd be even richer now inheriting Chanjori House. Would he eventually sell it?

He'd have his own children with Louise no doubt, so maybe they'd use it as a holiday retreat as Rick's work was in London. A picture of Rick with other children sliced her in two.

He would have come for her if he'd wanted her. But he hadn't. She needed to accept that instead of romanticising about a future with him in it.

Jo was sat on the front row on a chair decorated with a huge cream and gold bow. As they approached Jo, Eve's eyes were drawn to the back of Rick stood further forward a few metres from the rows of chairs with his best man.

He was wearing a light grey mourning suit and must have showered recently as his hair was still damp and was curling up at the collar.

Her tummy tightened.

Why didn't you come? We could have at least talked.

She encouraged Oliver to sit in between her and Jo.

Get a grip. He's made his choice.

She touched Jo's arm, "You look beautiful, stunning in fact. That colour really suits you."

"Thank you," Jo smiled, "you do too . . . as always." She put a loving arm around Oliver, "And what a handsome young man you are."

Oliver pulled a face, and shrugged her off.

"Did you have a nice meal with Rick last night?" Eve asked, fishing for any information about him. Just a glint he might not be happy.

"Yes, we did. We were up quite late having a night cap upstairs on the terrace. It's a gorgeous hotel, isn't it? Is your room nice?"

"It's beautiful." She playfully moved her eyes sideways towards Oliver, "*Mr fed up when are we going home,* isn't impressed though."

Oliver indicated towards Rick, "Can I go over and say hello?"

"No," they both replied in unison.

"You can't go waltzing over there," Jo told him firmly, "the bride'll be here in a minute."

Rick must have heard them because he looked over his shoulder. He winked at Oliver. Eve held her breath as his eyes met hers. Fleetingly, and just as quickly, he turned away.

She leaned across and whispered to Jo, "You did give Rick the letter?"

"Yes," she nodded, "I did."

So, he'd got it and was still getting married.

I can't bear you leaving me, not again.

*

Rick shouldn't have turned around.

Fuck. She wasn't supposed to come.

She was history now and he had to forget her. She was his half-sister.

God, he'd never get over that. That's why he'd brought the date forward to marry Louise. No-one was more surprised than her when he'd suggested it. Prior to that, he'd been stalling. Louise fell for the urgency, no doubt imagining his father's illness had made him think of his own mortality. Nothing was further from the truth.

He was marrying her to blot Eve out.

Since he'd been back to Chanjori, he'd never stopped thinking about her. He hated her for marrying his father, but when he went back and the old man was dying, the feelings for her were still there. And when they'd had sex, he still felt the same way about her that he always had.

A shudder ran through him. How the hell had he been fucking his sister? What sort of a pervert did that make him?

Eve had texted yesterday asking if they could talk, but he'd ignored it. She'd even got Jo to give him a letter, but he didn't want to open that. What was the point when he needed to distance himself from her?

He was going to have to speak to Ollie and tell him he was his dad, but he didn't want it coming out his mother was his half-sister.

What a fucking mess.

He'd have to speak to Eve to see if there was anything to be gained by disclosing that he, Jo, and Eve shared the same father. Not until after he was married though. That was safer.

The letter from Eve was still in his inside pocket. An innocuous white envelope that subconsciously burned a hole in his chest. It was more than likely a last-ditch attempt from her to halt the wedding. As if. There was no way she could do that. He was marrying Louise, any minute now. Or whenever Louise got her act together.

He glanced at his watch. Seven minutes late now. The vicar Louise had insisted on rather than a registrar didn't look concerned. He wouldn't be though with the amount he was getting paid. It wouldn't matter to him if she didn't arrive until midnight.

Lateness irritated Rick to death. Louise knew that yet she persisted in it. Countless times they'd argued over it. He was a punctual person himself, he had to be. He couldn't turn up late to court, *Sorry, your Honour, it took me longer than I anticipated to get here.*

Where the fucking hell was she?

The letter smouldered against his chest. Why he'd brought it unopened he didn't know. It was almost as if it was a personal test. He was marrying Louise and no late pleas from Eve would change that.

He checked his watch again. Ten minutes late, now.

Eve wouldn't have done that. She wouldn't have kept anyone waiting. She would have been on time.

The closest person he had as a friend stood by his side and winked at him. The sort of wink that said *there's no turning back now*. Rick wasn't a man that suffered with nerves or any weakness like that, but today he felt a restlessness inside that he couldn't shake off. His shoulders ached and his abdomen hurt, as if there was a huge knot inside him.

He glanced at his watch again. He needed a drink.

His fingers itched. Maybe he should open the letter? At least that would mean closure. He wouldn't have to open it after he was married then. It was only a letter, but the significance of it after he'd said his vows, wouldn't be right. It was different being single, it didn't matter how much Eve pleaded, but being married changed everything.

Or would it be better to give her the letter back unopened? That way, he'd have no idea what she'd written. Now she was going to be at the reception, he could discreetly pass it back to her. That would save embarrassment all-round for him and for her. Yes, that was the best option.

So why was he reaching in his jacket pocket and taking the letter out?

*

Eve heard a rustle outside of the room and turned around to the double doors behind her. She caught a glimpse of a bridal gown and her heart constricted.

Jo whispered, "She looks stunning. I love ivory. I'd like that . . . if I ever get married."

Eve couldn't speak. She was concentrating on breathing in and out.

"Here," Jo handed her a tissue, "I always cry at weddings too."

"Aw, no, Mum." Oliver shook her arm, "Don't start crying."

Eve took a deep breath in. What was she thinking of, coming to see him marry someone else?

42

Rick stared at the piece of paper in front of him.

The alleged father is excluded as the biological father of the tested female. The alleged father lacks the genetic markers that must be contributed to the child by the biological father. The probability of paternity is 0%.

The lying fucking bastard.

Chester Forrest wasn't Eve's father. They weren't related.

Fury raged through him.

The vicar gave a signal to the organist. Louise was finally here.

The first bars of the Bridal Chorus began and Rick heard the invited guests getting to their feet behind him. His stomach lurched as Louise made her way towards him on the arm of her father.

The letter had changed everything.

Fucking hell.

Give him the Old Bailey and a criminal to defend and he'd take that any day rather than this.

Louise arrived at his side. She looked beautiful and happy. In her shoes, she was almost the same height as him.

Eve was tall, but not as tall. Eve was the right size for him.

His heart hammered as he leant across, "You look beautiful, Lu."

"Thank you," she replied demurely.

She did look stunning, but he only knew one woman that was truly beautiful in his eyes.

Louise was wearing too much make up. And her hair was tied up with ringlets falling around her neck, which no doubt a hairdresser had spent hours doing, but to him it looked stiff as if hairspray was holding each curl. Her face looked orange which he guessed was the result of the spray tans she seemed to favour.

He reached for her hand and he lifted it to his face and kissed it. Her nails were acrylic and painted in a cream colour. Eve had beautiful hands and nails, and Louise's seemed false in comparison. Maybe he was just seeing it for the first time today, but the whole of Louise looked false with her coloured skin, pink lipstick, and heavily made-up eyes.

So unlike another woman, who was graceful, and didn't need a make-up palette to enhance her beauty, or colour on her skin to replicate a sun tan. She was simply beautiful with her pale translucent skin.

Shit.

Forget her. You're marrying Louise.

He needed to concentrate. The vicar was rambling on about the joyous occasion, and before the vows, they were to sing a hymn. Christ. He wanted this fiasco over and done with, not sing a pissing hymn.

The organ started up again, and the words of 'All things Bright and Beautiful' echoed around the intimate room.

Louise held the hymn sheet between them for him to follow.

All things bright and beautiful. More like, *all things stuffed and fucked.*

His eyes moved past Louise to her mother standing proudly in a green outfit with a yellow hat which reminded him of a budgie.

So that's what his wife to be was going to look like in thirty years.

He looked down at his feet. He needed to get a grip. The hymn was coming to an end.

The organ stopped. Louise gave him an *I love you* smile.

Shit, shit, shit.

"We are gathered here today to witness the joining of two people in holy matrimony."

The vicar smiled encouragingly at them both.

"But before we go through the legal ceremony, I need to call upon those present today to speak up if anyone knows of any reason why this couple should not be joined together in holy matrimony."

Rick took a deep breath in.

Yes, me.

I'm in love with someone else.

He had to stop this. Before it was too late.

He raised his hand.

The vicar smiled as if to say, it's okay, every groom gets nervous.

Rick swallowed. "Just a minute."

He turned his head to look at Eve. She looked so elegant and beautiful stood with his son who was looking intensely at him too.

Louise touched his arm, "Rick. What's the matter?"

The vicar lowered his voice, "Are you alright?"

No, I'm not fucking alright.

He kissed Louise on the cheek, "I'm sorry."

Her orange skin had turned a lighter shade of orange. "Sorry about what?" Her voice went up an octave, "Will you please tell me what's going on?"

He looked at her wounded face, she didn't deserve this.

"I can't marry you," he turned to look again at Eve who met him with a powerful stare. "I'm in love with someone else."

He swiftly moved past Louise and her father. Just a few paces and he was next to Eve and his son.

An astonished Jo moved her head from him to Eve as if the penny had just dropped.

He took Eve's arm, "Come on, let's get out of here."

"Yay," Ollie did a fist pump, "let's get out of here."

Rick indicated with his head for Ollie and Jo to follow, and marched Eve out of the venue, along the corridor with its thick lush carpets and heavily embossed wallpaper. He spotted someone on a ladder attaching a banner to the room where the reception was to be held saying, *Congratulations Mr and Mrs Forrest*.

He continued past it and didn't stop until they were outside the hotel in the gardens. They came to an abrupt halt but he still held Eve's arm. For the first time in weeks, the tension had gone from his body, and the knot in his stomach had finally come undone.

He breathed out, "That was close."

Her expression still looked stunned. "You're telling me."

Jo shook her head from side to side, a realisation of the two of them, together. "Come on, Oliver, let's go and pack up our stuff. It looks like we're leaving."

Ollie gave Rick a puzzled look, "Aren't you getting married now?"

He shook his head. There was so much explaining to do, but not right now. "No mate," he looked directly at Eve, "not today anyway."

"Why?"

"I dunno," Rick shrugged, "Maybe because I don't like wedding cake."

Jo rolled her eyes and laughed, "Come on, sunbeam, let's go and get our stuff," she gave Rick a stern look, "You need to get out of here too," and indicated with a gesture of her head towards the mess he'd left inside.

Jo took Ollie's arm and started to move away, but Ollie was watching them both curiously, "Why is Mum looking at Rick all gooey?"

"I'll tell you later," was the last thing he heard Jo say.

He took Eve's arm and led her to the side of the hotel that wasn't overlooked.

He hadn't wanted to kiss her in front of Ollie, but he desperately wanted to kiss her now.

He ran a finger across her cheek. "All gooey, eh?"

She widened her eyes, "You don't like wedding cake?"

"Ah, when I said I didn't like it, I lied. I do like wedding cake. It's just that I don't like it here. I'd like some at Chanjori though."

All the anxiety he'd seen in her face had disappeared. She looked happy. "Is that your roundabout way of saying you want to marry me, Rick Forrest?"

"That all depends on just how gooey you can be."

He kissed her then, and she kissed him back. He wrapped his arms around her and held her tightly. He'd nearly married someone else, but Eve hadn't given up on them and it made him feel incredibly humble, but there was something else. Holding her, he finally knew who she reminded him of. Evie Henshaw had the same qualities as another woman he'd loved. His mother.

She pulled away and asked cheekily, "How am I doing on the gooe?"

He shook his head, "Nowhere near enough. You'll have to keep practicing. I need much more than that."

43

They all got out of the car at Chanjori and Gilly opened the front door. She must have been surprised to see all four of them together.

Gilly frowned at Rick, "I thought you'd be on your honeymoon by now?"

Rick grinned that gorgeous schoolboy smile Eve loved so much as he opened the boot of his car. He certainly had some explaining to do.

They'd booked into a hotel the previous evening on the way back to Chanjori. Eve would have loved to have spent the night with Rick, but it wasn't appropriate with Oliver around. They'd spoken to him at dinner with Jo's support, and as gently as they could, explained things.

Her precious little boy seemed delighted that Rick was his father and beat them all to offering an explanation to Gilly.

"Rick's my dad and he's going to marry my mum."

"I beg your pardon…"

The sound of a car coming down the drive made them all turn. As it approached the house, Daniel Hurst who'd led the kidnapping investigation became visible behind the wheel.

They waited while he got out of the car.

"Good afternoon." He looked at Rick. "Would it be possible to speak to you all?"

"Of course," Rick answered, "Come in."

"Can we offer you anything to drink?" Eve asked.

Daniel looked at Gilly. "A coffee would be nice, thank you."

Eve smiled at her son. "Oliver, you go help Gilly and get yourself a drink as well."

Always the opportunist, "Can I have an ice cream?"

"Yes, I suppose so. Go with Gilly and she'll give you one."

She smiled at Daniel Hurst, "This way."

As they all made their way to the library, Daniel politely asked, "How is Oliver, he seems cheerful enough?"

"He's fine, thank you. For the moment, anyway. Rick thinks more will come out later."

"Yes, I'm sure he's right."

Surprisingly, Oliver seemed no worse for the ordeal. He'd said what had frightened him most of all were the masks the captor wore. Eve shuddered. Hopefully the detective was there to tell them they'd got the man that had escaped.

They entered the library and Eve closed the door.

The detective cleared his throat. "I'll get straight to the point. The kidnapper we arrested has been charged with abduction and false imprisonment and is in custody awaiting trial. It wasn't the most sophisticated kidnapping in the world, but nevertheless, it was kidnapping."

"What about the second man?" Rick asked.

"We now know his identity, and that's why I'm here really. I'm afraid to have to tell you, the second kidnapper is known to you."

Known to us?

"Who is it?" Rick asked.

"Your chauffeur, Niall Mann."

Eve saw the colour drain from Jo's face and rushed over to ease her into the armchair before she collapsed.

"It's alright, Jo. There must be some sort of mistake. You're alright, take some deep breaths." Eve turned accusingly to the detective, "Niall isn't capable of anything like that."

"I know it must be an enormous shock, Mrs Forrest, but he definitely was involved. We have the evidence to prove that."

"It can't be him. He's been in America," she turned to Jo, "hasn't he, Jo?"

Jo was becoming paler by the second. "Rick, get her a brandy, would you?" Eve tried to comfort her, "It's alright, we'll sort this. It's all a misunderstanding."

She glared at the detective. "Niall wouldn't kidnap Oliver. He took him to school every day. He drives us all around. We trust him. My late husband will have taken references when he took him on."

"As hard as it is to comprehend, he was definitely involved, Mrs Forrest. And I'm afraid there's some more bad news."

Rick passed her a brandy to give to Jo.

"What bad news?" Rick asked, "Don't tell me he's got away?"

Daniel Hurst looked awkward. "I'm afraid to have to tell you, Niall Mann is dead."

"What!" Eve clung to Jo. How on earth must she be feeling, she loved Niall.

Rick instructed Jo firmly, "Drink the brandy, Jo."

The detective cleared his throat. "Would it be better for you and I to talk in private, sir?"

"No," Eve answered sharply, "I want to know." She looked at Jo, "*We* need to know, however painful it is. I can't believe Niall did this to my son."

"Have you got a body?" Rick asked.

Eve didn't like the look on Rick's face at all. He looked as shocked as they were.

"Yes, we've retrieved Niall Mann's body."

"How?" Rick persisted.

"Rick," Eve said his name firmly. Jo didn't need reminding crudely that the man she loved was dead. She was barely holding on.

"Suicide. Carbon monoxide poisoning in his car."

"No." Jo sobbed, "He wouldn't. He loved life."

Eve held onto Jo. She couldn't comprehend their trusted driver was involved in any way with the kidnapping, "Are you absolutely certain? He's our driver. We trust . . . trusted him."

"I'm sorry, I know this must be hard for you. We do have a confession from the man we have in custody. Niall Mann had planned it. The trip to the US was fiction. He's been here all the time."

How could Niall do that to Oliver? Oh, God, the times her precious son was alone with him.

Eve remembered another thing that had puzzled her. "Who tipped you off about it all . . . you know, where to find Oliver?"

The detective shook his head. "I'm afraid I don't have the answer to that right now."

A knock on the door interrupted them, and Gilly entered with a tray of coffee. "Thank you, Gilly, just leave it would you."

She placed the tray down. "Shall I keep Oliver with me for a while?"

"Yes, if you would please."

They waited until Gilly had left the room.

"Nothing for me, Mrs Forrest," Daniel said, "I need to be going. I wanted to keep you all updated about developments before you saw it in the media."

"We appreciate that," Rick replied, "As you can see, it's been an enormous shock."

"Yes, I can see that. Incidents such as this don't always have a happy ending. I'm pleased for your sake this one has," he looked at her, "and your son was unharmed. You can never predict how these things will turn out."

Rick took the detective's outstretched hand.

"We will need to interview Miss Forrest when she's feeling better."

"Yes of course," Rick replied.

"Wait," Jo interjected, "Have you seen Niall's . . . Niall's body? You know it's definitely him?"

"We do, yes."

"Have you seen him . . . dead I mean, have you seen him dead?"

The detective nodded.

"Did he have a beard?"

"No. He was clean-shaven."

Eve held onto Jo while sobs wracked through her body.

"All the texts and emails were lies. He'd told me he was staying a bit longer in America and I believed him." She shook her head, "It all sounded so plausible. Oh, Eve, he never cared for me. It was all a set up to get Oliver."

Eve could barely comprehend the news herself. She needed to feel Rick's arms around her but he had walked the detective to the door.

She stroked Jo's hair while she continued to mumble.

"He made a joke once about a beard. Said he could commit a crime, shave it off and no-one would make the connection. Oh God, Eve, what a fool I've been."

"Shush, shush. We all have. He's duped us all."

Rick came back into the room clutching a small package wrapped in yellow paper with a bright red bow. He ripped the paper off to reveal a box of Cuban cigars.

"Where have they come from?" Eve asked.

"Gilly's just given it to me. It's been hand-delivered."

"But you don't smoke." She paused for a moment. There was so much she had to learn about him, "Do you?"

He didn't answer. Instead he opened the envelope containing the card and she walked towards him to read it.

Nelson was a poor sailor and look what he achieved.

Welcome aboard.

"What does that mean? Who sent them, Rick?"

"Someone I used to know. It'll be a wedding gift."

"But why send it here to Chanjori? Who would know you're here?"

"I don't know," he dismissed, "don't worry about it now. Let's just concentrate on Jo." His eyes darkened as if to say, no more now.

Jo was mumbling into her brandy glass. "None of it was true. It was all lies, he didn't care for me. He was only here to get to Oliver." She sobbed, "Thank goodness nothing happened to him, I'd never have forgiven myself."

Eve rushed to her again, "Hey, nothing did happen. Oliver is safe, and so are you, thank goodness."

"He's never even been to America. Oh, God, Eve, he used me."

The loud shrill of a mobile interrupted them.

Rick reached in his pocket for his phone and looked at the caller ID. "Sorry, I have to take this."

Rick closed the library door and made his way to the lounge to make certain he couldn't be overheard. Even though the number wasn't saved as a contact in his phone, he knew who it was.

He pressed accept. "Forrest," he answered.

"Ah, Rick, just the man."

Saul Boylen's supercilious tone gave Rick a thump to his abdomen. He could picture his smug, ugly face.

How did he know where to send the cigars?
Did he have some sort of tracker on him?

"Saul," he spoke curtly. It wasn't a social chat.

"We're just putting the finishing touches to your new office. It needed a bit of a makeover as it was full of junk, but we've got rid of all the shit like we said we would." He paused long enough for Rick to grasp his meaning. "I was hoping the first of September is acceptable for you to *come onboard?*"

Rick gazed out of the panoramic window across the lawn, and his eyes were drawn to the colourful array of flowers popping their heads up looking for some sunshine.

At long last he was home at Chanjori, his mother's precious house which now belonged to him. He could protect his sister and make sure no more toe-rags came anywhere near her.

Eve was his after all these years and they were going to make a life together. He had a precious son who he hadn't even known was his until recently. Maybe in the future there'd be more children?

It could have all ended so differently.

Ollie could have died. Now he would grow up into a man and eventually Chanjori House would be his.

It had all worked out.

So now it was time to sell his soul to the devil.

"Yes, Saul, I'll be there."

About the Author

Thank you so much for reading my book, I sincerely hope you've enjoyed reading it as much I've loved writing it. Please let me know, I love to hear from readers. joymarywood@yahoo.co.uk

If you are interested in reading any more of my books, I have two other romances available in paperback or electronic, both with a twist or two along the way!

For the Love of Emily
Knight & Dey